The Panopticon

Jenni Fagan was born in Livingston, Scotland. She graduated from Greenwich University and won a scholarship to the Royal Holloway MFA. A published poet, she has won awards from Arts Council England, Dewar Arts, and Creative Scotland among others. She has twice been nominated for the Pushcart Prize and was shortlisted for the Dundee International Book Prize. Jenni lives in a coastal village with her partner and son, and is currently completing her second novel.

Praise for *The Panopticon*

'*The Panopticon* is a breathtakingly poetic narrative about a troubled but humane Scottish girl in care of the state. Its big themes and uncompromising nature have proved too challenging for the literary establishment, trapped in their trivial and repetitive obsession with middle class couples in loveless relationships.'

Irvine Welsh, *Scotsman*

'Jenni Fagan's *The Panopticon* is not just uncompromising and courageous, I think it's one of the most cunning and spirited novels I've read for years. The story of Anais, a fifteen-year-old girl blasting her way through the care-home system while the system in turn blasts her away to nothing, looks on the surface to be work of a recognizable sort, the post-Dickensian moral realism/fabulism associated with writers like Irvine Welsh. But Fagan's narrative talent is really more reminiscent of early Camus and that this novel is a debut is near unbelievable. Tough and calm, electrifying and intent, it is an intelligent and deeply literary novel which deals its hope and hopelessness simultaneously with a humaneness, both urgent and timeless, rooted in real narrative subtlety.'

Ali Smith, *Times Literary Supplement*, Books of the Year

'The great Brazilian writer Clarice Lispector once wrote that she wanted her writing to be like a punch in the stomach to her readers, "for life is a punch in the stomach". This year the life in Jenni Fagan's debut novel, *The Panopticon*, knocked the breath out of me.'

Observer, Books of the Year

'Jenni Fagan is the real thing, and *The Panopticon* is a real treat: maturely alive to the pains of maturing, and cleverly amused as well as appalled by what it finds in the world.'

Andrew Motion

'Ferocious and devastating, *The Panopticon* sounds a battle-cry on behalf of the abandoned, the battered, and the betrayed. To call it a good novel is not good enough: this is an important novel, a book with a conscience, a passionate challenge to the powers-that-be. Jenni Fagan smashes every possible euphemism for adolescent intimacy and adolescent violence, and she does it with tenderness and even humour. Hats off to Jenni Fagan! I will be recommending this book to everyone I know.'

Eleanor Catton, author of *The Rehearsal*

'This is a wonderful book – gripping and brilliant. Anais's journey will break your heart and her voice is unforgettable. Bursting with wit, humanity and beauty as well as an unflinching portrayal of life as a "cared for" young adult, this book will not let you go.'

Kate Williams

'[A] confident and deftly wrought debut . . . Her voice is compellingly realised. We cheer her on as she rails against abusive boyfriends and apathetic social workers, her defiance rendered in a rich Midlothian brogue.'

Financial Times

'The most assured and intriguing first novel by a Scottish writer that I have read in a decade, a book which is lithely and poetically written, politically and morally brave and simply unforgettable . . . Anais's voice is an intricate blend of the demotic and the hauntingly lyrical . . . Fagan is exceptionally skilful with bathos, a notoriously difficult literary register; here, however, it manages to be funny and heart-breakingly tender at the same time . . . a rare achievement . . . As a debut, *The Panopticon* does everything it should. It announces a major new star in the firmament.'

Stuart Kelly, *Scotsman*

'Fagan's writing is taut and controlled and the dialogue crackles.'

Sunday Herald

'[The narrator] is engagingly drawn by Fagan, who has created a character possessed of intellectual curiosity and individual quirks . . . Written with great verve . . . Fagan has a clear voice, an unflinching feel for the complexity of the teenage mindset, and an awareness of the burden we impose on children.'

Scotland on Sunday

'What Fagan depicts in her debut novel, *The Panopticon*, is a society in which people don't just fall through the net – there is no net . . . Fagan is writing about important stuff: the losers, the lonely, most of them women. [Anais] maintains a cool, smart, pretty, witty and wise persona.'

Guardian

'Reminiscent of *Girl, Interrupted* . . . The novel is as bold, shocking and intelligent as its central character . . . The institutional details (magnolia walls, screwed-down chairs) anchor *The Panopticon* in realism, giving it a greater bite. Much of Anais' life is the stuff of tabloid shock stories and *The Panopticon*'s strength lies in giving you an insight into the lonely, damaged girl behind the headlines . . . This week's winner.'

Stylist

'An indictment of the care system, this dazzling and distinctive novel has at its heart an unstoppable heroine . . . Fagan's prose is fierce, funny and brilliant at capturing her heroine's sparky smartness and vulnerability . . . Emotionally explosive.'

Marie Claire

The Panopticon

Jenni Fagan

Published by Windmill Books 2013

4 6 8 10 9 7 5 3

Grateful acknowledgement is made to the following for permission to reprint previously published material:

Lines from 'Chapel of Love' words and music by Jeff Barry, Ellie Greenwich and Phil Spector © 1964, Reproduced by permission of Mother Bertha Music Inc/ ABKCO Music Inc/ EMI Music Publishing Ltd, W8 5SW.

'Chapel of Love' words and music by Phil Spector, Ellie Greenwich and Jeff Barry. Copyright © 1964 UNIVERSAL – SONGS OF POLYGRAM INTERNATIONAL INC., BUG MUSIC-TRIO MUSIC COMPANY and MOTHER BERTHA MUSIC, INC. Copyright Renewed. All rights for MOTHER BERTHA MUSIC, INC. controlled and administered by EMI APRIL MUSIC INC. All rights reserved. Used by permission.
Reprinted by permission of Hal Leonard Corporation.
UK Reprinted by permission of Carlin Music Corp, London NW1 8BD

While every effort has been made to obtain permission from owners of copyright material reproduced herein, the publishers would like to apologise for any omissions and will be pleased to incorporate missing acknowledgements in any future editions.

First published in Great Britain in 2012 by William Heinemann

Windmill Books
The Random House Group Limited
20 Vauxhall Bridge Road, London SW1V 2SA

Addresses for companies within The Random House Group Limited can be found at: www.randomhouse.co.uk/offices.htm

The Random House Group Limited Reg. No. 954009

www.randomhouse.co.uk

A CIP catalogue record for this book
is available from the British Library

ISBN 9780099558644

The Random House Group Limited supports the Forest Stewardship Council® (FSC®), the leading international forest-certification organisation. Our books carrying the FSC label are printed on FSC®-certified paper. FSC is the only forest-certification scheme supported by the leading environmental organisations, including Greenpeace. Our paper procurement policy can be found at: www.randomhouse.co.uk/environment

Typeset by Palimpsest Book Production Limited
Falkirk, Stirlingshire
Printed and bound in Great Britain by Clays Ltd, St Ives Plc

For Joe & Boo

Sometimes I feel like a motherless child.

Traditional US folk song from the 1870s, a time when it was common to take children away from slaves in order to sell them.

When liberty comes with hands dabbled in blood it is hard to shake hands with her.

Oscar Wilde

I'M AN experiment. I always have been. It's a given, a liberty, a fact. They watch me. Not just in school or social-work reviews, court or police cells – they watch everywhere. They watch me hang by my knees from the longest bough of the oak tree; I can do that for hours, just letting the wishes drift by. They watch me as I outstare the moon. I am not intimidated by its terrible baldness. They're there when I fight, and fuck, and wank. When I carve my name on trees, and avoid stepping on the cracks. They're there when I stare too long or too clearly, without flinching. They watch me sing, and joyride, and start riots with only the smallest of sparks; they even watch me in the bath. I keep my eyes open underwater, just my nose and mouth poking out so I can blow smoke-rings – my record is seventeen in a row. They watch me not cry. They watch me lie like an angel, hiding my dirty feet. They watch me, I know it, and I can't find anywhere any more – where they can't see.

1

IT'S AN unmarked car. Tinted windows, vanilla air-freshener. The cuffs are sore on my wrists but not tight enough tae mark them – they're too smart for that. The policeman stares at me in the rear-view mirror. This village is just speed-bumps, and a river, and cottages with window blinds sagging like droopy eyelids. The fields are strange. Too long. Too wide. The sky is huge.

I should be playing the birthday game, but I cannae, not while there's witnesses around. The birthday game has to be played in secret – or the experiment will find out. What I need to do right now is memorise the number stickered inside the back window. It's 75999.43. I close my eyes and say it in my head over and over. Open my eyes and get it right first time.

The car drives over a wee ancient stone bridge and I want to jump off it, into the river – the water is all brown whorls, but I'd still feel cleaner after. I slept in the forest for ten days once, it was nice; nae people, mostly. The odd paedo on the warpath like, so I had tae watch, but when it was safe, I bathed in the rapids. I washed my knickers and T-shirt in the current every morning – then dried them on rocks while I sunbathed.

I could live like that. Nae stress. Nae windows or doors. It must have been an Indian summer that year because it was still warm, even in September. I was twelve, and fucked, but not as fucked as now.

The policewoman lays her hand on my arm. She's dealt with me before. She cannae see my nails are gouged into my fist. I didnae even notice until I uncurled my fingers and saw red half-moons on my palm.

I hate. Her face. The thick hair on his neck. I hate the way the policeman turns the wheel. What is worse, though, is this nowhere place. There's nae escape. The cuffs chink as I smooth down my school skirt – it's heavily spattered with bloodstains.

We drive by a huge stone wall, up to a gateway framed by two tall pillars. On the first there's a gargoyle – someone's stubbed a fag out in his ear. I glance up at the other pillar, and a winged cat crouches down.

My heart starts going, and it isnae what's waiting at the end of the drive down there, or three nights with no sleep in the cells. It's not the policeman smirking at me in his mirror. It's a winged cat – with one red eye and a terrible smile.

Turn around and gaze back. That's what the monk sent me, drawn on a bit of cardboard he'd ripped off a cereal box. One winged cat, in pencil – no note. He sent it from the nuthouse. Helen's gonnae make me go and meet him, as soon as she gets back.

Look at it. A real stone winged cat! It's stunning. His wings would be a couple of metres wide if he unfolded them, and there's yellow lichen furring his shoulders. I'll draw him, later, alongside my two-headed flying kitten, and a troop of snails on acid – wearing top hats, with spirally eyes and jaggy-fucking-teeth.

A sign for *The Panopticon* is nestled in trees with conkers hanging off them. A leafy arc dapples light onto the road, it flickers across my face, and in the car window my eyes flash amber, then dull.

The Panopticon looms in a big crescent at the end of a long driveway. It's four floors high, two turrets on either side and a peak in the middle – that'll be where the watch-tower is.

'They'll not be scared of you in there,' the policewoman says.

She undoes the chain from her belt to my cuffs. I scratch under my ponytail, then my leg. I've one of those wandering itches that won't settle.

There is birdsong. The smell of wet grass filters in the window – bark swollen by rain, mulch, autumn, a faint wisp of wood fire. The car pulls away from the leafy canopy into a sudden glare of sunlight and the policeman snaps his sun visor down, but he doesnae need tae, clouds are already racing down from behind the hills. A light drizzle glitters in the sun. There'll be a rainbow after this.

Files marked *A. Hendricks: Section 14 (372.1)* are stacked on the front seat. My knees are itchy now. Funny things, knees, knobbly hunks of bone. The car stops outside a sign for the main entrance beside six shan cars and a minibus with *Midlothian Social Work Department* emblazoned on the side. I fucking hate travelling in those things.

Windows are open on the third floor but only about six inches – they'll have safety locks on, so they dinnae get jumpers. Three girls hang out, although only their heads and arms fit through. They're all smoking, and giggling to each other.

Up on the top floor, the windows are barred and boarded up. I bet there's petitions to close this place down already; there'll be people from the village writing letters tae their MPs. Mr Masters is right. He told us all about it in history – communities dinnae like no-ones.

Mr Masters said, in the old days, if a woman didnae have a husband or a family but she still did okay, people didnae like that. If there wasnae a male authority figure tae say she was godly – then they thought she was weak for the devil. Bound tae be bad. Or even if her crops were doing well, better than her neighbours, or she wasnae scared tae answer back? Fucking witch. Prick it, poke it, peel its fingernails off and burn it in the square for the whole town to see.

My shoes are tiny next to the policewoman's, and my heartbeat's too fast. I'm beginning to shrink, shrink, shrink, again! I fucking hate this. Everything recedes at the speed of light – the policeman, the car, even the white sun – until all that's left is a tiny pinprick for me to stare back at the policeman. He's saying something. His lips – move.

Gouge my nails back into my palms.

'Aye, they'll have you up on that locked fourth floor by teatime, Anais.'

Fuck off, wankstain. Stop looking at me. I need to just breathe, until this shrinking begins to give. It will give. It has to. The lassies are craning out their windows, trying to get the first look. They'll already know – about the riots, the dealing, the fires, the fights. They'll know there's a pig in a coma.

At the middle window the dark-haired lassie is laughing.

She's got a curly moustache drawn on her upper lip. Next to her is a small blonde with a pixie haircut. She's letting a long glob of saliva drool down, but it's still attached to her mouth. The lassie at the end is wearing a baseball cap.

A shoelace hangs off the bar on the blonde girl's window, but there's nae fag on it – just an empty knot. Curly moustache is smoking it. Each unit does that. We tie shoelaces to the windows, so you can swing your fag, or joint, or whatever along after lights out.

'Aye, you're no gonnae be the smart cunt in there!' the policeman says.

Focus on his face. It'll help keep the shrinking back. He's got green eyes, a squint nose, and the hair on his neck and forearms is thick as a fucking pelt. You're giving me the boak, fuck-pus. He's loving this. They've wanted me banged up away from town and their stations, for how long? They think if they put me far enough away then I cannae get in trouble. Aye. Okay. There's still buses, fanny-heads, I umnay behind locked doors yet.

The policeman is watching me in his rear-view mirror. He gave me a stoater of a slap yesterday. Old radgio el fuckmong, I call him, old cunt-pus himself.

'Smile, Anais, it's a palatial country house, this!'

He gestures at the unit. It looks like a prison. It was one, once. And a nuthouse. He smirks again. I wish *he* was in a fucking coma.

The polis dinnae get it – we compare notes just as much as they do. We know if there's a psycho in a unit, or a right bastard pig who'll always batter you at the station. We know if somebody's been stabbed, or hanged themselves, or who's on the game, or which paedos in town will lock you in their flat and have you gang-banged until you turn fucking tricks. We send e-mails, start legends – create myths. It's the same in the nick or the nuthouse: notoriety is respect. Like, if you were in a unit with a total psycho and they said you were sound? Then you'll be a wee bit safer in the next place. If it's a total nut that's vouched for you, the less hassle you'll get. I dinnae need tae worry about any of that. I am the total nut.

We're just in training for the proper jail. Nobody talks about it, but it's a statistical fact. That or on the game. Most of us are anyway – but not everybody. Some go to the nuthouse. Some just disappear.

The policeman unbuckles his seatbelt and checks there's nothing worth choring on the dash.

'Here we go.' He opens his door.

One of the girls whistles, long and low.

'Less of that,' he glares up.

'I wasnae whistling at you, pal,' she says.

The baseball-cap lassie spits.

'Dinnae give your mind a treat, we meant the hot one!'

They're still giggling when he rams his hat on and clicks open my door. The policeman guides me up, hand on my head, turns me around – beeps the car alarm on.

The blonde girl lets her long globule of saliva fall away. The polis walk either side of me. I keep my shoulders back, my gaze even – almost serene. I dinnae walk with a swagger, just a certainty. As we reach the main door, I look up and it passes between us: the glint, it's strong as sunlight and twice as bright. They can feel it in me. It can start a riot in seconds, that glint. It could easily kill a man.

I give the lassies my sweetest smile and lift an imaginary hat as a salute.

'Ladies!'

The blonde girl grins at me. The policeman takes my elbow and steers me under the porch where they cannae see, and he rings the bell and I stamp my feet lightly, once, twice. I already know what it'll smell like in there. Bleach. Cleaning products. Musty carpets. Cheap shite. Every unit smells the same.

There's wire through the front windows but not the side ones. They'll be easier tae smash. I try to breathe easy, but I want these fucking cuffs off, and my neck aches, and I'm starving. I want a milkshake and a vege-burger with cheese.

The policeman rings the bell again. My heart's going. I've moved fifty-one fucking times now, but every time I walk through a new door I feel exactly the same – two years old and ready tae bite.

It's open-plan inside. Nowhere to hide. That sucks. The Officer in Charge waddles towards us; she's got a shiny bowl-cut, stripy socks, flat red shoes, and a ladybird brooch on her cardy.

'Hello, hello, you must be Anais. Come in, officers, please come in. Did you get lost?' she ushers us through the door.

'Noh, we're later than intended, sorry about that. We didnae want tae hold Anais's transfer up, but it couldnae be helped,' the policeman says.

He smiles and takes his hat off. He's such a two-faced fuck.

'We thought Anais was arriving yesterday,' the Officer in Charge says.

She witters to the polis and I trail along behind them, turning around once, twice, looking at every single detail

– it's important to place where everything is. So nobody can walk up behind you.

This whole building is in a big curve, like the shape of a C, and along the curve on the top floor are six locked black doors. The two landings below have another six identical doors on each floor, but they've been painted white, and none of them are closed. I heard they dinnae close the doors in here except after lights out. It's meant tae be good for us, ay. How is that good? Even from down here you can see bits of people's posters in their rooms, and a kid sitting on a bed, and one putting on his socks.

Each of those bedrooms used to be a cell. Embedded in each door frame there are wee black circles where the bars were sawn off. I wonder why they kept nutters in cells? I suppose it was so each inmate could only see the watch-tower, they couldnae see their neighbours. Divide and conquer.

Kids begin to step out of their rooms and look down. I count them out of the corner of my vision – one, two, three, four, five. A boy with curly hair and glasses begins to kick the Perspex balcony outside his door. I dinnae look up. There will be time for all the nice fucking hello-and-how-do-you-dos later.

Right in the middle of the C shape, as high as the top floor, is the watchtower. There is a surveillance window going all the way around the top and you cannae see through the glass, but whoever, or whatever, is in there can see out. From the watchtower it could see into every bedroom, every landing, every bathroom. Everywhere.

This place has experiment written all over it.

My social worker said they were gonnae make all the

nuthouses and prisons like this, once. The thought of it pleased her, I could tell. Helen reckons she's a liberal, but really – she's just a cunt.

The ground floor is mostly open-plan; there's a lounge to the right of the main door, and opposite that four tables make a dining space in the corner. Three doors lead off the main room, probably to the laundry, interview rooms, maybe a games room – if that's a pool table I can see through there! There's a telly screwed to the wall so nobody can chore it. The DVD player will be in the office, same reason.

They've painted everything magnolia and it all smells like shite deodorant, and stale fag smoke, and BO, and skanky, fucking-putrid soup.

At the end of the main room, opposite the door to the office, there is a wee ornate wooden door, one of the only original things left in here. I'll investigate what's through there later. This place would have been nicer once, more Gothic. It's been social-work-ised, though, it's depressing as fuck.

The polis come tae a halt outside the office door, and the Officer in Charge goes in. I scan the ground floor, and tap my feet, and clink my cuffs together until the policewoman leans over and says: *Stop*.

The office door opens, and they let us in. The Officer in Charge must have been waiting on the staff finishing their changeover, but it's obvious they havenae. There's too many staff in here, last shifts, and this shift. I dinnae like it. I feel bare, like my skin's missing. My skin doesnae even feel like mine half the time. They shouldnae be putting me through a handover with this many staff in the office.

'Anais, sorry, I didnae introduce myself properly. I am

the Officer in Charge, my name is Joan. D'ye need a drink or anything?'

'No.'

She looks at the polis and they shake their heads.

'Okay, Anais, this is Eric, he is our student at the moment. This is Brenda, this is Ed, and this is your support worker, Angus.'

They all nod in turn, smiling. Ed has a frizzy ginger mullet and wee round specs. Slick. Ginger isnae the problem (all the hottest girls are redheads), it's not even the frizz; it's the tone, a pissy-orange colour, and it's waist-length and – a mullet.

The student prick is trying to dress like he's a casual. Twat! Brenda appears to be on Prozac and Valium, her eyes have that glazed dullness about them. My support-worker guy, Angus, has long green dreadlocks and knee-high Doc boots.

'I do apologise, you'll need tae excuse us – sorry, you caught us in between shifts. We were hoping to try and finish the changeover before you arrived,' Joan says.

The policeman puts my files down.

'Without disclosing anything directly, of course – can you verify that Anais has been released without charge?' she asks.

'We haven't charged Miss Hendricks, but she is under investigation. We need her school uniform in this, and you'll need tae do it as soon as we leave. We cannae give her the opportunity tae tamper with possible evidence.'

The policeman hands a clear plastic bag with a label on it to Joan.

'D'ye not normally do this at the station?'

'Miss Hendricks cited many, many regulations while she was detained. These included her right to only have her clothes removed, for a full search, if she has a female social worker present. She has this stipulated on her file.'

'Why's that?' Joan asks.

'There were previous allegations from Miss Hendricks about treatment during searches. We did try to get her social worker but she is apparently abroad, and of course we are only concerned for her well-being, so we decided tae wait until we brought her here.'

Old skelp-your-pus sounds well convincing, I almost fucking believe him myself.

'That's not a problem, officer.'

'I've arranged for our lab technician tae come out tomorrow. She'll do the final tests and collect Miss Hendricks's school uniform.'

He's shifting from foot to foot, he wants out of here – good!

'Can you tell us if the police officer's condition is stable, at least?' Joan asks.

'For now.'

'It is a coma, though?'

'An acute coma.'

'Is she expected to come out of it soon?'

Joan's not looking at me. All the staff are, carefully, not looking at me. Except the student. He's fucking fascinated.

'No, she's not, they dinnae know if she will.'

'But you didnae charge Anais?'

'No. We've no actual evidence that Miss Hendricks was responsible for the assault. Not yet.'

Joan puts the plastic bag in her drawer and signs a release form.

I hold my hands out and the policewoman unlocks my cuffs. It feels so good to be able to rub my wrists. Imagine a bath – that would be too good. A great big fuck-off thing on legs with a huge window next tae it, and bubbles, and views of the sky. Imagine a bathroom like that, with fluffy white towels and a bolt on the door.

Joan ticks more forms for the police, then they leave. Crusty reaches over to shake my hand.

'Hello, Anais, I'm your support worker, Angus. I'm really pleased tae meet you.'

'Hiya.'

'Are you no gonnae take a seat?' he asks.

I sit down.

The polis get intae their car, doors slam. The sky is azure out there now; azure means blue – it's nothing to do with Aztecs. The pigmobile trundles up the drive. Smell ye later, wankstains. The statues on those pillars are stark against the sky – the gargoyle's telling the flying cat a secret. His wings lift in the breeze.

'So Helen – it is Helen, your social worker?'

I nod and Joan continues.

'Good, Helen is not due tae arrive for at least another few weeks. She is really, really sorry that she has been held up like this, but it is completely out of her control. She asked me tae pass on her apologies.'

The cat's wings flex, just lightly.

Sit up straight and stare. It definitely moved, or it could be a flashback. There's nae tracers, though. I get the flashbacks a lot lately, I'm beginning to worry I didnae make it back from my last bad trip.

Mental note – quit tripping on schooldays. Keep it for special occasions: bar mitzvahs, pancake Tuesday, fucking Easter. Jay told me gangsters used tae dip their pinkies in liquid LSD so they were permanently tripping, but the clever bit was, if they got done, they only went to the nuthouse. It's because if you're permanently tripping, you're legally classified as insane. In the States, even if you only take acid like ten times or something, they still reckon you're certifiable. They'd think I was well gone.

I hate this. Handovers. New places. Staff. Files. What I want is a hole under the ground to live in. Or a treehouse. Somewhere nobody can see me.

My stuff's not arrived yet; well, it isnae in this office anyway. I asked for something other than bin bags – to move my stuff in – once.

'What would you like, Anais?'

'Matching Italian leather suitcases? Designer. Vintage if possible. And a trunk, a big old leather one with my name on it.'

They thought I was being wide. To be honest, I would have settled for a fucking rucksack! I'm not paying for one, though. Why the fuck should I have to pay to keep moving?

'Your room is forty-nine. The fourth floor is *totally* out of bounds for all clients right now. You will have access tae arts groups and counselling through your support worker. We practise a holistic approach tae client care in the Panopticon.'

Joan's been talking at me the whole time I've been sat here.

'Holistic?'

'Aye, that means we take into consideration all the needs of our clients.'

'All of them?'

'The ones we consider healthy.'

'Is it healthy getting locked up twenty-four hours a day, like?'

'You know why secure units are necessary, Anais, and you are not locked up in the main unit anyway.'

'Does that mean I umnay being put in the secure unit?'

'We cannae place anyone in there yet; there are delays because there's asbestos in the roof. The whole secure-unit renovation has been postponed, until we resolve funding issues.'

'Right.'

My heartbeat's fast, fast, fast. This is a score. I was sure they were gonnae get me locked up on the top floor straight away. This buys time. Maybe I'll no be dead for my sixteenth birthday. I'd rather be dead than locked up 24/7 – cos if that happens, the experiment will have finally, totally fucking got me.

'Am I getting put up there when it opens?'

'Well, let's hope not, Anais. But if you do get placed there at some point in the future, then rest assured you would actually be in one of the best small secure units in the UK.'

'Spiff-fucking-spoff.'

She just looks at me.

You dancer! It isnae open yet. Thank God, thank Jesus and Mary and Buddha. The student is fascinated. Subtle much? He wants tae measure me up – turn me around, knock on my head and peer inside my ear to see what's marching around in there. What a fucking womble!

'Are you gonnae ask me if I did it?' I ask him.

He doesnae know where to look.

'No, Anais! We are not going tae discuss it here.' Joan stands up.

'Aye? Well, he obviously wants tae, he wants tae so bad he needs put on a leash.'

'That's enough,' she snaps.

She's big, Joan. If she sat on you in a restraint or in a riot, you'd fucking feel it. Mental note – avoid bowl-cut next time there's a riot.

Mullet's reading a book in Chinese. He has skinny legs and knobbly fingers, and the way he holds his shoulders isnae what let me know. It's just something that's there. I cannae explain it, but I can usually tell on sight these days. Mullet doesnae do adults. No way. I'd put fucking money on it. Sometimes I think they should take me around schools and kids' clubs, like a sniffer dog, but not for drugs – for paedos. They'd never believe me if I told them? Hello, my name's Anais Hendricks and I can tell a paedo on sight – usually. Aye, right, they'd believe me! I can, though, I can tell if a lassie's been abused just by looking at her. They wouldnae believe it, though, there's nae point in telling them. Not about that. Not about the dreams. Not about flying cats.

Joan has twenty different religious icons up on the office wall behind her.

'Nae witch?' I ask her.

'You have a religious preference?'

'Pagan. Three-parts witch, white obviously – well, sort of!'

'Obviously,' she says.

'Seriously, white witch, 'cept on Sundays.'

'I shan't ask why not on Sundays.'

'Best not.'

'Well, we'll see what we can do, Anais. I'm sure there's a pagan symbol we can find tae put up for you. We dinnae want you tae feel excluded here. I know you've moved a lot, so maybe it's time for you tae settle down – for a wee while?'

I'm dizzy. I hate. Her red shoes. His ginger mullet. Paedos, polis, sniffer dogs, Chinese books, tits, dirt, the colour yellow, icons, cord-fucking-carpets. I'd rather be dead today, but I umnay – I'm fifteen and fucked.

'Wanker!' I whisper to the student, as I get up.

Eric stands with his soft posh hand on my files and looks hurt. Joan nods at him and he lifts up a big pile of folders with my name and number printed on them; he puts them on her desk.

'Brenda will show you tae your room. If you have anything sharp on you, it will be removed. And please, do not tell the other residents what you are in for!'

2

BRENDA HAS a fob-key thing for the rooms. I follow her through the main open-plan area; there isnae much in here, just ugly furniture, and crap carpets that urnay even a colour.

Count the steps to each floor – there are twenty-four. Six doors on each landing, I reckon there's about twelve of us in this unit. We go past the bathrooms and they have girl and boy signs on the doors.

We reach the third floor, and the three lassies are waiting. Brenda walks me along towards them. Moustache's tash is three fine brown spirals, on each cheek. She has wide brown eyes. Nae earrings – I dinnae even think she's had hers pierced. Her hair is long and she reminds me of Frida Kahlo. I like Frida Kahlo, ay, especially her bath and feet painting, and that deer, and the ones of her dreams.

We stop at a bedroom next to the girls, room forty-nine – it is right in the middle of the landing.

'I need shampoo,' Moustache says to Brenda.

'Okay, I'll let you into the stores in a minute.'

Next to Moustache, the blonde girl with the pixie haircut scratches her tummy. Her tummy's cut tae fuck. That's beyond normal. Normal is when someone just cuts their arms, legs or sometimes thighs – not slash marks like that right across their stomach. There's fucking hundreds of them, then there's thick white ones under the fresh ones. She's wearing low-slung jeans, and her hips have silvery stretch-marks. She must have a kid.

'Can you hurry up? We want tae go out, like today,' Moustache says.

'I'm settling our new resident intae her room, then I'll let you into the store. Anais, this is Tash – you choose tae be called Tash, don't you, love?'

The lassie nods.

'Aye.'

'Uh-huh, and this is Shortie. Shona does not like her Christian name, either.'

The girl with the baseball cap gives me a dirty look, takes her hat off and rubs her hair. It's curly, mousy and short. She pulls her hoody up and walks away, gesturing tae a laddie downstairs to meet her around the back.

'And this is our Isla. Say hello then, girls!'

They look, and I look, and Brenda pushes back the door to my room. I follow her in and she hands me the plastic bag. Great! Unbutton my school shirt, kick off my shoes. There's blood on my skirt – and my socks. There's some on my leg. Everything stinks (like the cells did for three days) of concrete, and bleach, and cold, and glass. There was a stone bog in my cell, with just enough water to flush, but no enough tae drown in.

'The bedroom doors are always open, Anais, but they can be pulled partially shut if you're getting dressed. Nobody can see in. Well, only the watchtower, and there isn't anyone in there unless the night-nurse is on duty; she can lock all the doors from a central locking system, if necessary – for the residents' safety!'

She shakes her head when I stop undressing.

'I need your underwear as well.'

Step out my pants and lob them into the bag. This room is smaller than my last one. There's banging out on the landing – that laddie must be back, he's really wellying that balcony.

'Most of the boys' rooms are on the second-floor landing. Nobody can see you dress or undress from the floors below, as long as you get changed tae the left of your door. We like tae keep doors open, to create a more trusting environment. There are no secrets here in the Panopticon,' Brenda adds.

I shove the bag out to her and I'm in the scud now, so I stand behind the door with just my head poking out. I fucking hate being in the scud in new places. Imagine a big fluffy dressing gown. I've not had a dressing gown since I was, like, ten! I wouldnae waste my clothing allowance, though. I like vintage stuff and it's expensive, I can barely afford even one piece a month.

Imagine, though, ay. Imagine soft new jammies, and an open fire, and a big dog I could set on strangers if they came anywhere near my house. Imagine having your own house? Imagine having ten big dogs and a gun. Tash is tapping her fingers off the balcony, and Brenda's trying tae ignore her.

'Is your underwear in there as well, Anais?' she whispers.

'Why, d'ye want tae sniff my knick-knacks?' I ask her.

Isla giggles. Brenda turns the bag until she locates my

scants. She smiles tightly and ties a knot in the bag. The wee laddie keeps kicking the balcony; he's got curly hair and thick specs and he's skinny as fuck.

'Brian, you have been asked tae stop doing that.'

'Aye?'

He boots the balcony harder and she marches away towards him.

'Brian, you need tae get, wait a minute . . .'

Shove my door shut but it still stays open about three inches. There's prongs in the fucking frame so I cannae close it. These doors really do only lock at night, and all from one button, up there in the watchtower! They say they dinnae use it to lock us in all the time. That's what they say.

I'm so pale my veins pop out all purple. My toenails are chipped. This room is cold. One window, one wardrobe. Everything's screwed to the floor so you cannae pick it up and throw it at the staff.

A tractor grumbles across the fields outside. Slide down the wall, drag the duvet off the bed and wrap it around me until I'm totally cocooned.

My bin bags are here, three of them. There's a hole at the bottom of one – I push into it with my big toe and a lipstick falls out. Pillar-box red, Dior. I bought it last week from one of the girls who go choring up town. There were three professional chores in my last unit. They'd come back, day after day, with big store bags full of stuff they'd nicked. It's a skill. I can do it but I dinnae, I have an aversion to being called a common thief. It's only worth stealing if you're in the big league. Diamonds. Rare artworks. Nuclear weapons. That kind of shit.

Pick up my lipstick and take the lid off. This shade of red

is absolutely perfect. I need tae get a pencil in a matching colour, or just a wee bit darker. Lips have to be outlined really, if you're not blessed with bee-stung. It's easy tae make a cupid's-bow-look more pout than it is. It's the same with a lack of right-angled cheekbones or supernatural baby blues or tawny owls. There are ways to make it work. Sometimes I make something so pretty, I dinnae even think it's me. It's not that I think I'm perfect. I'm so imperfect it's offensive. Totally and utterly fucked in fact – but I like pillbox hats.

Sun floods in my window, and a rainbow appears. I gaze up at it until the colour fades and the clouds turn grey.

The experiment are watching.

You can feel them, ay. In the quiet. In the room. Wherever you are – they're there. That's a given. Sometimes they're right there, sometimes a wee bit further away; when I want to hurt myself but I dinnae, I can always feel them then. They want me to hurt myself. They're sick like that. What they really want is me dead.

My legs are going numb, and I'm getting cold, but I still cannae be arsed unpacking. It's dark outside now. Those stars are way brighter than in the city. A bird flies by and there's a low hoot. I'm gonnae have tae go for a piss, I cannae hold it in any longer.

Stick my head out over the landing, there's a notice on the office door downstairs. The staff must be in a meeting. Score! If they were in the main area then I'd have to be dressed appropriately, even to go for a pee. As it is, I can shuffle along to the bogs in this duvet and hopefully no-one'll see me.

There's a girls' bathroom and a boys' bathroom – they just have toilets in them. I peek next door and there are two bathrooms with baths in them. Usually the staff make you bathe every day; no doubt they'll tell me to have one after tea. I go into the girls' toilet. Someone's been sick in here. There's a strong whiff of vomit, and sweat. Ming-fucking-mong.

Have a pee and look in the mirror and meet my own eyes, but quickly look away. It's funny when you make yourself feel uncomfortable. I do it all the time. Mirrors are best avoided, unless I'm getting ready, or on a really good E. Everything's fine if you've had a really good E. This bathroom is cold, I wish I was wearing socks or slippers or something. Someone's left a deodorant in here – bath in a can, ay. It'll do, for now. I spray it on and wash my face, then close the bathroom door quietly behind me. Shuffle back along the landing. Tash and Isla are arguing outside their room.

Isla nods at me, and I nod and pass around them, pretending not to listen.

'I dinnae want you tae come,' Tash says.

'I umnay letting you go by yourself.'

'Isla, I'll be more worried about you being there for half the night on your own – like a sitting-fucking-duck! What if you catch a cold?'

'If I umnay there tae take down the numbers, it'll be worse. I'll just worry.'

Isla scratches her belly. She's cut that again since earlier and she looks like she's gonnae greet. Tash has taken her moustache off, and put make-up on, and her hair is Pre-Raphaelite; earlier it was in a braid. She's wearing a wee skirt, and boots, and Isla has a pad in her hand. She touches Tash's cheek.

Slip into my room, and stand behind the door. They're whispering low now. They'll be heading for the docks, or wherever's closer. Isla must be taking down the licence-plate numbers, just in case Tash doesnae come back, then she'd have something to tell the polis about the last time Tash was seen. They scuffle by my door and down the stairs. I look out the window and a few minutes later they come out.

'Where's Isla?'

A laddie on the landing below is asking one of the staff, their meeting must be over.

'She's away on an outing with Tash. I think they were going ice-skating.'

I dinnae recognise the staff guy's voice. A door slams, then there's a thump as music blares out on the landing below.

Outside, Tash and Isla disappear to a wee dot across the fields. That's how Teresa started. Mother Teresa, where art thou?

Teresa began when she was right young. She told me she got intae a good sauna and stayed there for ages, but she got sick of giving away part of her cut. She was doing it from our flat by the time she adopted me. Her old man never knew. He thought she was in accounts. She said she tried for a straight life and it didnae happen, but she didnae regret it, cos that was how she got me. Her old man had had a normal job, normal life, normal family. She had Professor True. He was her oldest client and he gave all Teresa's refs for the social, saying she was his accountant, saying she was an exemplary this-and-that and the next thing. He loved her. Old True. Old likes-it-up-the-arse but dinnae tell anyone at the university, *or* his sainted wife – True.

Pull the curtains closed.

I cannae face lying down in that bed. I'm always getting in shit for not sleeping in beds. You dinnae know who's slept in your bed before you – it could have been a right clarty bastard. I got scabies off a bed in a unit once. It was itchy as fuck and I had tae slather on this pink ointment that smelled like chemicals, for like a week! It was fucking shite.

Snuggle back down, right in the corner of the room – so I can see if anyone comes in.

.

The hallway's lit with a dim blue light and my face hurts. It's the floor, under my face. Look along the carpet and see bin bags – and a single bed. Fuck! Shove myself up against the wall. I'm dizzy. Death-breath. Fuck. Fuck. Fuck!

'Bed,' someone calls from downstairs.

'But I'm fifteen!'

'You are twelve, Dylan. When you are thirteen years old you will get to stay up for ten minutes longer. Then, when you are fourteen, you will be allowed a further ten minutes! When you are fifteen, you will be allowed a full half-hour more.'

The laddie's on the landing below, by the sound of it, and he isnae giving up.

'I've got a tummy-ache.'

'No, you have not.'

'I miss my mum,' he pleads.

'I miss my mummy too, Dylan. Now, bed.'

I cannae believe the night-staff are on duty already, I must have been asleep for hours! I didnae sleep in the cells, though, so no wonder I'm knackered.

The night-nurse sticks her head around my door. The light on the landing behind her is a pale blue, and she's white. Like, white! I mean she isnae like Celtic pale-as-fuck white – she's albino. Try not tae stare. Her eyes look like they're a pinky colour, and they flicker from left to right.

'Get off the floor, and up into your bed, please. We do not sleep on the floor like dogs, Miss Hendricks.'

She has the most proper English accent ever.

'What time is it?' I ask.

'It's time for bed.'

She pads away down the landing. I stink. I want a bath. I want to cry and hit my head off the wall – and scream until I pass out, but I gave that up for Lent.

Grab the first bin bag; there's nae T-shirts for bed at the top, just my feather wings. I pull them out and rub my face against their softness, then hang them carefully over the window. They are the luckiest thing I own.

Rummage until I find a book and an old T-shirt, pull it on and climb into bed. At first, in a new unit, you always think of the bugs left from the last person who slept in the bed. Then you just think: Fuck it! I can tell that old albino's the type to put you in a fucking headlock if you urnay tucked up all neat and nice, ay. She looks in again.

'Did you eat today, Anais?'

'No.'

'The staff tried to wake you for dinner earlier on.'

'Could I get a glass of water? Please.'

I hate saying please, it makes me feel cheap. I hate saying thank you. I hate saying I need anything. If you had tae get up and ask for air every day – I'd be fucking dead.

'I'll go and get you something,' she says.

She glances towards my window and disappears. There's a murmur of chat coming from outside. The lassies'll be smoking before they crash out. I can hear Isla's voice, then laughing, and it sounds like the laddies are spraffing away from their windows downstairs as well. I umnay sticking my head out to join them, I cannae be doing with it. Not tonight.

Wind whistles along the roof of the building, and the whole place creaks. It's comforting. The night-nurse comes back with a tray, she places it on the chest of drawers.

'Okay, Anais, sit up, that's it. Leave the tray outside your door once you are finished, please. I would not usually make you a snack after hours. I am making an exception because you have not eaten, and I know you were detained for a few days before you arrived.'

She pulls the door slightly shut behind her. Detained. It sounds so polite – like there were cows on the road and we had tae wait until they moved on. Or maybe migrating deer. Something civil like that. Or like when the Queen visits Edinburgh and it's in the paper, and they always say that normal routes are closed until further notice. Folk on their way to work are late then, getting detained by the fuss. Everyone hates it when the Queen visits. You have to walk for miles the long way around – just to cross the road! If you cannae get straight over you might spend a full hour walking around the long way.

Suicides piss everyone off as well. Last week a wifie was gonnae jump off North Bridge, but she got stuck. Either she changed her mind or she just froze. She was there for two days, on this wee ledge – freaking out. I came out of a club and my skin was still all soaking from dancing, and I was right up – then I hear all these people shouting Jump, jump,

jump! That's sick, ay. It's sick to shout at a suicidal person – Jump, jump, jump!

On the tray there's a sandwich with white bread, cheese slices and a glass of milk. I pull the crusts off straight away. Milk gives me the boak unless it's on cereal, but I'm thirsty – drink it down in one go. A butty in bed and a book, sound! Today is pissing all over yesterday; yesterday I was beginning tae think the polis would never let me out.

Open my book, it's mostly vampire stories just now, before that it was witches. I could handle being a vampire, an evil one with huge mansions everywhere. I'd fly, and read minds, and drink blood, until I could hear wee bats being born right across the other side of the world. I hear other people's thoughts when I'm tripping, ay. I dinnae really know if it is thoughts actually, maybe it's just voices. They urnay my thoughts – I know that much. It's like tuning into a radio frequency that's always there, but when you're tripping, you cannae tune it back out. I get voices in my head that urnay mine, and I see faces no-one else sees, but mostly it's just when I'm tripping, so I mustn't be totally mental in the head yet.

The shadow from my feather wings is huge on the wall, it hunches like an old demon and a broken feather juts out like a crooked nose. The voices stop whispering outside. I hear windows being carefully closed, they must all be going to bed. Thank fuck. I put my book down and stretch, all I want is a smoke, in peace. I wish I had a joint, ay, but I dinnae.

Tiptoe to the window and open it, clean cold air – it feels so nice on my face. I still want to have a bath; a wash in the sink and spraying deodorant on isnae the same.

'Alright?'

I jump.

Isla's hanging out her window, and she smiles, I think she's been waiting for me.

'Alright.'

'You're Anais Hendricks, ay?'

'Aye, are you Isla?'

'Aye. D'ye want a wee smoke?'

'Aye, ta.'

She ties a joint to a shoelace and swings it along.

'I had a bit from Amsterdam but it's gone,' she says.

'That sucks.'

'Tash smoked the lot. She had six pipes, then she spent all night telling us about the clocks on the lawn, just down there. She says they're there all the time, just the shapes of grandfather clocks and grandmother clocks and wee baby ones, all across that lawn. All the time. Just ticking, tick-tick-tick.'

I cannae see jack-shit on the lawn, but that doesnae mean they urnay there. I've seen plenty of shit other people couldnae see and I knew it was real. Fact. I start tae tie the joint back onto the shoelace to swing it back along.

''S alright, I'm wasted anyway, you have it,' she says.

There's a crescent moon out now, and a cow moos in the fields. I double-drag the rest of the joint and flick the roach away.

'Ta for the smoke, I needed that.'

'See you the morn – night.' She ducks back in her window.

It's nice sometimes when you move somewhere and someone chats tae you. Sometimes you just want someone to say hiya. Like, before you batter someone. Like – if you're the hardest girl, you have to fight whether you like it or not. It's cos there's always someone else who wants to be the hardest, and they'll kick your cunt in tae get there if they can. I hate fighting. I'm a pacifist really, but if you dinnae fight – you'll just get battered.

The sky is a vast black. Each star up there is just a wee pinhole letting in pure-white light. Imagine if it was all pure-white light on the other side of that sky.

Nobody's up now. The night-nurse'll be in her tower – everyone else'll have crashed. It's quiet, the grass in the fields rustles and fir trees sway.

Now I can play the birthday game. I couldnae play it in the cells. The whole nearly-dead-cop-in-a-coma-did-you-do-it was getting in the way. Lately it's begun to feel more urgent, like I'm getting ready, but for what? I play it all the time now, I'll keep doing it until I get it right. Every time I play it has to be done exactly the same.

First – construct an identity, do it in order, dinnae fuck around. Start at a starting place, like being born. Not like the birth the social workers told me about; that's just something they made up and wrote down in a file somewhere so's they'd get paid.

In all actuality they grew me – from a bit of bacteria in a Petri dish. An experiment, created and raised just to see exactly how much, fuck you, a nobody from nowhere can take. It's funny having nothing – it means there's fuck-all to lose.

Begin, like always, with a birth. I pick a birth like I believe I was born once, I do it carefully, like it counts. Born in the bushes by a motorway. Born in a VW with its doors open to the sea. Born in Harvey Nichols between the fur coats and the perfume, aghast store-staff faint – story is printed in reputable Sunday broadsheet. Rich, beautiful, but tragically barren couple read it in bed in their palazzo in Italy. Adopt baby immediately. Harvey Nichols offer little baby Harvey Nicole a modelling contract for their Italian baby range. They promise the girl will have free perfume for life. Nice!

Born in an igloo. Born in a castle. Born in a teepee while the moon rises and a midsummer powwow pounds the ground outside. Born in an asylum to the psychotically insane. Born on an adoption certificate on a perfectly mundane Tuesday. Born in Paris. Gay Paree? Birthplace of one beautiful baby girl, Anais? That's the one, for three years now it's been a clear winner – I'm almost beginning to believe it. They'll interview me in Hollywood one day and I'll have tae tell them all about it.

'Where were you born, Anais?'

'Oh, you know, Paris, one early winter's morning.'

'Oh, right. What do your parents do?'

'They travel.'

Paris. Defi-fucking-nately. And me – just a tiny Parisian baby, prettiest the world ever did see. Done. Done. Done. Imagine being born so perfect and cool and lucky? Imagine Paris. Paris! Paris indeed. Close the window, dizzy now, climb into a cold bed.

I bet my Parisian mum wouldnae have one British bone in her. She'd never eat a pie. I like pies, but I wouldnae tell anyone in Paris that. I like fish and chips, macaroni, vege-haggis, deep-fried pizza, chips and chocolate. I dinnae eat much of it, like, but if I let myself – I could easy go like Elvis, fat as fuck! Still, my Parisian mum's culinary purity makes me mildly elated. I always knew my class came from somewhere.

If Paris is done – then next is parents, siblings, an upbringing, detailed memories of garden swings and pine Christmas trees and elaborate Halloween outfits! One year of the birthday game I had hermaphrodite twins as siblings. One grew up to be a physician, the other had orchards in Tuscany; mostly they were boring and gave rubbish gifts.

Another time there were four sisters and a brother who fought in the war. He was a fanny for signing up, but he was vastly preferable tae real-life foster-brothers. Pain in the arse, they are. They either want tae fight you, fuck you or pimp you out tae their pals, and sometimes all three – in that order.

I almost shagged my last foster-brother, I wouldnae have gone anywhere near him usually, but I was wasted. He was such a knob. He used to wear foundation tae cover his spots and he was always wanking in the loo; he was a wimp, ay, I could easily have battered him. We watched a porno and he tried to do it, but I shoved him off. It was totally lame.

There's a noise on the landing. It sounds like someone's walking along there, just slowly, peeping in the doors. It's a man. Wide-rimmed hat. No nose. He's sending back observations to experiment headquarters.

Place one foot out of the bed, then the other, pretend to put the tray out and glance out the gap in my door. I cannae see him. How many times have I stood in strange buildings – looking out a gap in the door? I slide the tray out quietly.

That surveillance window in the watchtower glitters in the dim. Dinnae look up. There could be anyone behind that glass. Five men in suits with no faces. All watching. They can watch.

I dinnae get people, like they all want to be watched, to be seen, like all the time. They put up their pictures online and let people they dinnae like look at them! And people they've never met as well, and they all pretend tae be shinier than they are – and some are even posting on like four sites; their bosses are watching them at work, the cameras watch them on the bus, and on the train, and in Boots, and even outside the chip shop. Then even at home – they're going online to look and see who they can watch, and to check who's watching them!

Is that no weird?

If they knew about the experiment they wouldnae be so keen to throw it all out there. The experiment can see every minute, of every minute, of every single fucking day.

I'm not thinking about the experiment again tonight – this is my time, and there isnae much of it. Pretty soon, I'll be sixteen, or dead. The funniest birthday game was two years ago, that was truly farcical. This year it will be straight reality – but that year! Powwow-wow-wow-wow-wow-wow. Bring it!

3

YEAR THIRTEEN of freakery. The birthday game begins in bed, under my flower duvet. My bed's a single. It got sawed off from a bunk when the other girl moved out. I dinnae share this room any more. It's nice, smells like lemon, and dust.

My foster-mum with the beard is two floors below. I live up here in the attic like a stoned mouse. I spent all this morning watching a spider weave its web in the eaves, it's amazing – so intricate. The spider wasnae bothered when it came back yesterday and found water droplets sparkling its web up. I took a photo of it with my imaginary camera – and stuck it up in my (imaginary) gallery.

Blow three smoke-rings. As the first one expands, I blow two smaller ones through it – it took me two years tae get as good as this. I only started getting the hang of it when I was eleven. Now I could win competitions. The ultimate smoke-ring is a boat, but I umnay a wizard, so I just do circles.

Cars drive by outside, people away on the school run already or going to work in offices in town. The postman clicks open the gate, and a phone rings somewhere. I pull down my pyjama bottoms and wank. The first orgasm is too quick and a bit rubbish, so I do it again slowly. I think of things I shouldnae, like the next-door neighbour, or my physics teacher, or the girl I shared a room with in the house before this.

There's a patch of sunlight on the wall, and it shimmers with raindrops from the attic window. I could stay in bed all day, but there's no way this foster-mum'd let me. I feel about under the bed for my parcel from Hayley. There are two immaculate cones stashed under there as well, one's pure grass, and a few trips from Jay. I look at the parcel from Hayley for a while, turn it around, smell it, shake it – I cannae work out what it is, maybe a top or something. Unwrap it carefully, so as not to rip the paper, and a brightly coloured feather headdress falls out.

For my Indian Squaw xx

It's so soft. Nobody else would think to buy me something like this, it's way cool. I rub the feathers on my cheek.

Three neat squares of paper are sat by my bed as well. Waiting. Jay's presents. The first has a tiny strawberry printed on it; I pick it up on the end of my finger and stick it on my tongue – strawberries for breakast it is.

I finish unwrapping the parcel from Hayley and at the bottom of it there's an old cigarette holder. It's like bone or ivory or something. Fuck! Just like in that film me and Hayley went to see last time I ran away.

Place the last bit of my joint into the cigarette holder, flick my hair back and inhale. The sunlight casts my shadow on the wall and smoke spirals out like curly grey hair. I practise balancing the cigarette holder delicately, like a Fifties movie starlet would. It elongates on the wall like I'm in a silent film. I make a shadow crocodile, and it chats up the silhouette film star – the silhouette film star kisses the crocodile. The credits roll.

My feet are pale on the swirly carpet, which is lifting and falling already – in gentle waves. It's sunny outside. Nice. Beardy weirdy is downstairs. She doesnae shave her beard; it's a totally obvious one, but she isnae bothered how it looks. Me neither, it's kind of debonair on her. Why should women have to shave? I do, like, cos pit-hair is gross, but tae be fair, if I want to grow a beard tomorrow and stubble comes – then that's my business.

I slip on my school skirt, button it, grab a clean shirt. Put the other trips in my shirt pocket, knot my school tie in a bow and wear it at an angle.

The other trips are dancing test-tubes on golden platters, I got the test-tube bits of the print. The squares of paper urnay too thin, or too thick. I float downstairs.

'Morning.'

'Morning. Anais, are you getting yourself intae school today or d'ye want a lift?'

'I'll walk.'

'You better leave soon then.'

The clock reads 8.36 a.m. The breakfast table is odd. The teapot stands with its spout tipping away – handle on its hip – and the checks on the tablecloth shift left, right, left, left, right. Our sugar bowl is blue with yellow chickens on it, and it's heaped high with sugar; each white grain stands out.

My foster-mum places a cup of coffee down in front of me. She's sound, Beard is. I place the second trip on my tongue, let it dissolve in my saliva, then chew methodically.

I jam the wee bit of leftover paper in the gap between my teeth.

Beard puts down some toast and I butter it, add marmalade and eat. I count each chew, the toast is getting bigger in my mouth, chew, chew, chew. I cannae swallow it down! Beard goes out the room and I gob the toast out into the bin.

The sugar granules keep making a high-pitched weeeeee noise.

I smoke three cigarettes in a row and watch them. Beard is okay about the smoking – she's kind of ideal as foster-folks go. I like that she lets me stay here cos she needs a wee bit of cash and she doesnae hide it, it's honest. I've got a deep respect for that kindae honesty. We both nod at the social worker when she comes around. Beard washes my clothes, makes my meals and other than that we stay the fuck out of each other's way. I stub out the third fag and put my plate upside down over the sugar bowl. You cannae be too careful.

'Bye,' I yell and slam the front door shut.

There's a world outside, it's moving so I have a choice – count things, or name them. I'm like that, ay. I always know how many seats there are on a bus. How many poly-styrene squares are on the roof of each classroom at school. When I'm in the cells I know how many bars there are, and if there is a pattern anywhere (flowers on wallpaper, squares on a blanket) I'll count them. I cannae help it. If I umnay counting when I'm tripping, then I'll name things. This morning – I'm naming things. It happens like this when I'm coming up, and sometimes when I'm coming down. It's like I have to name the things I see, just to be sure they are what they say they are.

The curtain lifts between this place and the next, and I name things on the way out and the way back in again. Gate. Path. Door. Gate. Path. Door. Gate. Bin. Dog. Ugly old man. Lamp post. Tree. Three trees. A carrier bag. A turd. A postbox. Boy on a skateboard. Cyclist.

Streets are weird. Maybe they urnay weird, it's hard to tell, but it is stunningly beautiful out this morning. The flowers are pink and white, and it rained earlier, so the air is that super-fresh way.

I walk down through the field, then over the road; the woods are exceptionally elvish this morning. Hayley's waiting by the stile and she's had her hair bobbed, she is so totally gorgeous. She has different-coloured eyes, one blue, one green. That makes her a chimera, that's what it means when you have two different-coloured eyes.

'Alright.'

'Alright.'

'Ta, for my present!'

She grins, gives me a kiss. I feel like a total idiot, I wish I wasnae so high already.

'What's he following you around for?'

I nod behind her and Wankstain glowers at me. Hayley shrugs and kisses me again lightly. She strokes my arm – then there's a flicker as her tongue touches mine, and her fingers brush quickly across my top, it's so quick I sometimes wonder if I dream it. She smells like a good clean thing in a good clean world.

I sometimes think if there is a God and he found out that I was going out with Hayley, he'd shoot a cherub. Some people urnay meant to know the true shitness of life, it isnae meant to be that way for them. Hayley's one of those people. I'd never have her near the kind of folk I know, I'd never let her meet Jay, no way. It's not about other people, we are just for us. We kiss and we walk and we watch movies, and she treats me so sweet. She's never made me feel embarrassed to be me. Not once.

'Do you know much about surgery, like cos of your dad?' I ask her.

'A bit, not much really.'

'I was thinking about women surgeons, like are there many? Like not even here, like maybe in Paris? Brain surgeons, tae be exact.'

'Are you playing the birthday game, Anais?'

'No!'

'Did you give that up?'

'Aye.'

I forgot she knew. She's the only person I ever told about that, she got me to tell her about it one time when I was pissed. I informed her that real birthdays are overrated. Mine are anyway. Well, I get my birthday money off the social worker, obviously, but I dinnae wait for cards, or cakes, or wee fucking sing-songs. I denounced real birthdays when I found Teresa – I dinnae tell anyone about them any more. I cannae believe it was nearly two years ago already that I found her dead. Mother Teresa – where art thou?

Stabbed hen. Fucking pissed off about it as well, ay.

Dinnae think about it. That's the trick. I wonder if my biological mum thinks of me on my real birthday? Or maybe a scientist just looks fondly at a test-tube.

Hayley takes my hand and we lean back against the stile and she kisses me again. Breathe her in. I want to forget. Everything but this.

'Are you okay?' she asks.

'I'm fine.'

'Are you thinking about Teresa?'

'A bit.'

She strokes my hand. That's all. She did that for hours one night – we were camping in her back garden and it was warm out; we lay holding each other, her stroking my hand, our heads poking out the end of the tent so we could watch for shooting stars.

'D'ye want one?'

I offer Hayley a trip but she shakes her head. I wish Hayley wasnae so square, but she is, she's far too square to be a circle. I am a circle. Circles are infinite. I umnay meant for Hayley and we both know it. She's just a perfect kiss.

Tracers begin to materialise across the sky, wee bright wriggly things everywhere.

'Are you coming tae school, Anais?'

'Nope. Dinnae tell anyone you've seen me.'

'As if I would!'

She gives me another kiss and then wanders away down the woods with Wankstain. I cannae stand that prick. He totally tried tae rape me after the school disco when I passed out in the bog. I woke up as he was trying tae yank my knickers down, so I battered him. Arsehole. He'll no try that again.

I wave at Hayley when she reaches the road and look up at the sky tae let God know – he can put the gun away.

Kick up leaves, swish, swish. They swirl around my ankles, a river of them, all different colours. Ochre. Gold. Red. My tree stump's empty and there's nobody around, they'll all be in school. I pull off my shoes and shirt, slip my skirt down and shove it at the back of a bush. My plastic bag is still here – bonus. I keep all sorts of shit in this bush, it's my only permanent chest of drawers.

Undo the knot in the plastic bag, and inside there's a pair of damp shorts, platform shoes I bought last month, a vest and a cardigan. I pick leaves off my cardigan until it's all pristine. You can see veins on the leaves that look just like the lines on your hand, especially if you hold them up to the sun.

Pull out my new feather headdress from my school bag, and fasten it at the back so it fits perfectly. The leaves whisper – I know exactly what they mean. Nod my head and the feathers ruffle out around me. I pick a flower and admire the tiny hairs on its stem. The clouds begin to race, and I decide on who my parents were, right there and then.

I am a love-child, conceived during a ritualistic peyote shaman trip. I am the sole offspring of Timothy Leary's spirit-guide (an Amazonian eagle-woman) and a forest nymph. Teresa met Leary once. She walked his dog. I wasnae ever really sure what she meant by that.

Lay down and run my bare feet across the grass. I'm on the bank near a river, I can smell wild garlic and wet ferns, water and deodorant. I've run out of perfume, I'll need to buy some when my clothing allowance comes in; that's the only perk of being in care, ay, a monthly (pitiful) clothing allowance. Some foster-parents dinnae let you have your clothing allowance, though, they just keep it for themselves! Beard gives me mine. God bless Beard.

Flip onto my stomach and weave a daisy chain. I make it super-long, so I can wind it around twice. Lace the flowers through my hair, lay back and watch the clouds drift.

The third trip sits on my tongue at noon. It's here I begin to tip, everything goes a little bitty sideways, so I walk kindae crab-like. My arms feel strange and my skin goes all see-through, and it feels dirty and just like – wrong hair. Just wrong. Hair so wrong it's not funny, it feels big on my head, and fluffy. Like a mane. Long and fluffy. Long dark fluffy hair. Fuck!

'Alright, Anais?'

I sit up and shake my headdress. It takes a minute tae remember his name. Little gnome. Odd wee gnome in a tracksuit. He's wearing two-stripe trainers and gold rings. He's short. I bet his balls are bald. Man, the birds are loud up there in the trees. 'S like the fucking rainforest. 'S so pretty.

'Mark?'

'Are ye going somewhere, Anais?'

'Nope.'

'Noh? No like, a fancy-dress party?'

He's staring at the headdress.

'D'ye like it?' I ask him.

'Aye, I s'pose so. You dinnae want any gear, do you, Anais? Hospital speed, like?'

'Aye! Sound. Can I get it on chucky?'

'Cash up front.'

'How much, like?'

'Seeing as it's you, I'll give you three grams fir a tenner?'

Three grams for a tenner's alright, though it's probably cut. It's still cheaper to buy it in bulk but I cannae get bulk any more. I count the money out. I've been saving up from my outing allowance; on my outings I'm meant tae go and do shit that will help heal me after seeing Teresa dead. Okay, then. I'll bowl myself better. I'll ice-skate tae fucking happiness every Friday fucking night.

I dinnae go on outings with the money. I just get wasted and go and rub up and down on Jay when we're kissing, I prefer that to the other stuff, but he prefers the other stuff.

'So what have you been up to?' I ask Mark.

'Just kicking aboot, Anais – wee bit of this, wee bit of that, keeping my fingers in plenty pies, ay, hen. I've been working for they guys Jay knows, d'ye ken them, fae the top flats?'

Jay cannae stand they guys, he's always owe them money. Now I think about it, he cannae stand Mark. I take the wrap off him and stuff half the money I should intae his hand.

'Ta, Mark, see ye.'

'I thought you werenae going anywhere?'

'Later!'

'Wait a minute, are you busy the day?'

'How?'

'Well, you could pick up some stuff for me. I'll give you a few pills for going, like? The guys name's Roo. He lives here.' He holds out a scrap of paper with an address on it.

I read the address. It's about a million miles away. I take the piece of paper and turn to walk away and Mark goes to walk in step with me. I stop and stare at him.

'I'll get away the now then, Anais. See you later, ay.'

He crosses the road and smirks back at me. Loser. Fucking troll. I stuff the bit of paper with the address in my pocket, and unwrap my speed. What a weird wee envelope. He's folded it wrong. I do mine way neater than that. He's used a porno mag tae make his wraps with – I've got a bit of some guy's knob on mine, mid-cum-shot, gross. Unfold it and breathe in the cat-piss smell and wonder if it'll take the edge of the colours. Lick it clean off the wrap, it's bitter, but easier than snorting.

Everything accelerates. There is a bicycle ride. A coffee cup. A bus. A boat. A train. There's a toilet on the train so white and cold I begin to wonder if I'm dead. This cubicle feels like a fridge. I bet a body kept in here would take years tae decay.

Listen tae the chug and hope I umnay dead. What if I'm dead and I just think I umnay?

Dead on a train.

Dead-dead.

Chug chug chug chug.

Train station, ooh, be quiet, breathe quiet. I laugh, but my laugh jumps back at me. It's fucking freaky. Chug. Chug. Chug. I sit on the loo and stare at the door too scared tae make a noise. I try to breathe right quiet, but my breath grows as loud as the train chugs, and the chugs say ridiculous things.

Lift up the toilet lid. Dinnae look at hands or veins. Sit and take a long nervous piss. I pick a scab on my knee and close my eyes.

Flashes. Fluorescent. Witches flying to and fro on the inside of my eyelids, they cackle and fly up in packs of twelve. One sticks her fingers up at me, winks, then does a skid out of sight.

Open my eyes. Tiny screws on the door handle stare at me. I stare back at them but they dinnae look away. They spiral round and round and round. The lock mouth below them grins. I might never be able tae leave this cubicle. Fact.

Heart really begins tae pound and I dinnae like this any more – I need to come back down. Shit! Red spots of blood splash onto the floor, my nose is heavy, and blood streaks down my chin. I grab a wadge of tissue, shaking. Who gets a nosebleed on acid? Shit. Shit. Shit!

My hands are see-through in the mirror. Fuckfuckfuckfuck. Veins sticking out. Take another long pee, it's lime-green. I drop a bloody tissue down the bog and flush twice. The train stops. This is it, if I'm getting out – this is it.

Pinch nose hard, tilt head back and walk. The platform echoes and the announcer warbles and something crackles and a man in an orange waistcoat gnashes his teeth.

Nobody stops me. I make a phone call in an old phone box with one windowpane left and roach cards all over it. Call 07926145601 for a good fuck. The black Madonna – £10 a massage. Girls, all ages, no short visits. Transsexual gives good massage, water sports extra.

There is a street and another, a high-rise and a lift. All I need to do is ask for the bag. Get the bag. Go.

The lift pings, then there is a door. Knock. Knock. Knock.

'Are you a shaman?' he asks me.

'Aye.'

I shake my headdress.

'Come in,' he says.

The guy opens the door wide. There is a hall but no carpet, there's no anything really. I'll not embarrass him, so what if he squats. In the living room a muscular iguana turns around on the windowsill. His claws tap, tap, tap.

'This is Chief.'

'Alright,' I say.

Chief the iguana blinks.

'You urnay bleeding, are you?' the guys asks.

'No.'

He's a sly fucker is Chief. I know it and Chief knows it, and the guy tries tae kiss me but his breath smells like sick. I shake my feather headdress and begin to do a war dance. It's the only way.

'What's your name?'

'Anais. Mark sent me, ay.'

'Did he now?' He looks me up and down.

'What's your name again?'

'Roo.'

He's still looking me up and down. He's a right skinny cunt and he fucking stinks. He folds down onto the floor like a fucking locust (two-parts insect), it's in his legs. It's in the exposed knots of vertebrae along his neck. He should put a top on, his tummy is fucking concave. He soaks a wee ball of cotton wool and looks up at me.

'D'ye want some?'

'No,' I say, but I dinnae think he hears me.

He's boring as fuck. Heroin makes people like that, ay, it's dull as shit – so's crack, the whole thing's lame, there's nothing there tae learn. It isnae like psychedelics. Every time I take a trip I return tae a world that waits for me. Trips are just the ticket in. Lately, the experiment have began to follow me through, I'll have to stop soon.

Roo gestures at the bag of Es on the windowsill. I pick it up and turn it over. All the wee pills have a stamp on the front. Bonus. I take one and continue tae stomp the floor.

'No, that's all wrong!'

He's looking up at me, he drops his spoon. It's empty now anyway. His gear's in the needle.

'Noh, really, noh, I'm sorry, it's not your fault; noh, dinnae get upset now, just wait a minute,' he says.

He's tightening the elastic around his arm, takes his shot, then he's away. I'll take the bag when he wakes, or I could leave him a note . . . *Taken bag* . . . but I just feel like dancing.

The man nods and I powwow-wow, and Chief taps out a beat. A while later insect-oid-us-smack-a-dick-tus comes to again. I keep doing my powwow-wow and Chief is beginning tae get freaked out. Mr Locust puts his lighter down.

'You are unbelievably fuckable,' he says.

'Really?'

'Really. You're so fucking . . . wasted, look at you! I think I love you.'

'D'ye know what I love?'

'What?'

'The clouds, and the stars, and the grass – it sounds silly, ay. But I do. I fucking love them.'

I do, I love them, I love this feeling. He pads out of the room, then he comes back in and holds out a jellyfish. No, it's not a jellyfish, it's a bikini with polka-dots on it.

'Try this.'

'I dinnae like polka-dots.'

'Aye, but there's a cool skull and crossbones, right there,' he says.

There is as well, just there, a skull and crossbones right on the arse. Just a wee one. It's cute. I change in the kitchen and start my dance again in bare feet.

'That's better!' He grins.

'Tell Chief tae stop watching.'

'He's not watching, honest. Best keep at it, though!' he says solemnly and so I do.

He goes in the kitchen at one point and grabs my shoes. He opens the window and lobs them out, then he throws away my shorts, my vest. Chief edges away from him. Powwow-wow-wow-wow-wow-wow. A clock on the wall spins time, and in the other world an ice-cream van tinkles and children shout and the sun is clearly furious, but we dinnae pay it any attention.

Roo takes his cock out, it's got red marks, all up and down it. He puts a needle down and swoons.

The windows are so bare. There's a high-rise across the way and there's three down the hill and they all point at the sky. Look at that ice-cream van – seventeen floors below, d'ye think they can see me from down there? Me. Up here. Arms raised, doing an Indian war cry. Whoop, whoop, whoop!

He won't wake, I kick him, but he doesnae move.

Me and Chief stare each other out, we circle around slowly in the age-old voodoo way, and when I get to the door for the fifteenth time I escape. The hallway's dark and smells like pish. Pick a door. Any door. Bathroom, okay.

Pull the light, there's no knob on the end of the string, just a knot someone tied. Dirty knot, dirty string.

Must find fire.

I kneel down on the dirty lino, and it's sticky, so I shove a damp towel under my legs. Must find fire. Quick. Must find fire, must find fire. Find fire. Fire, fire, fire. The word sounds weird, how weird does it sound? Shit! My reflection is in a round cracked mirror by the toilet. Stiff nipples, dirty skin, strange neck, see-through veins. There is a large bruise on my thigh and thunder in the hallway, huge claps of it. It sounds like a storm that shouts.

I use a teaspoon to unscrew the front from the radiator cabinet. I lift bits out and yank bits away and I'm almost there, inside, where the fire will be, when the door is flung open. A man in black stares. I push my headdress back up on my forehead and the feathers wilt tae the left.

'What?'

He looks at me. Maybe he's here for Chief, or maybe he's having a party? Pick up the bag of Es and offer him one, but he reaches a long arm out and takes them all.

'That's fucking greedy,' I tell him.

'What's your name, love?'

'Cloud.'

The plebeian is clearly impolite, but it's better to let it go, for that is the shaman way. He doesnae know I was born in a trance witnessed only by an Indian chief and his daughters, but I was. I am above greed.

The man stuffs the bag of pills in his pocket, then he shouts in thunder to somebody else. Somebody else appears with Chief in a cat basket. Chief grins at me.

'What is going on here then?'

The man holding Chief seems to be asking me. What does he mean by *here*? Here as in where?

They both keep gazing at me and I blink. They are definitely expecting me to say something. What? What are the plebeians expecting? Perhaps they are awed by my shaman aura – probably they are.

'Fire.'

Gesture at the radiator and pull off another bit of metal. The slow people are just standing there. Maybe they are humbled, yet confused by meeting the daughter of a shaman and a forest nymph, here, in this bathroom. It's most likely. I must be kind tae the simple mortals, for that is the shaman way.

'D'ye have fire?'

I ask it politely but they dinnae answer – fucking toss-pots. Chief rolls his reptilian eyes, his nails tip-tap loudly on the plastic cat basket as he turns himself around, then grins at me again.

'Skin up then?' I say.

I hold my hand out for an E, cos shamans should be happy, everyone knows that. The people dinnae seem tae get it, though. They pick me up off the floor and walk me out to the lift, draping a big black jacket around me. I'm shaking. It's cold. I cannae quite remember why I'm wearing a bikini.

One of the men goes back into the flat, then he comes out with the guy's trainers.

'Put these on, I cannae find yours and there's broken glass in that lift. Put them on!'

I shove the trainers on, they are twice as big as my feet. In the lift I do a powwow dance, but the trainers have given me big clown feet. I try one more powwow-wow, but it's horrible and klutzy and the trainers trip over each other. I'm sad now. Really fucking sad.

When we get downstairs, Roo is being taken away on a stretcher.

'Where's Mr Locust going?'

'He isnae well. D'ye know him?'

'Nope.'

As we walk through the car park one of the guys tries tae take my headdress off.

'What the fuck d'ye think you're doing?'

'You need tae take it off and get in the car!'

'Dinnae touch the fucking headdress!'

I scream so loud that windows open as far up as the eighteenth floor. I scream harder. Curtains twitch. Lights go on. People look down and point until the men just shove me in the back seat with my headdress on. We drive out of the estate in silence. Chief's in his cat basket next to me. The slow people have a blue light. They're fucking odd ravers.

'Can you put the radio on?' I ask.

'No. We cannae. Are you gonnae tell us what you've been up to today then?'

'It's my birthday.'

'Having a party, were you?'

I grin at them, cuffed, in my bikini, headdress squint, watching spirals of light dance across the sky. I cannae quite remember where they are taking me but fuck it, ay – maybe it's a better party where we're going, hopefully there will be fire there.

When we get there, there's nae music. Just a drunk woman sat on a plastic chair in a room with a bright light. She's pished herself.

'We are booking you with possession and intent tae supply – do you have anything tae say?'

'This party's pish.'

4

IF YOU stare at the watchtower long enough it looks like a bug. Especially if the sun is reflected in it, like wee golden irises. Or if the moon is in it, like last night. Then it has white eyes that follow you around. All the floors and bedroom doors are reflected in the window. Even me, I am in it too, looking up at myself.

I'm sitting on the third-floor landing – in the lotus position, throwing up a rubber ball and catching it. I took it off the curly-haired laddie; his name's Brian and he's a freak. I have thrown the ball one hundred and seventy times without dropping it. If I drop it – the pig will die.

If the pig dies, I'm getting put into a secure unit until I'm eighteen. Then jail. Except I won't make it, I won't make sixteen – I'll be dead. Then it'll be me and the pig, and Teresa, and Jake from the last home with the noose around his neck. All of us sad bastards sitting playing poker in the last cell before Sheol. Jake in the last home was a fucking arse. He's better off dead. It's sick, but true – some people take living out on anyone who'll let them.

The thud when I catch the ball is a perfect rhythm. The

bug-eyes are watching. That watchtower wants its face smashed in. It wants a smile drawn on it and a petrol bomb up its arse.

Throw, catch, throw, catch. It's the only sound.

Everyone is at school apart from Brian, cos he gets collected by a taxi and taken to a special school cos he has special needs. Translate that as – cannot be trusted with civilians.

There's a cute guy downstairs in the breakfast area, he's eating toast and staring at a wall. He keeps scratching his balls through his trackie bottoms and he's wearing Adidas two-stripe trainers; they look like an original design, but they urnay, they're just a retro reissue. Jay used tae wear the exact same style.

I wonder if PC Craig's eyes were open, when they found her on Love Lane? Do they stay open if you're in a coma? When you go into hospital – if you're in a coma, do they shut your eyes like what they do if you're dead?

The polis kept asking me where I was that morning and I cannae remember. Well, I remember being in a park, and the waltzers in town. The last thing I can mind is the waltzers – then nothing. It was the ketamine that did it, Troll Mark's fucking ketamine and four days caning it. I didnae tell the polis that. I didnae tell them I was so fucked up I couldnae even mind my own name.

They kept on going on about a kosh. I've never even held a kosh. I saw mad Chrissie swinging one once – but that was years ago. Me and Chrissie were on acid in a house with black and white checks all over the walls and her bloke had just died of Aids, and there was a paedo with money following us about, cos of me. I was eleven, I know that cos it was before Teresa died. I cannae even mind how I met mad Chrissie. I cannae mind that – and I cannae mind how I got blood on my skirt.

I keep getting wee flashes. It'll come back, I'll remember, you always remember something eventually, ay. The pigs dinnae give a fuck if I did it or not; they just want me locked up and that's that, they dinnae care what it is they put me away for. It's not just cos of the death-threats. She deserved them. They fucking know she did.

I drop the ball. Shit!

Pig's dead.

I'm dead.

It rolls along the landing. The cook opens a hatch downstairs and the radio clicks on in the kitchen, and some tinny song plays. Thank fuck! It's like a fucking tomb in here.

I am not wearing any socks, my feet are a size two – my feet are quality. Nae knobbly bits. They might be my best feature, or my eyes. Or probably it's my hair, black, long, thick and wavy. I'm gonnae bump down these stairs on my arse. Fifteen-going-on-two, I am.

Bump.

Bump.

Bump.

Cute looks up and I cross my eyes, make a mongo face at him and he grins. He'll tell me what I need tae know. Whenever you arrive at a new unit the staff always tell you to not say what you're in for, and it's always the first thing you get asked. Usually one person tells you what everyone else is in for – then they go away and tell everyone else what you're in for.

The breakfast hatch is open and there's a carton of milk,

cold, icy-cold, perfect. Cornflakes, brilliant. Pour cereal until it's *almost* spilling over the edge. Then milk up to the rim. Walk with it held out like precious treasure – do not spill!

I sit down with the stealth of a vampire. Begin to eat. Crunch. A perfect crunch. Mm, mmm, mmmmm. The cook isnae looking at us, he rolls out pastry and listens to his radio. He's wearing blue football socks and he's got the aura of a man just out of jail. I lift what's left of the fresh coffee while he's not looking; it must have been made for a staff meeting earlier. Score. Cute watches while I pour myself a mug of black coffee, dump three sugars in and stir. I start on my cornflakes again.

'Are you gonnae be in for dinner later, Anais?'

Eric has creeped up behind me and asks this while staring at my cereal, not at me. My cereal evidently has some secret information on me, that it's about to reveal. I didnae even know he was in. Fucking wankstain. He doesnae notice the coffee pot. Ha. Nil points to the student, one to me. No fresh coffee for your break later – fucking loser. He looks nervous and he still won't meet my eyes; he must be reading my files.

'Anais, are you in for dinner? I asked.'

'Depends on what it is.'

'It's chicken.'

'I dinnae eat meat.'

I drink the rest of the milk out of my bowl, but keep my pinky tipped all posh like Teresa used to do. Teresa went to a private school when she was younger, so did Pat. Airs and graces. I slam the bowl down and Eric shites his pants. Cute laughs.

'You'll have tae eat the same meal, just without the meat then, if you have an aversion,' Eric says sullenly.

'I dinnae have an aversion.'

'Are you a registered vegetarian?'

'Why, d'ye need a licence?'

'You need tae be registered.'

'Are you a registered prick?'

'I won't take cheek, Anais. I'll bring this up in changeover.'

'You do that.'

Eric's right angry. Fuck him! His casual clothing is wrong as well, somebody's ironed his jeans so there's a line in the middle.

Brian is in the lounge area. He balances a school bag on his ankles and lifts, then lowers it, for weights.

'What are you waiting for?' Eric asks him as he heads towards the office.

'Taxi.' Brian pushes his glasses back up his nose, they are held together with silver tape on the right arm.

A car beeps outside.

'Your taxi is the next one, Brian!' Brenda calls down the hall.

He glances over. He wants his ball back. I roll it over the table and he looks at me out the side of his head. He's a foetus with teeth. Brenda walks out the front door; the beep must be her lift, she must have been on sleepover last night. I need more coffee, and a fucking smoke.

'So, you're Anais Hendricks?' Cute smiles at me.

'Nope.'

He grins wider, he's got dimples. I smile back. I cannae help it. It's one of they awkward ones where it seems like you like somebody *that* way, but actually you dinnae! You're just smiling like that cos you're a moron!

'I'm John, pleased tae meet you.'

He shakes my hand. That's unnerving.

'So, you've been in care a while, ay. How long?' he asks.

'I got taken in when I was born, moved through twenty-four placements until I was seven, got adopted, left there when I was eleven, moved another twenty-seven times in the last four years.'

That's that out the road. I've said it so many times it's like reciting a wee bunch of words that dinnae mean anything. I could be reciting the ingredients for cornflakes. There's some football chat programme on the radio in the kitchen. I fucking hate football – it's the most depressing game in the world.

'D'ye never meet your folks?'

He swings back on his chair. He likes me, I can tell.

'No, I didnae meet Mummy and Daddy, or anyone else like that.'

I debate whether to have a slice of toast. I didnae eat one meal in the cells, I dinnae trust anything they give you in there.

'You never got adopted again then?' he asks, and he's not even being that subtle about checking me out. He grins at me and, despite myself, I grin back.

'Have you ever heard of an eleven-year-old being adopted?' I say.

'I suppose not, ay. Guess you're fucked then.'

He'd make a stunning vampire. Wonder what he kisses like.

'What's he in for?' I nod at Brian.

'His mummy and daddy had enough of him being a naughty boy. Running away. Nicking things. They used tae bring him Tupperware tubs full of cakes, tae share with his pals, ay. Except he's no got any pals. I think they thought we all had midnight feasts and went on adventures. They dinnae come now though, ay. They dinnae come *now*, Brian, your folks, ay?'

'Why?'

'You dinnae ken yet?' John swings back on his chair.

'Ken what?'

'Brian's sick.'

'What, like good sick?'

'Noh, no good sick; like fucking very fucking bad sick,' he says.

'I'll try not tae faint,' I tell him.

'He raped a dog,' John says loudly.

'He fucking what?'

'Last Thursday. Raped a dog – ay, Brian?' he shouts.

The curly-haired laddie turns away, his cheeks flaming.

'Aye, the cunt kidnapped it, raped it, threw it off a wall – broke its fucking legs.'

We both turn to stare, but the laddie's face is blank. No emotions. Nothing. Sick as fuck. I mean I can be a cunt, but I dinnae batter someone unless they go for me first and I'd never, ever pick on a kid, or an animal, or some old person.

I'll pick on the polis, aye, but only when they ask for it. PC Craig went tae war with me, not the other way around. Brian rams his index finger up his nose; he knows we can see him doing it, he's liking it cos we're watching. He inspects the bogey and then flicks it away.

'What the fuck's he in here for then? He should be in secure,' I say.

John raises his eyes to the locked fourth-floor doors.

'Jesus Christ!' My heart sinks.

I'm not going up there with that. Or up north with the kiddie-killers. I'll not make it. I'm hard, but I'm nothing like them; they urnay even hard, they're just scum. There's nothing good in them. Teresa used tae tell me that all the fucking time.

Aye, hen, you cannae reason with scum, you cannae talk tae scum, you cannae associate with scum, cos if there is anything good or nice or decent in you – they'll break it.

I used to think everyone had some good in them. They don't, though, do they? I have no empathy for scum. None. I mean, I could kill a kiddie-killer. Easily. It wouldnae make me feel bad, I dinnae think it would make anyone feel bad, not even God.

'Joan said the secure unit is on hold for now – asbestos or something?' I ask John.

'Aye, the staff are gutted, though. I heard in a meeting, they wanted you right up there, you were gonnae be their star pupil.'

Brian has lifted up his top and is picking fluff out his belly button.

'He's giving me the boak,' I say.

'Aye. He has that effect on people.'

'Was it a big dog?'

Brian cranes to see if his taxi is coming. He's pretending not to listen in, but he can hear every word.

'I dinnae think so! That wee bastard wouldnae pick on a big dog, it was a wee fucking runt, ay. He'll move on, they start off with animals, then they move on to people – he'll do a pensioner before the year's out. He'll end up with they kiddie-killers up north. Your support worker, Angus, drove the last two up there, did you ken that?' John asks.

'No, I didnae.'

'Aye, the two in the paper.'

'They should just fucking shoot them.'

'They give Angus the ones nobody else can handle.' He smiles at me.

'Aye, I fucking bet they do. How'd they know Brian raped a dog?'

'Shortie and wee Dylan saw him; they were just walking back from school, and they see that! Shortie took a run at him just as he pulls his knob out of its arse and throws it off a wall. She leathered him while Dylan ran tae get the staff. They didnae find the dog's owner, but they've got the name-tag, they had tae put it down, like. Probably did it a favour – who'd want tae live after being raped by that?'

I cannae face cereal. Toast. Nothing.

'So, what are you in for?'

'Battered my grannie,' John says.

'That's not fucking funny,' I say.

'Noh, she didnae think so, either.'

'Are you fucking serious?'

'I'm kidding, Anais, calm down – fuck! I'm sorry, okay, bad joke. Nothing major, I used tae do over shops with my mum, and my aunties, down in Leeds. That's where I was moved from.'

'You dinnae sound English.'

'I umnay. My ma and all the family are from Glasgow, they just moved down there a few years ago. Mum's got an appeal tae get out the jail in a few days, fingers crossed.'

'I hear the homes are worse down south.'

'They are. I was only in one, though, so I dinnae know really. They kept me there for six weeks before they sent me here.'

'Where were you before that, like?'

'Some loopy teacher was fostering me, until she had a breakdown. I burnt down her work, ay.'

I begin laughing, I cannae help it. That's the best placement-breakdown story ever, mine isnae such a good one. Prozzie mum gets stabbed – it doesnae have the same funny vibe.

'Where did she work, like?'

'She was a teacher in a disabled school.'

'You burnt down a disabled school?'

'Aye. I did.'

He looks sad, and I begin laughing again – it's so wrong you couldnae make it up. I'm beginning to like him.

'I umnay proud of it!'

Brian's taxi pulls up outside. He jumps up and hurries out the door.

'You're gonnae get battered later,' John shouts after him.

The door slams.

'Aye, so then I burnt her hoose down, flat tae the fucking deck, pal – you should have seen it! She'd pissed me off by then, though, d'ye know what I mean?'

We're laughing so hard the cook looks out. Some woman pulls up outside, jumps out of her car and then posts something through the front door.

'Christ!' John says.

'What?'

'She's a local mum, ay. They've got a campaign down the village tae get this place shut already. They're worried we'll fuck their children. Contaminate their bloodline.'

'They should be so fucking lucky. Have you seen their kids – nobody wants tae fuck them!'

John laughs and, just like that, I know we'll be mates.

'Did you move here from a foster placement?' he asks.

'No. I've not been in a family for,' I count back on my fingers, 'about ten months. I prefer units anyway, they're less hassle.'

It's a relief just to chat with someone. In the cells I thought I'd go mental, I hardly ever speak to police in the interviews. Hayley used to be the best person to speak with, until she moved away to Singapore with her dad. She still sends e-mails but it's not the same. I used to speak to Jay, but not since he got put in jail; now it's just texts and him being weird.

'D'ye never find a family you liked, Anais?'

'Families are overrated. They're like elephants.'

'Elephants are sound, aye, with their big ears and that,' John says.

'Elephants are cunts.'

'Noh, they urnay, nae danger!'

'Aye, they are. I mean, look – if you're an elephant, you're only alright if you belong! Like if you're *in* the pride or the tribe, or whatever the fuck it is they live in.'

'What's the pride?' John asks.

'It's like the group, the family; if you're in that and you've got a ma and a da, or some auntie elephants or some cousins

– then you're alright. They'll play football with you. They'll protect you if the lions come, and if you drown in the river they'll be right sad about it; they'll stand over your body and sing you some nice fucking songs. They'll even bury you with branches.'

'Aye, exactly!' John says.

'Aye. But if you're an orphan? Ye'll starve. Tae death. Alone.'

He doesnae say a thing for a good minute.

'That's no nice.'

'Noh, it's not fucking nice,' I say.

'What, they'll no even feed you? What if you're, like, a three-month-old baby elephant?'

'You'll stand there until you're fucking emaciated. If you approach them, they'll kick you in the pus, and tell you tae get tae fuck.'

'Maybe it's a strain on resources if they need tae feed an extra mouth?' he tries.

'How? Are leaves expensive?'

'Maybe there urnay enough leaves?'

'Aye – well, maybe it's not that. Maybe elephant matriarchs are just mean old fucks, maybe they dinnae *want* tae share their bananas.'

The cook glances out the hatch and keeps wiping bunkers down. John shakes his head and grins, and it's infectious. I have tae look away. Jay would be pissed off.

'I umnay fooled. Not by families, and not by fucking elephants.'

'I can see why they want you banged right up on the top floor!'

'Aye?'

'Aye, they're gonnae get you up there and throw away the key, mate. And you put a pig in a coma – I mean, if she dies! If she dies, you're fucked, mate.'

I've already finished my coffee, so I just look at the bottom of the mug. I'd rather be dead today. I'm bored of places, tables, windows, shite food, cheap deodorant. Same pish, different unit. Families with their wee petitions. I want to live in a hotel on a side street in Paris – I dinnae belong, not here.

I put my mug down and he rubs his hair and sighs. He's stunning with the morning sun coming in the window.

'I mean, they say you put a cop in a coma,' he adds quietly.

'Do they now?'

'Well, first they said she was dead.'

'Right.'

'Then we figured they'd have put you in John Kay's secure unit if she was dead, ay. I didnae mean tae put you on a downer. Sorry.'

He takes his bowl over to the hatch. His narrow hips are bare, and his trackie bottoms sit low. His hair is shaved short and his skin is light brown. He wears a gold ring on his left hand, and a gold bracelet, and a chain.

'You're prettier than they said, like a lot prettier,' he says.

I cannae speak. My chest's all closed up. I want to sleep.

'It's really nice tae meet you, Anais. If you need anything, just gimme a shout, aye?'

He wanders up the stairs, slams one of the bathroom doors fully open. The shower blasts on and he starts singing in the bathroom. 'S some crappy dance tune that came out last month.

Steam rises out the door and I want tae go up there, follow him around with a camera. Take photos of his hands, and his sneakers, his hips, and the indent on the small of his back. I love that indent on a guy's back.

Boner Brian. That's disgusting. No wonder they've already started a petition trying to get this place shut down – I might take a walk down the village hall myself, and autograph the thing twice.

John is back out the shower already. Dance music booms out from his bedroom. He drags on jeans, and a hooded top. The whole door thing, supposedly giving you privacy if you stand to the left, doesnae work. Cannae see in from the ground floor? As if. I can see right in, especially if he's standing in the middle of his room.

I look up at the watchtower. They can see in, but they can see everything, whether you're left, right or in the corner.

John sprays half a can of deodorant on, then he wanders back along to the bathroom. He leaves the door open as he rubs some wax on his head, looks at himself this way, then that way. He knows he's good-looking. How could he not?

It's freezing in here, these old buildings are always totally Baltic. The skies are blue today, but it's blustery, autumn's well settled in already. I'm gonnae go over and check out that wee ornate door with Fire Exit written above it – just as soon as John fucks off.

'Where you off to?' I ask as he heads towards the office.

'Clap-clinic. Later, Anais.'

His eyes are blue and his hair's black. If you met him like at school, or hanging out somewhere getting wasted, most people would just think he looked like a radge, but when you see him up close, and look at him – not his trackies or that – he's graceful. He just is.

He gets money off the staff, then swaggers out, walks away down the drive.

It's just me now. Chef's in the kitchen. Eric's in the office. Everyone else is at school. The watchtower windows reflect the sun, and the big bug-eyes stare, and it's totally obvious that watchtower doesnae even need staff in it; it just watches – all on its own.

5

LIFT BOWL, put it through hatch, smile at the cook. Anyplace you live, the cook isnae a man to cross. He unties his apron and switches off the radio. I walk past the dining tables, then the living-room area, past the watchtower, over to the fire exit on the furthest-away turret. You have to practise walking quietly, you have to will yourself silent – barely even breathe.

Place my hand on the wee ornate door and push. It gives. My heart skips as I slip inside the turret; it reeks of damp in here, and it's dim. There's a wooden gate on the bottom step and a No Entry sign. Bags of concrete are stacked along the wall. I shove the gate and stumble up, following dusty footprints on worn steps. Round, round, round.

The spirals get smaller, the stairs narrower. I need tae stop smoking so much, I'm wheezy. It isnae the fags so much as the joints – cardboard roaches are a killer. One hundred and seventeen steps; one more floor and it's the penthouse. The hairs on my arms rise.

Fourth landing, fourth floor, there's a black door. I shove it hard but it won't give. It's locked. It's only a wooden door, with a Yale lock. I could get that open if I had my metal card, but I dinnae, cos the polis taxed it off me.

Keep glancing back down the stairs, it's like someone's there but when I look they disappear. It's dark and cold and musty. My heart thuds, it's a dull sound. Lay against the door, flatten my hand and listen. What if someone's waiting on the other side of this door – their hand where my hand is?

My breathing is loud. Somewhere outside someone shouts. I press my whole body weight on the door and rattle the handle. It won't budge. Fuck!

That's rubbish as fuck, I really thought I could get in there for a minute. Fuck it! At least I found a joint in my school jotter, it's flat but smokeable. I had to add another few skins to tighten it up. Light it and blow three smoke-rings; they hover in the still air. Inhale and it glows all red in the dark. The first smoke of the day is always the best one, especially if you double-drag it back-to-back.

This turret's well draughty. A window leads out onto the roof further up. I open the latch on the wee window and pull myself up so I can look right out.

Wow! It's amazing – I have never seen skies this big. The fields go out for miles and miles, and there's a flat attic ledge-thing tae sit on. Slate roof tiles, though. If you fell off from up here, you'd be dead.

This window would be the only escape if they got me into the secure unit. If they get it built while I'm still here, this turret will be the main Fire Exit. Turn around and look back up at the locked door, the only access to where the secure unit will be. Imagine if the experiment were just waiting behind that door to welcome me in.

'Welcome, Anais, we knew you'd figure it out in the end!'

Then they would inject me in the head – with a big needle full of shit that makes your skull see-through. Then they would put me in a box. The box would have a light switch that'd make my thoughts glow a different colour, in my see-through skull. So they could read them. Forced telepathy – it's the last step for total mind control.

Imagine them waiting to hand over a wee award for finally catching them out! They'd clear it all up.

'Yes, yes, Anais, we grew you in a Petri dish – you got us!'

'I did?'

'You did, you got us! We knew you would.'

'How did you make me then?'

'We grew you, yes. Clever, isn't it!'

'Not really.'

'Now we're going to keep you in a cage, next to Brian. You can read Brian's thoughts in his see-through skull. See, Brian's thoughts are as warped as your own.'

That gives me the shivers. Brian's thoughts are clearly more warped. Is it more warped tae rape a dog or tae think of murder? Thinking of murder isnae the same as murder – it's not even like I think about murder a lot. I just think whatever the fuck it is I shouldnae think.

Like, on a train platform, the train rushes in and I always think – Jump! Just fucking jump. Or some wee radge will be standing there, or even some nice wee old lady, and I'll just picture my arm slamming out. Then – them dead on the train track. I dinnae wantae, I dinnae wantae think stuff like that. Probably there is something fundamentally wrong with me. Thoughts are not actions, though, thoughts dinnae mean anything – unless they do. Then you're fucked.

I can never work it out. Why do I think thoughts like that, unless I'm bad? Probably there's something in me that's gonnae come out one day and everyone will see it. I mean, even though I umnay a Brian, really – right where no-one can see – I'm rotten. There's something wrong with me.

It's why nobody kept me. Except Teresa and she got murdered, and whose fault was that? The therapist said it wasnae mine, but I could have checked on her, I could have made her come through for lunch. I could have knocked on the door after her client left and asked her if she wanted a cup of tea. But I didnae, I sat in my pyjamas and ate crisps and watched cartoons while she lay there for a full fucking hour.

The experiment know.

They dinnae know this, though: I'd die before I'd pick on someone. I would. You dinnae bully people, ever, cos all bullies are cowards and I umnay a fucking coward, I never was. And I'd take my own life, I mean totally fucking kill myself, before I'd hurt even one hair on a bairn's head. I wouldn't think twice. I umnay a Brian – but they cannae tell the difference, and I'm beginning to get less sure by the year.

Turn so my ear is pressed against the door. What if they're behind the door? The experiment. Maybe some of them have made a bet that I'll get in, but some have made a bet that I won't. They could be sniggering into their test-tubes right now. They'll ask me about it one day, on the radio, when I invent something dead useful.

'So, did they grow you, Anais?'

'No.'

'Liar.'

'Am not.'

'Are too. Just like in the nightmare!'

It is always the same. In the nightmare they grow me from a pinprick, an infinitesimal scrap of bacterium, study me through microscopes while wearing radiation suits and masks. There's a stupid tune in my head. What is it? It's that nursery rhyme Teresa used tae sing about what little girls are made of. Sugar and spice and all things nice; whatacrockofshit – I knew I wasnae all things nice, even then.

'What did they make you out of then, Anais?'

'Sugar and fucking shite, mate.'

'No, really, what did they make you out of?'

'Bacteria. Bacteria they scraped off some dead motherfucking alien, you prick; now get out my fucking way!'

The nightmare happens in the daytime. It happens in the night. It happens in the shrinking place or especially the falling place. First the tongue expands so fast you cannae blink, then it kicks in, too fast to grab a hold, or breathe, or form thoughts. Shrinkingshrinkingshrinkingshrinking. Nothing – gone.

There's nothing to hold onto out there. Not a single thing. Fuck all – you are just floating in space. It's worse than back-to-back panic attacks. It's worse than psychosis. It's worse than getting fucked after you said no, and it's worse than not knowing anything about who you are or where you're from.

It's worse than the polis fucking with you just for fun, or cos they see you as a nothing, a no mark, easy meat – just like all the other freaks do. It's worse than listening tae kids you dinnae know cry themselves to sleep, or watching your twelve-year-old pal go on the game. It's worse than your ma jagging up on Christmas Eve. Or not knowing anything about someone other than their da raped them, or their uncle abused them, or their brother's been fucking them up the arse since they were three. The shrinking can take you from person back tae a pinprick in seconds, and once the pinprick disappears you – are gone.

Nothing but empty space.

I have tae get in that door. I have to look. It could be full of fuck-all, or it could be the experiment, holding up test-tubes of champagne, ready to toast their long-lost specimen – finally come home.

I stick my head around the office door. Eric's sat behind Joan's desk with his feet up.

'I need Tampax.'

'Okay, Anais.'

What a tosser! Don't be cool about it, Eric, you hate blood, you hate fannies – I can tell.

'Like today would be good.'

He's looking at me like he cannae believe something I've done, and I realise he has my files half-open on the desk. He's reading year five. He's not got tae the good stuff yet, he's still on the phenomenon bit. The psychologist bit. The child-that-cannae-show-love shite.

'Uh, okay, Anais, when I'm ready.'

Eric's relishing the power. He's on the lamest power trip in the world – the decider of how long it takes for me to get a tampon. Wow, Eric, the heady fucking heights your degree is taking you to!

I'm glad I never had to ask him for a fanny-pad. I started a right good fire with a bunch of fanny-pads once, but that's all they're good for. I even hate the way it sounds . . . fanny-pad. I umnay keen on sanitary towel either, or pants – or vagina. Vagina sounds like a venereal disease. Or like the name for some snobby rich German countess's daughter; her entry into society would be announced in some glossy magazine, and underneath it would read . . . *Vagina Schneider at the débutante ball, wearing an electric-blue Vera Wang – a true glory to behold.*

Vagina. It's a shit word, ask anyone. It's not like cock. Cock is a good clean word. Pat was a big fan of the word cock. And cunt. She said if two words ever got married, it should be cock and cunt.

Eric shuffles around, he makes sure the petty cash is locked up, he puts a pencil back in Joan's pen mug on the desk.

'I'm bleeding like a fucking haemophiliac here.'

'Can you spell that?' he snaps.

'Can you spell, fucking arsehole!'

'Dinnae swear, Anais.'

He picks up a large set of keys and walks ahead of me. At the store cupboard he shoves a key in, but he cannae get it to turn at first.

'What kind of sanitary products would you like?'

'The kind you stuff in your fanny to stop blood?'

He steps away from the door, his cheeks burning. Seriously – this cunt's a total retard. Has he never had tae get Tampax for any of the lassies before?

'Go and select one then.'

'I umnay picking a diamond ring, Eric. You dinnae select *one*, you need the whole fucking box.'

'You have an attitude problem, Anais.'

'No fucking shit, Sherlock.'

Step into the big old cupboard. Toothbrushes, bonus, two in the back pocket; four combs, a bag of rubber bands. Further down, at the back, there are some tools for the Hoover and a flathead screwdriver. The screwdriver will be perfect.

'Are you alright in there?' he calls.

'Aye, just a minute.'

Grab a box off the shelf and walk out. Eric closes the cupboard door and locks it twice.

'I know that Angus is your support worker, but if you ever want a chat, I'm totally happy tae listen. Any time.'

'Sound.'

'We could chat today, if you like?'

'Are you doing a dissertation, Eric?'

He doesnae answer but he's pissed off, he disappears into the office and shuts the door. Back out the fire exit, close the gate and run up the steps.

When I get to the top floor I take the screwdriver out of my sock, jam it into the door frame, hard – harder. Fuck, I wriggle it around, then I manage tae wedge it right in. Take my sneaker off and belt it; the sound echoes off the stone walls. Fuck it, if they hear it, they hear it. Boot the door and it ricochets open.

Fuck! It's black in here. Feel my way across the floor, pushing my sneakers out in front of me, so my feet will hit anything before I do. I bump around things, they feel like big boards of MDF or something. I reach the big old windows and it's hard to undo the first shutter, but I get the clasp and pull it back. A shaft of sunlight floods in. Particles of dust rise up, all golden in the sun.

There are white sheets draped everywhere – it's a snow scene in a derelict theatre. A faceless, dusty sheet is a polar bear, arching up a paw. Beside him there's a snow sleigh. A snow wolf thrusts his nose out, sniffing for blood.

Sneeze. Shit! Sneeze again.

This room is amazing. I pull a white sheet off the sleigh shape and underneath there's a leather bench. Thick ankle-straps dangle off it, and wrist ones and another for across the forehead, which has teeth marks on it. Run my fingers across the stained leather. That's how they used to hold patients down, so they could fry the voices out. If they fried my mother's voices out, did she still know who she was afterwards? They found her naked outside a supermarket supposedly. In labour. Psychotic. They never did say what supermarket.

This bench must be from when this place was a nuthouse. It's not my first time near this kind of stuff, not if you believe the social workers, ay. They reckon bio-mum squeezed me out on the nut-ward, then jumped. Like from the window. They said the staff couldnae find her on the grounds, and they never saw her again. Like ever. She didnae leave a thing – no forwarding address, no hand-knitted booties, no wee gold bangle. Not even a name.

I touch the leather softly. They would fry patients' memories as well as their voices, and sometimes they'd even fry out their names. Fry it all out, boys, every last drop.

'What did you get fried out, Anais?'

'Nothing.'

'Oh, come on, it must have been something – a birthday? Bar mitzvah? Your first time?'

'Nobody fried anything out, so fuck off!'

What if they fry out the wrong voices? I bet they do as well. They just fry everything, they dinnae just pick the bad things to fry out and leave the good things. They urnay that clever, they just fry it all, willy-fucking-nilly. Then they say you're better.

My old social worker was the one who went to the nuthouse after Teresa was gone. She decided it would help me with my *identity* problem – you know, like if I trace my roots. That's how she found the monk; he talked at her for half an hour about flying cats, and apple crumble. She said it was the flying cats he was really passionate about, though, and she said he'd seen my biological mum and did I want tae meet him? Aye. I do. I wonder if I should take him an apple crumble?

The snow wolf and the snow polar bear are silent. There are bars on the windows. I open another shutter and look down: the car park's half-empty and trees framing the lawn bend softly. The light is neither this nor that.

You can see for miles. Past the driveway there's fields and a thick patch of forest; a couple of farmhouses are tiny specks up towards the hills. Down to the left there's the village, then a wee loch. A boat's going out on the water, someone fishing maybe, and behind the trees there's a wee house. Smoke curls out its chimney. I didnae see that on the way in.

Step away from the windows, in case any of the staff come out and see me. I lean across the bench in a perfect spanking pose. 'S just like my old postcards of Victorian girls in stockings, with wooden paddles. They're hot, hot, hot. I need touch. I need tae fuck and kiss and dance, and get out of my head – like now. That's the best thing about shagging, when your mind leaves your body. If it wasnae for that, it wouldnae be as good.

Swing my legs and let my head hang upside down. There's a rusty base holding the bench up, it must have been here for ages. Years ago they'd cut people's memories out and keep them in a jar, just hunks of grey tissue preserved in formaldehyde. Sometimes they pickled them, but more often it was formaldehyde.

If you look at a brain in formaldehyde you wouldnae see

preserved memories. You wouldnae see Christmases or first presents or snowy days or a red bicycle. Memories must still be somewhere, though – like just because the tissue is dead, the things that created the memories still happened! So where are they?

Maybe if there's nobody else that remembers them, then it's like they didnae happen. They're just gone then. If they fried out my memories it'd be like I never existed, cos there isnae a sister, or aunty, or da who's gonnae say: Oh, remember when Anais broke her ankle? Remember when she cried on her birthday? Remember when she ate a whole cake and was sick at the back of the bus!

I saw brains in jars on a school trip to the College of Surgeons. There was even a pickled two-headed baby. I'd love a two-headed baby in a jar. If I ever grow up I want tae be a vampire with a two-headed baby. As if. I'll never grow up.

Imagine all the people getting their memories fried out cos they were too sad to live, or their voices were too loud or too mean or too many? In the old days they'd do it just because you had a baby but not a husband. That was enough back then. They'd fry your memories out so you couldnae remember the baby or the no husband. I want Jay. I want touch. I lie back on the bench and unbutton my jeans.

Run my fingers over the leather strap, then use it to tickle my tummy. It feels good. I always do it just before my period. Well, most days really; actually – it's every day. If I think about it, it's everyday. My name is Anais Hendricks, and I'm a wanker.

Some days it's just once, but sometimes it's two or three times. Sometimes if I cannae get to sleep I'll just do it again and again – it gets harder to make it happen after a while; the most in a row's fourteen or fifteen. The first time I did it ten times. Nobody said how to do it, it's just something you do. I had a Sunday job in the paper shop for five weeks once. I kept shutting the door so I could wank in the loo with porn. Magazines are fuck-all like the stuff online, they're less hardcore.

I point my toes and everything recedes: sound, colour, temperature, words. Then there are flashes – Hayley's perfect tits, sucking her nipples. Jay watching, telling me to lie down. The physics teacher and tongues, up and up, and up until there is nothing, no thoughts, no time or space.

My legs go slack and my feet fall out to either side. Sunlight's warming the room. I button my jeans up.

They cannae have my memories, not even the bad ones. They dinnae belong to them. They cannae get me up here when the locks go on those doors, cos they'll never let me back out. Fact. I'll spend eternity drooling down my chin while Erics do their theses, then fuck off to have lives with houses and kids and gardens and holidays and cars and dreams.

Someone should take photos of all this shit before they clear this room out. The white polar bear and the white wolf. The bars. The straps. The teeth marks. I wantae photograph them all and hide the photos in a box – then even if they do fry me, someone will open the box one day and find them. Then they will have the memory. The snow wolf and the snow bear will live on.

6

RIP OPEN the first bin bag. All my posters are worn along the creases. Jim goes above the bed, Teresa's original Chanel photo under that. I had to break into our flat and chore the photos after Teresa died. It's funny to say it like that. Like she just died.

In our kitchen there were forty boxes of teabags, and a vintage photograph of French girls smoking cigars. A blonde and a brunette – bobbed hair, wearing face masks. I fancy them both. Imagine going to a ball wearing a fancy face-mask and a beautiful dress. I Blu-tack that one up by the side of my bed, then a picture of Teresa, smiling like nobody will ever hurt her.

There are other important things that must be checked. I need tae make sure that everything has survived the trip here. There's my robot badge, an igloo postcard, a Lego dragonfly, an art-nouveau ad for absinthe. A photo of me holding a plastic bucket on a beach, topless and blank-eyed. I was called another name then.

'Anais, the lab tech's here.'

'Shit, Angus, d'ye not know how tae knock?'

'Sorry.'

'Can I finish emptying this bag?' I ask him.

'Two minutes. I have tae see Dylan, then I'll be back.'

I tip the other bin bags upside down. My floor's strewn now, with earrings, sandals, sneakers, books. Some novels have bits ripped off for roaches, or cartoons drawn in the margins, or notes I've made. Things like: Be Happy. Quit Chocolate. Become a Movie Star. The Revolution Will Be Televised and Streamed Live Online.

One-eyed teddy, boot him under the back of my bed; hairdryer, make-up bag, eight journals filled with drawings. A guide to Paris. My old brace in a box.

'Come on, Anais, let's go.'

'Alright, I'm coming.'

My phone beeps.

Wank me.

That's all it says. Prick! The only person that'll be wanking Jay is some guy in the jail.

Go to the safe-house. Split the profit. 50/50.

I read his text again. He would never split the profit 50/50 on the outside, and he'd usually get one of his guys to sell his gear, not me. I could use the money, though.

What are you wearing, kitty cool?

I'm naked. Turd-breath. I text it back as I follow Angus downstairs. A lawnmower hums outside and I can smell fresh grass, and Angus reeks of patchouli.

Really?

I'm ignoring that.

'How'd ye get your hair that bright green, Angus?'

'Organic dye. I get it from India.'

You are giving me a hard-on.

Angus hangs back until I catch him up. Downstairs the

entire unit are eating their tea, it looks like shepherd's pie. It's too quiet. There isnae even a murmur coming from the dining area, just the click-click of forks.

Text me a photo of your tits.

'I told the chef tae keep some dinner back for you, Anais.'

'Dinnae bother. I'm a vegetarian.'

'We can accommodate that.'

Why, so you can sell it in the jail for a quid?

Are you kidding? I'd need a fanny shot for a quid.

Fuck off, Jay.

Noh, you fuck off I'm in DEBT. Send me a fucking PIC.

I switch my phone off. He keeps making out like it's my fault he's in debt or I should help him out, cos what? Cos he hid me when I was on the run? Cos he thinks I owe him – owe him fucking what?

Me and Angus walk past the dining tables, Brian is watching me, out the side of one bespectacled eye. Shortie glances up as well. Angus opens a door on the right turret. There's a wee corrider, then another door – he gestures at me to go through before him. I step into the interview room and a tall woman wearing a blue plastic pinny looks up.

'I've been waiting for you, Miss Hendricks.'

'It's just Anais.'

I fucking hate formalities. Angus shuts the door behind him, clomps away back down the corridor. On the table there's a row of glass jars lined up, and a marker pen.

'Could you please be quick, Anais? I'm running late. Chop-chop!'

Chop-chop? Chop fucking chop-chop? I hate. Her face. Those jars. My socks. How many miles is it to Hollywood?

I should go there and make like Marilyn, take my kit off and see if anyone'll let me on their film set.

There's a great big lump on the lab tech's left ring-finger, under her plastic glove. Now that – is a diamond. Will anyone ever buy me diamonds? Who cares. I'll never wait for anyone, if I want a fucking diamond I'll buy it myself. I dinnae want any of those blood ones, though – people die for them, and that's well sick.

'Open your mouth, Anais. Open it a bit wider, please!'

She runs a long cotton swab around my gum, and she smiles at me and her teeth are fucking immaculate. I open my gob wide and show her my two straight big middle teeth, surrounded by squinty ones.

'They did this already.'

'I am sure they did, Anais, but *in* these situations, you know.'

'What – these *being*-accused-of-putting-someone-in-a-coma situations?'

'Exactly those. This will prove you didn't get yourself into any naughty trouble.'

There are so many wee jars on the table, must be about thirty. Each has swabs in it, invisible bits of skin, strands of hair. Saliva. It's clarty.

'You can close your mouth now, thank you, Miss Hendricks.'

'How'd you get a job like this? Did you have tae get a degree in, like, swabbing?'

'I did indeed, three of them actually.'

Fucking smart-arse. She rubs some funny-looking paper on my skin, then drops that in a jar. Then she holds up some tweezers.

'Can I take a hair sample – just one strand will do?'

'No.'

'It's not negotiable.'

She advances with the tweezers and I hold my hand up. I pluck one hair from my scalp and hold it out to her.

'Merci beaucoup,' she says.

'Do you speak French?'

'Oui, oui.'

'Have you been there?'

'Yes.'

'Have you been tae Paris?'

'Yes, I go to the South of France most summers, but Paris is beautiful at any time. Would you like to go there?'

'Nope.'

'Would you like to go anywhere, Miss Hendricks?'

'No. I heard they had a revolution there once, though, in France, ay; they killed the rich people because they were really beginning tae irritate the fuck out of the poor.'

'Vive le révolution,' she mutters.

'Exactly. Viva la revolution.'

'Did you get a degree in mispronunciation, young lady? "Viva" is Italian; "vive le" is French!'

'Whatever.'

Vive le. Vive le. I say it in my head and remember it. That's how you learn. Fuck school, ay, just listen, and google, and read like fuck.

You can learn a lot on Google, but some of it's lies. Like the rumour about the chickens that are grown with four legs – for the fast-food places. I believed there were four-legged chickens for ages. Knowledge is power, and what fucking other power do I have? None. Fuck-all! I'm stashing up facts and figures and words and reasons. One day I'll use them. I'll learn tae master mind control and take over the fucking world.

Teresa used to say school was an uneccessary form of social control.

Aye, sweetie, everything you will ever need to know can be found in songs, books, art, films and lovers.

The lab tech drops the strand of my hair into a wee jar. She scribbles something on the label. It's like another me is going to be grown in there – a wee DNA Anais in a glass jar. They can grow it until it gets to about five centimetres long; that'll be big enough so that they can tip it out onto the table, poke at it with a toothpick until it does a dance.

'You've got enough DNA in there to grow a new me.'

'We're not growing new people yet.'

'Not legally.'

'We grow organs, Anais. Sheep have been cloned successfully, pig hearts – that kind of thing.'

'If you grew a new me, you could experiment on the old one.'

'Now there's an idea!'

'I bet you did really well at school, ay?'

'Yes, I did quite well. What are you going to be after you leave school?' she asks me.

'Spaceman.'

'Sounds fabulous,' she says.

'If you grew a new me, would it have better skin than I do?'

'Don't worry, we never clone anyone new on a Wednesday.'

She packs all the wee jars into special compartments of her fancy flight-case.

'Have you met many murderers?'

'More than I'd have liked to,' she says.

She clicks her case shut and walks out.

There's a sticky circle on the table, where a jar sat. She's left a piece of paper as well. I feel like starting a fire – one match is all it takes. I could start a great fire, with just one match and that piece of paper.

I watched a documentary once, about Hindu wives getting shoved on the pyre after their husbands died. It's cos they're meant to want to jump on the flames on top of their dead husbands, but some of them dinnae really fancy it. They dinnae want to burn themselves alive – just so's their husband can have someone to make them a cup of tea in the afterlife. They reckon that sometimes the wife just gets shoved on, like if she doesnae jump on herself, ay. Someone in the family will do it. An elbow in the ribs and a boot up the arse. In you fucking go.

Angus sticks his head around the door.

'Sorry tae leave you in here, Anais. I had tae see Mrs Patterson out. I've got you a vegetarian option, come on.'

'I want tae be alone.'

'So did Garbo. You do know what happened tae her, don't you?'

'I dinnae give a fuck what happened tae her.'

'Nobody wants tae be a recluse, Anais, we all need friends.'

'Fuck off, Angus.'

'That's not polite, and I can tell you are a polite girl really.'

I stare at him.

'It's sad tae eat on your own,' he says.

'It's sad tae get done for an attempted murder you didnae commit.'

'You didnae put PC Craig in the coma?' he asks.

It's funny how many things you never get asked. Things that are totally obvious. He closes the door quietly. I dinnae want to go out there, I dinnae want to sit, with people, in rooms. I just don't. Why is that such a fucking problem?

My nails look nice today – red, no chips, not like when I flake them away for hours in the cells. I do that, then I organise all the wee red bits of varnish intae upside-down smiles and leave them on concrete benches. Maybe the next person in the cells walks in and sits down and sees them. Maybe they don't.

'Okay, Anais, here you go, service with a smile. If you want more cheese, just shout. I put butter on your tattie and I poured you a fresh orange juice. Is that alright?'

Angus slides a tray in front of me, then touches my shoulder just lightly, like he didnae, but he did. He closes the door behind himself again, really quiet and careful like. I look down at the tray and I feel like crying.

7

TWO DRAGONFLIES flutter by, then come to rest on the window frame – their wings are metallic blue in the sunlight. I adore dragonflies. I adore the sea, the moon, the stars, vintage Dior and old movies in black and white. I adore girls with tits and hips and class, and old men in suits who have that dignified look about them. Sometimes you see a decrepit old man, and his hop-along mangy dog, and you can tell the dog is hanging on for the old man, it won't die before he does. The two of them creak back from the shops together every day.

I adore guys who talk in a way that makes you wonder about their smooth cocks, or that narrow perfect ridge along their hips. I'd like to paint guys like that, in a studio in Paris, somewhere above a bakery where I'd wake up every morning to the smell of fresh croissants.

Teresa ate cakes from the French pattiserie when she was depressed. She'd sit in her bed, in a kimono, drinking gin and reading. Sometimes I think she's still here, but she's not. Pat has the ashes, and me and Teresa never did make it tae Paris. We had the passports ready and everything. She's so dead, it's more than a full stop.

If I lived in Paris, I'd sit in cafés by the river smoking

coloured cigarettes and I'd never speak. Or, only rarely – I'd be mysterious.

'You fucking silly cunt!'

Step out my room and look downstairs over the landing. It's Shortie. She's giving this lassie it tight, but really it's me she wants, she's chuffed that I've come out to look. She's making out like she's hard, but right now she's just being a fucking bully. She glances up and I go back in my room quick as. I've been here over a week now – to be honest, I'm surprised it's taken this long.

Earrings out. Hair scraped back. Boots on. Laces tied.

'D'ye want a smack in the pus?'

There's a thud from downstairs, then the girl, pleading.

'I didnae,' she says.

'You didnae what?' Shortie hollers in the lassie's face.

I take the stairs two by two, clocking who's around, hardly anyone; Isla, Tash, they're watching me descend.

'I dinnae know,' the lassie whimpers.

'You dinnae know what you didnae?'

'No!'

Shortie smacks her.

'Leave her alone, she's fucking leaving the day,' I say.

'What the fuck's it got tae do with you?' Shortie snaps.

'Ssssh.' Tash jerks her head towards the office where the staff are. She's sitting on the back of the sofa thing. Isla's lying back on her.

I step between Shortie and the lassie. The lassie doesnae need tae be told; she edges out the front door to wait outside, where it's safer.

'If you want a fight, Shortie, all you have tae say is pretty please.' I shove past her.

'Aye?'

'Aye. I dare you. I double-fucking-dare you.'

She's getting edgy now. Flexing her fingers. Psyching herself up, summoning up the worst memory she's got in her head, so she can try to batter me. Up on the second floor Brian squats down and grins.

'Stop being a tit, Shortie,' Isla says.

Isla tries to stand up, but Tash puts a hand on her shoulder.

Shortie's heavier than me, and taller, but not much. She's game. Game is good, it'll get you a lot further than hard will. I can feel her behind and I turn, slow as. Here it comes. Right. Fucking. Now. She's pulling her head back tae head-butt me and I swerve – just out of her way, up two steps, and boot her right in the pus.

Spit flays through the air.

'D'ye think that hurt?' she gobs as she pushes herself back up.

Grab her by the back of the head, smash my skull off her skull. *Crack*. She makes a glutty pit-pit noise in her throat.

Tash is standing up now, but she doesnae step in. I can taste blood. Shortie's pupils are black, and I see it, just for a second – her behind a rose bush with her Granda standing over her. She punches me right in the face, so I grab her hair and smack her face off the stairs, once, twice. John walks in the front door.

'For fuck's sake, you could try to separate them, Tash!'

'Are you gonnae step in between those two, like?' she says.

'Fuck off, John, fuck off. I mean it, I'm fucking fine,' Shortie says, holding her nose.

The office door opens. Brian snickers up on the landing

above, his hands splayed on the Perspex. Me and Shortie untangle and limp towards the stairs.

John stoats across the room and up into the staff's faces. Isla sprints up behind him and makes sure they're distracted – so they cannae see what's happened.

I'm up the stairs first, Shortie's behind me; when we get tae our landing I push her towards the boys' toilet and she slaps my hand away, slams the door.

'Noh, I want tae see my social worker now, ya fucking radge!'

John harasses Mullet, keeping him in the office.

Step into the Ladies, turn on the cold tap. There's blood. Stop shaking. Stop it. Dinnae look in the mirror. I hate fighting, it makes me feel sick – if I never had tae fucking fight again, ever, that would be such a relief.

Clumps of hair are stuck to my fingers. Flick them away so they swirl around the sink and settle at the top of the plughole.

Red knuckles. They fucking hurt, and there's a bruise in the middle of my forehead. I yank off a wadge of bog-roll, and run it under the cold tap so I can dab my face.

The bath's empty. Dinnae think about it. Not about *that*.

My breath sounds loud, and wee flashes of Shortie behind a rose bush just make me feel – sad. Nobody should go through that. No-one. Shortie's alright really; she just wants tae be hard, but she isnae, but it'll not stop her. She's a social climber.

'Are you okay?' Isla opens the door.

'Aye. Are the staff away?'

'Aye.'

'Ta, Isla.'

She pulls fags out her pocket. 'D'ye want one?'

'Aye.'

'C'mon.'

I follow her down the stairs and through the open-plan area.

'Where is everyone?' I ask.

'They've all just been dragged away in the minibus. You should think yourself lucky you've missed it. These weekend trips tae the park that Joan's trying tae get us on are truly pish.'

'The social-work minibus!' I say.

'Everyone stares!' we both say.

'They want us tae go boating soon,' Isla says.

'Fuck that! They sent me on a therapeutic canoeing trip once and I got charged for breach of the peace, and assault.'

'Anais, that's too funny. Tell!'

'The guy was wearing an orange wetsuit and a What Would Jesus Do wristband.'

'The God Squad – sinister.'

'Exactly. He went mental cos I was having a fag in my canoe.'

'How – does God hate smokers?' she asks.

'Aye, cannae fucking stand them!'

Isla checks the staff urnay around, then she opens the fire exit and runs up the turret ahead of me. Fuck – I thought it was just me that knew it was here.

On the fourth-floor landing she opens the wee window and climbs straight out. It's windy as anything today. I climb out behind her and try not to look down.

'So what happened then, did you stop smoking?' she asks.

'No. I double-dragged it down tae the wood and flicked

it in the water, and he's all, like, the fishes, the fishes, cos my dog-end's floating on the water, and I'm, like – fuck the fishes! Fuck the fucking fishes!'

'What did he do?'

'He spits!'

'What? At you?'

'Right in my face. Fucking cunt!'

'What? Fucking hell, what did you do?'

Isla grinds out her fag and pulls another two out for us.

'I hooked him.'

Isla is giggling so hard she slides forward. I grab her back without thinking. I dinnae like the height up here, but the view is all fields and clouds and autumn colours on the leaves, reds and oranges, golds and russets.

'So, what happened then?'

'I thought he was gonnae punch me out.'

'What a prick!'

'Exactly, he pulled back his hand like he was gonnae, so I pulled the paddle back – knocked the cunt out.'

Isla's laughing now, tears are flowing down her face. I cannae help but laugh as well.

'He was flat out across his canoe and I'm like, fuck – I've killed Gaarwine.' The two of us roar with laughter. It's so funny it's not even funny any more.

'Why were they sending you on a healing canoe trip anyway?'

'I found my adopted ma,' I say.

'What, dead like?'

'Aye. In the bath.'

'Suicide?' Isla asks.

'Noh. She got stabbed.'

I dinnae know why I said that. I feel stupid now. I normally dinnae say that.

Bring me some gear in, and wank my cock while you're here. Dinnae be square, kitty cool. We'll get high as fuck again soon as I'm out, just you and me, and nothing else.

'Boyfriend?' Isla asks as I switch my phone off.

'Not really. He's inside, keeps hassling me to take him stuff in. He's in debt though, ay, and I think he's getting shit inside, but I cannae tell.'

'Really?'

'Aye.'

I like Isla. I really like her. She's one of those people with manners; she doesnae ask me anything else, and she knows I'm not – you know – a total arse that just fights with people.

'Shortie didnae really mean it,' she says.

'Did the staff see anything?'

'Noh, John kept them occupied. He fancies Shortie like fuck.'

'Aye?'

'Aye. He doesnae admit it, but he does.'

'Does she like him?'

'I dinnae ken. Shortie's the only virgin I ever met in a home!' Isla giggles.

'Is she?'

'Aye. She's frigid. She says she doesnae like guys, but she does. She's not like me. I wouldnae shag a guy if you put a gun tae my head. I mean I've shagged a guy, for a while, but I didnae rate it.'

'Are you and Tash together?'

'Aye.'

'She seems nice.'

'She's amazing. She takes a while tae get tae know people, though.'

'How come she wears the moustache? Like it's cool, it reminds me of an artist,' I say.

'She likes lassies with a wee bit hair, but she's not really got any – a bit on her legs, aye, but she's got tae shave them for work. The moustache she can put on and take off when she wants. Mine's too blonde.' Isla touches her upper lip. 'She'd like it darker.'

'Have you got a kid, Isla?'

'Aye. Twins, they're with foster-parents. They dinnae let me see them much, ay. Tash's saving up money for us tae leave care and take them.'

'Aye?'

'Aye. She's saved quite a few hundred already. I really want them back. Their foster-mum's nice, but I miss them and she cannae understand it, no like I do.'

'Understand what?'

Isla flicks her fag away.

'We've – we're all living with the same condition, ay. Like you can live a long time with it now, like a lifetime.'

She looks out over the fields. It's so quiet up here – we listen tae the birds, and she looks unbearably sad. I've seen her getting her meds, ay, the same one's Teresa's pal used to take.

'What age are they?'

'Two,' she says.

Fuck! Fuck, fuck, fuck.

'Modern science,' I say.

I cannae speak now, I'm an arse-piece, I know nothing

about nothing and I should probably be strapped to that turret over there and shot.

'You get an owl out here at night.' She grins, changing the subject.

'No way. I heard something hooting the other night but I've never actually seen an owl.'

'Me neither, until I moved here. She's beautiful, really wee, we called her Britney; listen out at night and you'll hear her. Did the social workers ask you if you wanted tae live away out here in the sticks?'

'No!'

It's amazing what the social work dinnae ask. They dinnae ask about the terrible baldness of the moon, they dinnae ask about rooms without windows or doors – and they sure as shit dinnae ask about flying cats. I bet they didnae ask Isla what her dreams are as a mum. They didnae ask me about blood in an empty bath, and they didnae ask about what Teresa was gonnae do when she got out that bath – she was gonnae curl up with me and watch a movie. We were gonnae make microwave popcorn.

8

THE WATCHTOWER's even more sinister when it's dark. The staff urnay around, so I put the big light out and I've angled my chair so I'm facing away from the watchtower, but I can feel it behind me. I keep imagining men in suits sitting behind that glass watching, and they're all wearing shiny shoes – and none of them have noses.

I'm watching a documentary in Japanese with subtitles, and it feels like there's no-one in this building but me and the experiment. It's almost a relief when Shortie stomps in from outside and sits down. She smells like rain.

'Alright,' I say.

'Alright, what's this pish?'

'It's a documentary.'

'Aye, I can see that, but I cannae understand what the fuck they're spraffing about,' she says.

'Read the subtitles.'

'Fuck that! What's wrong with them anyway? Why can they not speak English?'

'They're foreign, Shortie.'

'Fucking tossers.'

She fucks off upstairs. The Japanese presenter is gesturing

excitedly cos the Sumo Baby Champion is about tae be decided. The last two babies face each other: one is in a green jumpsuit, the other baby is wearing a headband. All the parents get really excited and clap. Bets are in. Yen flash up; it's big money. My cash is on Green, he's a fat one. Fat babies rule.

The camera pulls out to a big gym hall with, like, two hundred other sumo babies. They've all been set up in twos, and each baby stares at the other until one baby cries. The first baby to cry is the winner, gaining honour for their family and grace for their future. They're down to the final two contestents now. The mums step back and wait, but neither baby does a thing.

The first mum yanks her baby's hair to try to make him cry, and then the judge guy makes faces at the two of them and flaps his hands around. Nothing. Especially not from Green, he doesnae even fidget – he just stares. He's Buddha, but harder. He is the total nut. If I ever had a baby, I'd want one just like him.

The presenter gestures at the two babies, and the other parents are all trying to see over each other's heads, as the judge snaps at one of the mums.

The judge flaps his hands. Green's bored. He's clearly intelligent beyond the idiocies of social decorum and he quite obviously doesnae give a flying fuck about the honour of his family. The baby opposite him starts crying and his mum lifts him up, shows him off. They reckon he's the winner, but he's not. Green's the winner as far as I'm concerned. That attitude'll take him far one day, he'll see.

I still keep feeling like I'm shrinking, but I umnay giving into the fear. All I have tae do is breathe and bide my time, and this will pass. I shouted about the shrinking – at a panel of social workers a few years ago. That started a great big ball of shit. Antipsychotics. Post-traumatic stress disorder. Flowcharts. Borderline personality. Hooroo-kooroo. Fucking murk! That's when the social work started.

'We think you have a borderline personality, Anais.'

'It's better than no personality.'

Wrong. Apparently – no personality is the correct answer. Borderline not so much. It was all cos of that canoe trip and Gaarwine, the instructor. The social workers sat about after Gaarwine had me charged; they were all sipping herbal tea, and acting disappointed, cos that trip could really have healed somebody.

'He was traumatised!'

'I'm traumatised.'

'But he was really traumatised.'

'How – did he find his ma dead?'

They didnae like that.

Identity problem. Funny that. Fifty odd moves, three different names, born in a nuthouse to a nobody that was never seen again. Identity *problem*? I dinnae have an identity problem – I dinnae have an identity, just reflex reactions and a disappearing veil between this world and the next.

Someone's crying, upstairs.

Tash comes out of Isla's room and goes along the landing. There's a hoot outside, then another, long and low. That must be Britney. I go to the window and rub it, but I cannae see much; it's weird that hooting out there, coming from nowhere.

I wonder what my mum, or dad, would look like? I've never even seen a photo of someone I'm related to. I dinnae know a name, there's just a great big void, black as night. I dinnae understand how they cannae work out where you're from by, like, your blood, or your eye colour – or the way you hold a knife and fork or something?

'It's impossible, Anais.'

'Really?'

'Totally impossible. You have to accept that you will never meet anyone you are related to, or see a picture of them, or hear their voice, or know what their name is, or where they live, or who they are. You have to accept this, so you can be well and whole. You do want to be well and whole, don't you?'

'Fuck off!'

I dinnae trust social workers or their stupid stories. I'm a bit unconvinced by reality, full stop. It's fundamentally lacking in something, and nobody seems bothered. Like – if we're in the middle of the universe, *one* of the universes, and there's nae proof heaven exists, and religion is just used mostly to control people, then the real fact is: nobody knows why we're here.

That means really, we all come from nothing. A great big fuck-all that will never have an answer, and it bothers me. I want tae ask the woman in Tesco about it, when she says – That'll be £4.97, I want to say to her . . . *We're in the middle of the universe, right now, right at this exact minute! Does that not bother you?*

It bothers me. It really fucking does. Nobody talks about it, though, that's the thing. We live, we die, we do shit in between, the world is fucked up with murder, and hate, and stupidity; and all the time this infinite universe surrounds us, and everyone pretends it's not there.

I'm suspicious of silence, and reality, and social workers. I'm suspicious of teachers, and police, and psychologists, and clowns, and apples, and red meat, and cows. Cows are too big and they're telepathic. You walk past a cow field and they all just turn as one being, and stare. And they do chase people. I've fucking seen them. Bovine grass-munching hippies – my arse!

Authority figures are broken, and they're always bullies as well. Red meat is just an arm, or a leg, or a face – without skin on it. I cannae deal with raw meat. I walk past a butcher's and begin tae see everything as meat. Meat hands. Meat feet. Head meat, heart meat. There's a meat moon and a meat tree. Some bloke drinking a meat margharita, in a meat bar on meat street.

Clowns are vicious – they're all nefarious grins – and if you hang out with a bunch of clowns in a bar, pretty soon it would turn into a horror movie. Nefarious means evil. It's nothing to do with Rastas.

Apples fall from trees. The sound an apple makes when it hits the ground gives me needles in my spine. Teachers, shrinks, pigs, staff, they all do the same, and so does life, without being able to think about who I would have been – if I'd actually got to be me.

I wouldnae have been this. This was a mistake. I'm gonnae get it straight in my head again later, play the birthday game and finish it this time. It's the only thing keeping me sane right now.

'Telly off now, up tae bed, Anais.'

'Okay.'

'Did you put the big light off?' Angus asks me.

'Nope.'

He flicks the big light back on. I put my cornflakes bowl through the hatch; that's all I ate today, tomorrow it will be normal food. The day after that – crisps only. Angus goes through tae the office and comes back out with the keys for the watchtower. He opens a door round on the back of it.

'Can I have a look up there?' I ask him.

'No, Anais. The watchtower is out of bounds.'

I knew he wouldnae let me look up there. No fucking way.

9

THEY WON'T let me in the office yet, cos Isla cut herself again last night. There's a doctor in there cleaning her up – it must have been a bad one. I want to take her something, a magazine and Lucozade, or Valium and Victorian porn.

'Alright?' Shortie asks me.

'Aye, you?'

'Aye.'

It's a truce now. I knew the fight wasnae anything personal.

'Where are you going?' John asks her.

'I'm getting my head shaved.'

'Dinnae get your head shaved, I like it like that,' he says.

'Twice the reason tae shave it then, ay?'

Shortie disappears out the front door.

'Anais, come on, we'll use one of the interview rooms.' Helen appears.

She's been in the interview room collecting herself. Meditating. Reading up on my putting-a-cop-in-a-fucking-coma-might-get-done-for-murder-if-she-dies case.

What are you wearing?

Press delete on my phone, follow Helen into the interview room.

Strip for me, baby.

Bolt!

'Okay, Anais, sit down.'

Helen closes the door behind us.

That's no very nice. I miss you, d'ye no even miss me?

'So. Where were you?' I ask Helen.

'I was totally unable tae get back home! You wouldn't believe it out there, Anais, there was a terror alert and all the planes were stopped, then there was flooding and we couldnae even leave our region. It was a nightmare.'

'What, you mean you couldn't leave your five-star all-inclusive hotel? For three more weeks?'

'I ended up stuck in India for another three weeks, yes. We couldnae fly anywhere, then I got ill. I think I had dengue fever.'

'Here's hoping.'

'Don't be rude, Anais. All I could do when I got home was rest and sip tea. I know, I really do understand that you have been having a nightmare. I am really, really sorry I wasn't there for you.'

Send me a fucking picture.

I stare at the LCD. He's getting pissed off cos I'm not like what I was at eleven, or twelve. Everyone changes, though, ay. I should just tell him to fuck off, but he's the only person who ever held me *that* way, stroked my hair. After Teresa, after she died, that was where I went. Jay's bed. Jay's drugs. Jay's arms. I don't think I would have made it otherwise.

'It did give me another few weeks working in the elephant sanctuary – you would have loved the elephants, Anais!'

'I fucking doubt it.'

'Anyway, I've been given all the details by Angus. He seems nice?' she says.

'He's alright.'

'He told me that PC Dawn Craig's condition is not improving; she's not in a vegetative state, but she is still in a coma. You know if she doesn't improve, Anais, and they find any evidence, you will be detained in a secure unit until you're eighteen.'

'I didnae do it.'

'You're sure?'

I think she must have been doing some hardcore meditating over there; she's finally fucking grown a pair.

'So, how did you get all that blood on your skirt, if you didn't get in a – altercation that day?'

'Ask the police, they've got the swabs; they should have proved by now that the blood on my skirt is fuck-all tae do with PC Craig,' I say.

'We're going tae have to go down there this morning.'

'Why?'

'They want to do some additional questioning, Anais, and they would like to speak with me as well, and I would like tae speak with them.'

'I umnay going.'

'It's not optional, and there is a policewoman's life at risk here. You might want tae think about that, maybe, rather than just yourself.'

'If they put me in a secure unit like John Kay's, with the kiddie-killers or the paedos or whatever the fuck it is they keep up there, do you think there is *any* chance that I won't just fucking hang myself, Helen?'

'Calm down, Anais!'

'I'm not spending my life inside, for something I *didnae* fucking do!'

She takes coconut hand-oil out of her bag and rubs it into her hands. She doesnae think I'm getting out – she thinks I'm in the system now, all the fucking way. Foster care. Homes. Young Offenders. Jail. Where to when I graduate? Experiment headquarters – so they can pickle my fucking brain.

'Secure units really help some kids, Anais.'

'I need tae get changed.'

'Okay, I'll meet you outside. Don't be longer than ten minutes, please?'

'Fucking whatever.'

Run up the stairs, grab a pre-rolled skunk cone – John brought some back into the unit last night. It's fucking lethal shit. I go into the toilet, double-drag the entire spliff. Fuck, it reeks, I haven't smoked grass for . . . I cannae mind. Months. Flush the roach down the bog, cold water on face, go.

I'm trying not to pay attention to the way the floor rises up and down in waves. I feel fucking queasy. I hate this station.

'Hello, I am Helen Stevenson, Anais Hendricks's social worker. We have a meeting at 2 p.m.?'

'Take a seat, please.'

'They'll see us soon, Anais.'

She sits down. There are posters on the wall: how tae put someone in the recovery position, what to do if you've been mugged, and an advert for self-defence classes. Sit down and scuff my feet. I'm too stoned. Too, too, TOO – stoned. Dawn

Craig used to lift me in this police station all the time. Her fiancé works here, he's an even bigger cunt than she is – I wouldnae be surprised if he'd koshed her, he's got a right look about him. Like a wife-beater. Or a rapist.

'Hello again, Anais.'

'Alright.'

I cannae mind his name, but he's lifted me before. He comes out from behind the reception bit.

'Are we going tae do the interview straight away?' Helen asks him.

'We received notification that you would like tae speak with us on your own first, is that right?' the policeman asks her.

'Yes, if that's possible?'

I'm looking at Helen.

'Is that okay, Anais? We'll come and get you soon.'

Helen doesnae wait for an answer; she disappears into an interview room and I am left in reception where it is too bright, and the coffee machine hUms. hUm. hUm. hUm. I'm gonnae go insane. Fact. What the fuck is it about this place? Last time I was here I thought I'd die, right in front of PC Craig.

The cell's cold. It stinks of bleach and the rubber mattress, the loo never has a lid, and it's concrete, same as the floor and the walls. The concrete has wee glittery blue flecks in it. There's thick glass square windows, and blurry shapes of trees outside.

The toilet pan has skid-marks, someone else's shit.

Shivery, shivery, shrinking, shrinking. The light hUms. I'm gonnae have a whitey. No, I'm not. No, I'm not. Don't panic. Don't freak out. Fuck, fuck, fuck! Sweating. Shit, here it comes, fuck, I cannae breathe, I'm gonnae be sick. Shit!

I squeeze my eyes shut so I dinnae have to look at skid-marks splattered with sick.

The cell door has a small straight line in its middle, a wee hatch of an iron mouth set in a grim grin. That mouth can open any minute. Then an eye will stare through it. Tears mix with sweat and I'm embarrassed to cry, even in front of myself, so I dinnae.

My heart is gonnae come out my chest; I cannae fucking breathe in here and they know it. I sense them before I see them. In the concrete, across the floor, and the ceiling – wee faces materialise. One appears in the bottom of the toilet, another looks up from the pipe; they swivel tae peer out at me, squint noses, thin lips.

Traffic zooms by somewhere out there. I cannae breathe. What if this is it and I've gone psycho, just like bio-mum? Clinical psychosis. Schizoid visions. Permanent insanity or suicide? What do you do? Stay permanently crazy or just fucking jump? I dinnae believe in suicide. I dinnae – not one bit – so if it's permanent insanity, then that's just what it fucking is. And those faces in the walls: spies, the lot, sent straight from experiment headquarters.

'Can I fucking help you?' I hiss.

They turn away in alarm. One pretends to whistle, another one gazes nonchalantly at the floor.

'What the fuck are youz looking at?'

I try to touch the nearest concrete face and he pulls away, horrified. Good. Flick it on the nose and it sinks into the wall. They mutter quietly to each other. Fucking let them talk – they can do their thing, I'll do mine.

I lay back and stare. Chip my nail varnish off bit by bit, and pile it into smiley wee faces on the concrete bench.

Footsteps clap down the corridor outside. They stop at the door, and the narrow mouth snaps open and an eye looks through. Then there is a key in the lock, click, click, click. The door swings open, and she walks in. PC Craig. She's straightened her hair. She closes the door behind her and turns around. I dinnae sit up. I dinnae look at her. I feel sick.

'Get up, Anais.'

The faces watch closely. Glare back at them and they contort, their nostrils flare and their eyes narrow. I push myself upright.

'Up, Anais, come on, stop fucking about.'

I will have to leave my upside-down nail-varnish smiles on the bench, but I dinnae want her tae see them.

Let my feet fall off the bench; the floor seems too far away and things are spinning – the world is turning on its axis just that wee bit too fast.

'Take everything off, Anais. Hurry up.'

She points to the middle of the floor, and I stand there, like a dog that has got used to orders. Unbutton my school shirt, slip off my skirt, my sneakers, my socks. I have goose-bumps all over my arms, and I can feel my teeth want to clatter together and there's a roar in my head. She steps forward and begins to walk around me. Round. Round. Round.

'What makes you think you're so special, Anais? D'ye think you're above the same rules as everyone else, is that it?'

She stops in front of me, runs her finger under my bra, then she pulls my knickers out and takes a long look tae see what's down there. She lets the elastic snap back.

I stare through her. I have perfected this, staring through people. I have been here, all the fucking time lately. Thursday, 12.02, me on a come-down, middle of the cell, stripped. Sunday, 22.17, me with a black eye, to the side of the cell, partially stripped. Wednesday 3.14 a.m., bent over. Monday, 13.10, me with a coldsore, too thin and too frazzled, with bruises on my arms and cut marks on the inside of my thighs and a total inability to conceal my hate.

'Take off the bra, Anais.'

'Fuck off!'

'What did you say?'

'I said fuck off.'

'I dinnae think so, Anais – fuck off is the wrong answer. You just say *Yes* in here. *Yes*, PC Craig. *Thank you*, PC Craig.'

'Someone's gonnae put you in a fucking grave.'

'What did you say?'

I made six official complaints against her, and not one of them has been resolved. I bet I wasnae the only person she pissed off on the job.

'Anais? Are you coming through? We are ready tae interview you now.' The policeman is standing at the door.

PC Craig. I wonder who did have the honour of koshing her? The faces are here again, they glance slyly at me. Mind-readers. Dinnae think about them.

Paris. Remember Paris? It doesnae sound right. Paris. Paris. Paris. *Paris*. Fuck!

10

THEY'VE GIVEN me warm tea in a styrofoam cup, with lots of sugar in it. An empty bin has been placed by my feet – in case I'm sick again. Remembering that last whitey in here, with PC Craig, it sparked me right into another one. Cold. Clammy. Dizzy-feel-sick-want-tae-puke. Shouldnae-ever-smoke-skunk. Fuck!

One policeman's sat in the corner, the other one's at the table eyeballing me. Helen had to leave. Another emergency – maybe there's an elephant at the zoo needs some fucking Reiki or something. He clicks the Record button to begin the interview.

'Can you say your full name, please?'

'Annette Curtains.'

'Dinnae take the piss,' he says.

I lean into the recorder.

'Minnie Mouse, address: Disneyland,' I squeak.

'Recording started at three seventeen, 1st October 2011, interviewing Anais Hendricks, who evidently has no middle names,' he says, unimpressed.

The recording light flashes red.

'Her body lay on Love Lane for hours,' the first policeman says.

The light glares down and a sign on the wall reads Exit Only.

'Where were you on Wednesday 23rd September at eleven a.m., Anais?'

'School.'

'That's not true, we checked with your school. Where were you?'

'Skiving.'

'Doing what?'

'Wanking.'

'Have you any witnesses tae that, Miss Hendricks?'

I shake my head.

Cold skin. Shivery. I dinnae feel right and it isnae the skunk, that just opened the door. Truth of it is I'm mental, or I'm gonnae be mental. Maybe I should just say it. I'm Anais Hendricks and I'm mental in the head.

Sweating. I hate it when this kicks in. They should just lock me away. Stick a needle in my vein. Fry it all out. Fry out rooms without windows and doors, and red bicycles and Teresa's kimono. The policeman reminds me of a dog. I'm scared of dogs. What a fanny, ay? Scared of dogs. I'd never tell anyone.

'Are you okay, Anais?'

'I think I have flu.'

'Really. So, what did you hit her with?'

'I didnae hit her.'

'Then who did?'

'I dinnae know, do I? That's your job.'

'Dinnae get lippy, Anais.'

'We know you did it,' the one in the corner says.

'Noh, you dinnae, or you'd have charged me by now.'

He leans over the table into my face and his breath stinks of curry. Dinnae breathe. Just remember what the wishes look like, down the woods in summer. Wee silver orbs. Totally magical.

'Speak!' the policeman roars.

Wipe the spittle off my face. I'm done answering now.

Say nothing. Just stare. The pigs' nerves begin tae fray. They get angry. They get calm. They offer me a smoke. They try bullying, threats, bribes. I'm not shrinking any more. It went. It does that. It just goes. You think this is it – permanent psychosis – then it goes. I will beat these pricks. I dinnae give a flying fuck how long they keep me here.

The faces look from me to the policeman, like we're at Wimbledon, but there's nae umpire. The thing is to think of other things. That's the thing. Like when I was a kid, things were different then – even when it was shit, it wasnae shit. The sun smelled like the sun, and summers were warmer. I remember I had this amazing bike, a chopper with a flag on the back. I had tae use stabilisers even though I was nine; I learnt to ride it so late it was embarrassing.

'Why did you not learn before you were nine?' some kid asked me.

I wobbled around him with one stabiliser lifting off the ground.

'My mum was too busy tae teach me.'

'Too busy doing what?'

'Your da.'

'What?'

'And your brother.'

'What?'

The kid skidded his bike intae the gravel and clenched his fists.

'Aye, and anyone else who'll fucking pay.'

Helen should have come back for the rest of the interview, but they've said she's still called away. She'll be uploading elephant photos on Shitebook. Just focus on enunciating. It will all be okay. Just enunciate.

'You have a long history of violence.'

Paris, think of Paris. New York. Florence. Think of Jay. Think of kissing Jay. Think of being held that way. The policeman begins to shrink; first it's his head that seems the wrong size, then his nose elongates and he accelerates – further and further away.

'Possession of marijuana.'

'Mmm.'

'Possession of hydroponics, one harvest in a school shed.'

Focus on the space between his eyebrows.

'Possession of an offensive weapon. Let's see, three times: one hammer, one baseball bat and a nineteen-millimetre easy-gauge gun.'

The second policeman begins tae shrink.

'Possession of seventeen grams of heroin.'

'That wasnae smack and it wasnae proven,' I say.

'Seventeen grams of heroin, charged fully for. The hospital speed was the other one, Anais, can you no even remember what you were charged with?'

It wasnae heroin. It wasnae my heroin. Fingers look weird. Don't fingers look weird? They think I'm scummy as fuck, maybe I am? But I bet I know more about paintings than they do. I dinnae know much, like, but I bet it's more than they do. They dinnae know I know about sub alterns. Old Professor True specialised in that, he was my favourite client of Teresa's, old True, even if he was old and fat and ugly. I know what the meaning of empathy is. I know how to outline my lips in red liner.

I umnay meant to be here. I was meant to be born in Paris.

'Over one hundred charges in the last sixteen months, Miss Hendricks. Now, the Ecstasy tablets and, let's see,' he runs his pen down a long list, 'three sheets of LSD, a half-ounce of ketamine, a quarter of hash, an eighth of sinsemilla, a nine-bar in December. How have you stayed out of secure?'

Because I get grade As at school, when I go. Cos I move so much that each department forgets where I am and where I've been. Because the experiment find me amusing.

'Two drunken disorderly, seven breaches of the peace – oh, and of course your weekly absconding phase, how can we forget that, Anais? Let's see: forty-eight times you have absconded, only caught once?'

I know what the experiment would like tae see. They'd like to see me hang myself in a secure unit. One knot. One neck. Vertebrae. Snapped.

'How were you only caught once?'

'Luck?'

The faces are gone. Almost. They are fading all over the walls. I focus on the bit between the police officer's eyebrows; you can sometimes get a shrinking person back if you look at that space between their eyebrows and focus. Or sometimes, like now, it just makes their head a minuscule fucking pin. Tiny Head shakes from left tae right. His tiny eyes glare. His tiny mouth squeaks.

'You're in a bit of a mess, aren't you, Anais?'

There is nothing at the end of the rainbow. Not a fucking thing. Fact.

'Battery of an eighteen-year-old.'

'She was picking on a kid I know.'

'Two broken bones, a broken nose, broken ribs. Stolen property. Shoplifting. Destruction of social-work property. Brandishing a hammer at an officer of the peace. Joyriding. Smashing the window of Continental Jewellers. Inciting a riot in Valleyfield children's unit. Inciting another riot in The Braids children's unit. And, oh, this is lovely, Anais, destruction of police property – a prolonged campaign of terror by one Anais Hendricks of 13/9 Loam Terrace, Handerly Estate, against one officer now in a coma, our own officer: PC Dawn Craig.'

Tiny Head turns a laptop round. The CCTV footage is in order of dates; he presses Play. It's me. I'm a movie star, Mama, are you proud? Me walking through the police-station door with my arms full. I know what's coming.

I chore the first polis light off PC Craig's pigmobile at 6 a.m. It is February. It's still cold and the ground is frosty. Foam the CCTV with cheap-as-shit shaving foam, climb on top of the car and unscrew the bolts holding the light down. Wear a Buddha bag on my head, with holes cut out, so I can see. They know it's me, but they cannae prove it.

Run up to my dealer's after and chap on his window until he wakes up. He's the vicar's son. Hold out the police light for him, it's a love-token. He's well impressed. He stashes it under his bed and says he always wanted some genuine police memorabilia for a keepsake. He fancies me, and he's totally – hot.

Do the next car at 3 a.m. This one is double-screwed and an extra CCTV camera is on the roof. Spray the camera with fluorescent-pink paint. Dawn Craig strips me twice that week.

Strip the third car at 4 p.m. on a Sunday while the church bells ring. This one has two screws and has been glued down, so I have tae use a Stanley knife tae get the light off. Almost give up, but I get it off in the end. Strip the stickers off the side of the car. Take the hubcaps off. Remove anything I can get. Climb up on the roof of the car and surf for the cameras; my Buddha bag is squint and over the eye-holes I'm wearing star-shaped sunglasses.

Three more searches from Dawn Craig.

Wait, wait, wait. Three long weeks pass, then I do two more cars.

Five visits by the police to the children's unit. My room gets searched. Staff quizz me. The polis look in the woods for stolen blue lights, and give me a lecture on how much money vandalism costs the average taxpayer a year. They talk to me a lot about the taxpayers. The taxpayers hate me. Why am I costing them so much money? I am selfish and personally responsible for their high taxes – they would like to see me hanging from the old oak tree.

They ask if I'm a Buddhist.

'Are you a Buddhist, Anais?'

'Do I look like a fucking Buddhist?'

They come again, the next morning – just before breakfast

– and say there is a witness. They show me my bag with the Buddha and the holes cut out. I have no fucking idea how they found that. They're so chuffed to have caught me, they're almost being chatty. They are cowboys and I am the only Indian left now. They have my tomahawk and they're gonnae burn my settlement to the ground.

'It will be better for you if you can return the stolen police goods, Anais. Can you do that?' the police officer asks me in the station. They are so smug in their victory of catching me that they probably didnae even spit in my tea.

'Can you give me half an hour?'

'Ten minutes, no more.'

He's the only nice policeman I've ever met. I run all the way to my dealer's; from outside his window I can hear his spotty bird laughing in his room. I shagged him last week. I didnae know about Spotty until after the shag, like. When I was putting my jeans back on he told me Spotty was his bird, then she turns up at the door and just knows we've been shagging.

Hammer on his door.

'I need the lights back, all of them – they've fucking caught me, ay.'

She's sniggering and he's telling her to shut up, and he goes to get the lights out from under his bed. I cannae fucking believe it when he hands me them. The two of them are in hysterics, but I umnay laughing. I can still hear them roaring away to each other as I run down the road.

Me and the two policeman sit watching the footage on his laptop. Me spraying the CCTV. Me crouched on the roof of a police car with a knife. The next bit of footage is the last one they've got, and the policeman turns up the brightness on his laptop.

I walk into the station, up to the counter. I am holding an armful of police sirens. A wee boy and his mum are sitting in the waiting room. The wee boy stops crying when he see's what I'm carrying. The pigs all watch from behind the reception desk, their cups of tea poised in mid-air as I line the police lights up carefully. Six of them. Official police lights. Neatly placed in a row. Each one has been spray-painted fluorescent-pink and covered in glitter.

It still makes me smile.

The policeman stops the footage.

'So, your vendetta against PC Dawn Craig started over a year ago?' he states.

'I didnae have a vendetta.'

'You threatened tae kill her. Is that friendly behaviour, in your world?'

'When's Helen coming back?'

'She's not.'

11

IT'S PEACEFUL on the roof and there's a big yellow full moon. I've been listening out for Britney, but she's not around tonight. I keep thinking about my biological mum – it's probably cos Helen's finally taking me to the nuthouse I was born in. She wants me to meet the old schizo who supposedly saw bio-mum when she got committed. I still have the monk's wee pencil picture, a scrawl of a cat with wings.

I don't know what to think about it: someone who actually claims to have seen me, actually being born. Well, not actually being born, but he reckons he was there (in the building) when it happened. Helen says the old guy actually saw *me*, when I was a baby. Like not in a test-tube, or a Petri dish, or a lab, not growing in a glass jar. He saw me. A real wee baby, born the usual way, and this wee frantic part of me is hoping – for what?

I've been thinking about the experiment growing me for so long – I almost cannae imagine anything else now. Maybe this is just a ruse. The experiment urnay fucking stupid. Helen thinks it will help my *identity* problem. I fucking doubt it. She keeps saying she's leaving the social soon, tae go and help people in other countries. Wish she'd fucking hurry up about it.

7652.4 – Section 48 was my first name. Seriously, they couldnae even give me a name until they'd filed me and discussed me and decided what I came under for sectioning. I hate the first name they gave me after that one; I wouldnae even tell anyone it, ever. It was shit. At least Teresa picked something better: Anais – she named me after one of her favourite writers.

A glow from the window below spills out into the dark and stars appear. Pull a half-smoked cigarette out my jeans pocket, spark my lighter, the silver bit hurts my thumb, but it catches. Inhale until I'm dizzy. My jeans smell now, that burnt-umber kind of way. I'll have to put them in the laundry tomorrow. I might just quit smoking. Why follow the crowd?

The wind is picking up, trees rustle all the way down the drive. Malcolm, the flying cat, is waiting for me tae go and say hello.

Are you fucking ignoring me?

I look at the text twice. Mind-games. Delete the message and look at my photos. There's a beautiful one of me and Hayley, one night up on Calton Hill, with the Beltane behind us, fire-breathers and drummers and me – feeling like a white witch on LSD.

I'm in debt, the pigs are saying I grassed someone. They're gonnae kill me, Anais.

Cold. Cold in my heart. I dinnae know how tae tell him that, since I've been away from him, I see things differently. All the times he – I dunno, it's like he manipulated. But maybe he didnae. Maybe I'm just being a bitch? Maybe everyone deserves a second chance.

Hang on xx.

I tried to get in the watchtower again, but it's locked. The experiment are like the watchtower: they can see in everywhere, but nobody can see them. But they're even cleverer, they can see you anywhere you are. You could imagine them like a man with a wide-rimmed hat staring in your bedroom window while you sleep. Every night he comes and watches your dreams like he's watching the telly. Sometimes he sits by your bed and whispers words to rearrange them, so you might start out dreaming of something nice, then he'll whisper tae you about something bad. It's always something bad. The experiment are like that.

I was in hospital once, and I saw them – just under the curtain, four guys in suits; all I could see was the bottom of their trousers and identical shiny shoes. Then Teresa. Kimono. On the floor. Blood. The walls. Her cigarettes. Kraft macaroni cheese congealing in a pot while Tom chases Jerry and a siren roars. They'd been there then as well.

If you sit really quietly and focus, you can feel the experiment. You will. You'll feel them right fucking there, in the room. Just watching. Dinnae ever let them know that you know about them. If they find out that you know about them – then it will just be a matter of time. Just a matter of time. You'll walk down a street one day and a bus'll fly by, and where you were stood – just a second ago – there'll be nothing but empty space!

Gone.

Game over.

It happens all the time. There are hundreds of thousands

of people go missing every year in the UK, never-seen-again. Gone. A few come back, like. Most dinnae. It's getting worse every year, and it's not just nobodies; I mean mostly it's nobodies, but in all truth, they'll take anybody. They hate. You. Me. Everyone really.

Like ming-bag Elaine last spring, I watched the final footage of her on some train's CCTV on the local news. They never found her body, just her bag at some dump.

Then there was Brendan, in fuzzy footage – shoplifting, just before he climbed into some taxi. A taxi where? Nobody knows, Your Honour.

'Who was driving the taxi?'

'I dinnae ken.'

'How not?'

'Didnae ask.'

'Did anyone ask?'

'Nope.'

It could have been anyone driving that cab. It could have been Elvis. It might have been some sick cunt with a space in his sex circle, who knows? Maybe Brendan is cement under a patio right now. What a waste, ay, he was a fucking great shoplifter. I bet he didnae look at the number on the back of that cab when he got in. I bet he didnae memorise it. I memorise every number in every car I get in. I memorise nameplates. I did it on the docks for Mary when she went on the game, and Mary never went missing on my shift, not fucking once. She used to give me twenty fags tae keep track of the registration numbers for her, and a drink at the end of the night. It was better than a paper round. Teresa went fucking mental when she found out.

Disappearing, ay. It can happen alright. Any time,

anywhere. Even from a nice leafy street, or a dark cinema, or the dinner queue, or the back of the bus, or straight from bed, all cosy in the morning.

I could be stood out on somebody's car sunroof on a summer's night, a fat bassline vibrating, my arms flung out wide, and just as the driver turns to shout something up and touch my bare leg – he finds nothing. Only air. Gone.

People in care are always disappearing. Nobody finds out where they go.

The office is warm. Angus's got one of those hot-air heaters on. I turn it around so it blows on my legs.

'I want tae file a counter-complaint for harassment.'

'Okey-dokey.'

He crosses his legs. The soles on his eighteen-hole Docs are almost worn through. His army shirt's frayed and his knees poke through his jeans, and his dreadlocks are tied up at the back in a kind of weird green bun.

'Is that your phone buzzing, Anais?'

'Aye.'

Part your legs.

He's fucking bored in that jail.

'D'you think I should file a counter-complaint against the polis?'

'That's not what I said, Anais.'

You are the most beautiful girl I've ever seen. Marry me.

'They arrested me without cause, and kept me for three days.'

'Two and a half days.'

'Whatever.'

I stretch an elastic band I found on the desk.

Will you meet me, Anais?

He's really putting the pressure on lately, and I'm just trying not to answer.

'They only kept you for four hours today,' Angus says.

'Aye. Great.'

I take out my voucher to top up my phone and tap it in.

'The police will want you tae make another statement,' Angus says.

'They're harassing a minor.'

I'm getting out the jail, they told me this morning.

What?

In about three weeks, meet me at the safe-house? You better fucking come!

'I have some more bad news, sorry. Helen has decided tae take annual leave. She's not gonnae be your social worker any more.'

'That's not bad news.'

'It's not?'

'Eh, no!'

'Okay. Well, I'll be your main point of contact through the investigation. Helen will be back in for an end-of-client-care review, and she says you have a trip booked to go and see a Mr Jamieson?'

I love you.

I cannae believe he's getting out, and despite myself I'm thinking – of moving into his, of painting his living room, of getting a flatscreen, and a dog. It's not that long until I'm sixteen. If the polis dinnae get me in secure, then the social cannae keep me. Fuck that, though. I'd rather go into homeless accommodation and wait to get my own place, then nobody can ever kick me out again.

Will you meet me?

'Anais, are you with me?'

'Aye.'

'Come on then – enlighten me, please?'

His eyes are bloodshot.

'Angus, are you stoned?'

'I dinnae take drugs, Anais. So, who is Mr Jamieson?'

'Read my files.'

'I could, or we could attempt the archaic habit of conversation.'

'We're gonnae visit the nuthouse tae see some schizo, who supposedly met me when I was a baby.'

I ping the elastic band across the room.

'I see,' Angus says.

'Helen thinks it will help if I say hello tae the drooling old fuck.'

'Help you or him?' he asks.

'Are you taking the piss, Angus?'

'No. No, I'm not. For the record, *drooling old fuck* is now known as mentally ill, or aged and infirm, or special needs.'

'You're special-fucking-needs.'

'Okay, that's us done. Are you coming for dinner, Anais?'

'What is it?'

'Macaroni.'

'Sound.'

Everyone is eating already in the dining area. Mullet is sat at the top of the table. I collect a plate and sit opposite Isla and Tash; Dylan and the new boy are on the next table, Brian's next to Mullet, for safety.

'Alright.' Isla smiles.

She looks better than she did yesterday.

'Alright.'

Mullet peers under the table. 'Brian, what's wrong with your trousers?'

'Nothing,' he says.

'That doesnae look like nothing?'

Brian crosses his legs tae cover up a hole that's been cut in the crotch of his school breeks.

''S that for easy access, ay?' wee Dylan asks.

The new boy sniggers; he seems alright, quiet though. He only got brought in cos his mum's got cancer and there's no-one else tae take him. Dylan's looking after him. It's good he's got a pal.

Shortie wanders in and grins at Tash and Isla, and half-smiles at me.

This macaroni cheese really is – the business. I want seconds. John throws the front door open, it bangs off the wall and we all turn around tae look. He marches over and, *smack!*, he punches Mullet clean off his chair.

'You fucking liar!' John roars at him.

Mullet thuds off the wall. Fucking hell! Wee Dylan and Brian snigger, Tash's mouth falls open, and Isla steps away from the table.

Mullet puts his arm up. 'Calm down, John, what the fuck are you doing!'

'John, what is it?' Angus asks, looking edgy, like he already knows the answer and it's not a good one.

Brian skulks intae the kitchen. He takes two puddings and disappears upstairs.

Mullet launches himself up and ontae John's back, and they hit the deck. Mullet yanks John's arms back in a restraint. Tash giggles.

'This is not acceptable behaviour, John. Calm down, we can talk about this!'

Mullet shoves John's face further intae the carpet so he cannae even reply. He drags him up off the floor and marches him off towards the interview rooms; they tussle through the doorway, then another door slams and there are thuds, and *Fuck's sake*, then silence.

'I need a smoke,' I say.

Wee Dylan nods and follows me out, he's started to do that recently; he likes my stories, he likes me, ay – all the kids do. I've never lived in a unit where they've not. We walk around the back and it's a nice day out.

'D'ye want one of my fags, Anais?'

'What are they?'

'Regals.'

'Aye, alright. Gimme a few for later.'

'Here.'

He gives me five, I give him two back. He's wee and freckly and cute.

'I cannae believe John smacked Mullet!' He grins.

'I know, it was a stoater unnaw.'

'D'ye ken what he's pissed off for?' he asks.

I shrug.

'So they made you go canoeing?' he asks me.

'What?'

'Isla said it was a funny story. The social workers sent you canoeing tae heal you.'

'Aye.'

'From what?'

'Everything,' I say.

Wee Dylan rolls a joint carefully.

'Is that a good one?' he asks me.

'Aye. Okay, when you exhale, click your jaw, like this – look, can you see my jaw click?'

I blow a perfect smoke-ring.

'Aye, I've got it!'

Wee Dylan opens and shuts his mouth à la goldfish in a bowl.

'No, you have to exhale and click, click, fucking click! Here, put your hand on my jaw, feel – can you feel that click?'

'Aye,' he says.

He blows a reedy smoke-ring and jumps up and down. That's how I got started, he'll never stop now. He blows another one, but it's totally pish.

'That was a good one, Anais, ay?'

'Nope.'

'Was it pish?'

'Keep practising.'

Brian skulks around the corner, the new laddie Steven is following him. Wee Dylan nods to Steven.

'See you later, Anais.'

They follow Brian around the back of the building.

It's quiet inside. I go upstairs wondering where everyone's fucked off to. My room's well sorted these days. Along one wall are my books – arranged small to big. Then along the next wall are shoes, wedges, plimsolls, espadrilles, a pair of Chinese slippers.

I love you.

I stare at the text for a long time. He used to say that. He used to say he loved me. He'd say it in the middle of the night, in his bed, naked and in the dark, just one candle, his eyes black and nothing else in the world but us, and the gear, and kissing, and him pushing me down, and the shadows on the walls. That was before he went inside. Lately I'm beginning to realise that Jay isnae what I thought he was when I first met him. He's pushy. He's interested in himself, not me, and sometimes he's really fucking mean. I need to get my shit together and it won't happen with him.

I love you too, but I cannae be with you again. A Xx.

I press Send.

12

THE WHIRLY washing line in the back garden sags. Brian's tied to it by his wrists. Steven hauls the whirly around in circles so that Brian is dragged along with it, his feet flapping away like dying fish.

'Spin on it, cunt-pus!'

He's trying not to get dragged along in front of Dylan again, but it's no use. *Crack!* Dylan punches Brian a fucker and his head flies back. Then he snorts up a greener and gobs it right in Brian's face. A flood of pish darkens his crotchless breeks. Thick yellow snot drips off his glasses.

I'm in the second-floor bathroom; nobody else is watching. Some people are down in the open-plan area watching TV, but you cannae see the drying green from there. Angus walks by below, but he doesnae look towards the back door. He's been in a meeting with Mullet.

Steven drags the whirly all the way around again, to where they started, and Dylan belts Brian again and he drops, his legs give and his head falls forward.

He's still getting battered daily, and nobody gives a fuck, not even the staff. It's not just the dog-thing. He stinks. He's got yellow crap in his teeth and you feel dirty if you have tae sit next tae him. John saw him hanging around Cherry Lane yesterday as well. Bad, bad, bad. Old people live down in they cottages, and they dinnae get it. Brian looks like he's just walked out of one of their old school novels. He steals pity – like golden eggs – then he sucks them dry and places them back real gentle.

It's just a matter of time.

Cold fish. Spineless. Amphibian. Dylan walks away, wiping blood off his knuckles. Brian's dank hair sticks tae his face, his arms are bound up, he looks like a pale-faced bug-eyed Jesus.

Dylan glances up and gives me a wave; he's relieved to see it's not the staff watching. He told me that he's in here cos his uncles kept putting him through pub windows – like the toilet ones or even through the beer hatch if they could. He can unlock any alarm system quick as.

Squeeze a spot. It's just a wee one. I end up making a red mark where there wasnae really anything before. I really need to stop doing that.

'Tash!'

Isla's shouting out on the landing. I glance out and John slams his door shut – he's so angry he's booting it hard from the inside, and it actually closes all the way.

I step out of the bathroom, fascinated. A closed door? A totally closed door that isnae a staff door, or the watchtower. It hasnae been locked by the central locking system that the night-nurse uses more and more lately. She says it's keeping us safe and snug, but it actually means we are unable to come out and riot. Glass is being smashed in John's room. Angus runs past me, up the stairs. Tag along behind him.

'John, open this door, now!'

'Fuck you, Angus.'

'John, step back, I cannae have this door closed. Have you stepped back?'

'Aye, I've stepped back, ya fucking prick!'

Angus tries to push the door, then he ushers us to move away. He throws his whole body weight at it twice, before it gives. Tash comes out of her room and stands beside me.

'What the fuck is going on?' she says.

He's smashed his bedroom window out. I like it, the feel of fresh air right on my skin like that, and one of our windows, all the way open – it's sort of beautiful. John's climbing up onto his windowsill and he's only wearing a T-shirt, he's not even got socks on, or boxers. He sways on the window ledge, his balls showing below his T-shirt. Angus puts his hands up to show him he isnae gonnae step forward.

'Calm down, John,' he says.

'What's your fucking problem? I was trying tae have a fucking sleep!' Shortie snaps as she stoats down to the boys' landing as well. This day is beginning to feel odd.

'Can you leave us, please, girls?' Angus asks.

We dinnae move. John bunches his T-shirt in one hand.

'Jesus Christ! What's his problem? You better hope he's not got a fucking match,' Shortie mutters.

Angus glares at her.

'What? At least he fucking doesnae, mate, or you'd be going up in fucking flames, ay! John, look at me, it's alright!'

He's swatting the air, he's out of it – I can see it now, and I dinnae know what he's taken, and I dinnae know how long he's been freaking out, but he doesnae look right. I feel a lump in my throat. This isnae like him.

'Anais, get back out of that room right now. It's against

policy tae approach someone when they're threatening tae jump!'

'Fuck the policy, Angus.'

I hold my hand out and John smiles at me, but it's not really a smile, it's a grimace. He slows down, dazed, and points to the back garden.

'What the fuck's that?'

'I cannae see from here – what is it?' Angus asks him.

'It looks like Brian.'

'Okay, now climb inside the windowsill, come on, pal.'

'It looks like someone's fucked him right up!'

'What?'

Angus leans over the balcony. Eric's on the phone downstairs tae the police department: you can hear him reporting all the details back to an officer.

'Can you check out the back, please, Eric?' he calls down.

'Come down,' I ask John right quiet, holding my hand out for him to take it.

He's flapping his hands, twisting his torso. I can see the gear in his veins; they are big and purple and pulsing and he gives me this evil stare and I get the fear right in my gut. He points at all of us one by one.

'Fuck you, fuck you, fuck you, fuck you and fuck you!'

He points at Angus last of all, and jumps.

13

THE COLD tap is dripping. My bath water's not hot, but there's still a haze and the taps are reflected in the water – so is the wall, and the window and the door. I love looking at reflections in bath water, any kind of water in fact. They're like wee surreal paintings. I might photograph reflections, in water, in kettles, in things other people dinnae look at, like bins and shit like that. My tits are perfect in water. When I stand up they sit lower, cos they're heavy, and I cannae put a pencil under one and have it just fall away – that's only if your paps are medium or small. Sink down until only my nose and mouth stick out. Blow three neat smoke-rings, one shoots through the other. I'm floating up as my mobile begins to ring.

'Hello?'

'Alright,' Jay says.

'Alright.' Fuck – my heart totally goes. He hasn't rung me for months and he's not texted since I said it was over. I curl my toe around the tap.

'How's you?' he asks.

'I'm alright, how are you?'

'Anais, I wanted tae tell you something.'

'What?'

'You're just a wee fucking dirty from a fucking kids' home, hen, ay?'

I press off, and my heart's beating now, I cannae believe he phoned just to do that. It rings again straight away.

'Who the fuck d'ye think you are?' I say.

'Come on! I'm only kidding – you're too over-sensitive, nae sense of humour, that's your fucking problem.'

'What do you want, Jay?'

'I want you back. D'ye not want me back, Anais?'

'I need tae be on my own.'

'Aye, that's not what you used tae say all the times you came tae get wasted, when your old dear fucking died, ay? Who took you in, Anais? Who hid you from the polis a million fucking times?'

I drape my legs over the side of the bath, and steam rises up off the bath in wisps.

'Aye, and all the other lassies made you happy too, Jay.'

'That's a low blow, Anais, and it's not like you were some wee virgin, were you?'

He's not saying anything, but I can hear him breathe.

'So, d'ye want tae see me or what?' he asks.

'Maybe.'

'Maybe? They're letting me out, Anais. Meet me at the safe-house, I *need* you tae come.'

He's making me feel like I'm all wrong, until I'm confused – I hate it when he turns up and does this. I'm trying not to let my phone get wet from the bath, and I feel like crying. I wish that would stop, it's a new thing – this teary shit lately.

'Why are you no gonnae meet me? Are you fucking someone new, Anais?'

'Fuck off!'

I launch my phone off the wall. The back scuds along the tiles, spins and stops under the back pipe on the toilet. The battery lands under the sink. I slide up, tears hot on my face – not real tears, I dinnae do real tears – blink them back, blink them right fucking back. Fuck! I want to hurt myself. I want to cut or bite or hit my head off something, cos it hurts – it really, really fucking hurts. There's a knock on the bathroom door.

'Are you okay in there?'

Christ! It's Joan.

'What?'

'Are you alright in there, Anais?'

'Aye, sorry. I was just washing my hair.'

'It didnae sound like it. It sounded like you threw something?'

'I dropped the soap.'

'You are aware that bathtimes don't begin for another two hours?'

'Sorry.'

Stick my fingers up at the door. Fuck off. Fuck off. Fuck off. Fuck off!

'Okay, I'll see you later on.'

'Okay.'

I hate it when a guy makes you feel cheap. It's like that in fights. It's like that when you say no and they do it anyway. I've not let that happen for a long time, I learnt – the worst way.

Turn the cold tap on with one toe and let it run until the bath's almost cold. I turn the taps off using both feet and rummage behind my head for a roll-up. Spark the lighter three, four, five times, cos my hand's damp; eventually the flame catches.

Sink back under the water. I wiggle my toe in the cold tap, so rivulets trickle down my ankle. The fire alarm is ripped off the ceiling, half of it is sat in the sink – I'll need to try to shove it back up later.

I like being underwater like this. All I can hear is my heart. Thud. Thud. Thud. It's muffled like the soundtrack of sharks in a documentary I watched a few weeks ago, thud, thud, thud, thud, thud – I'm just a girl with a shark's heart.

Mullet's in. I try to get around the landing without him seeing but he clocks me right away.

'Anais, it's not bathtime yet.'

'I know.'

'So, why did you have a bath?'

I shrug.

'I'm putting this on report,' he says.

'Have you got a girlfriend?'

'That's none of your business, Anais.'

'I bet you only do fresh meat.'

I stare at him and he flinches, and glances around – but nobody else heard.

'Are you having an outing later?' he asks.

'Why can you not just say – are you going out?'

Tash comes out of her room. 'Has John been seen yet?'

'No, Natasha, he's not. Did you give a description tae the police of what he was wearing?'

Mullet is glad to have someone focus his attention away from me.

'Aye, he was wearing fuck-all but a T-shirt with a monkey DJ-ing on the back!' Tash says.

He walks off, shaking his head.

Shove my door as shut as I can get it, put all the bits of my phone back together, get the battery in and turn it on. Messages flash.

I'm sorry. I want you. I'm just being a dick. You are the most stunning girl I've ever met. I need tae see you, I miss you, it's alright if you only want tae be pals – please, I am begging you, Anais, come and see me when I get out. I'll send you a time and date, be there, it's important.

'Anais, what are you doing later?' Shortie sticks her head around my door.

'Nothing, why?'

'You couldnae do me a huge favour, seeing as things are, like, alright with us now?'

'What?'

'I've got a date, tae piss John off, not that he's fucking here tae see it now, likesae, but it's a doubler – you wouldnae?'

'No.'

'Please?'

'I'd rather chew my own arm off, Shortie. I'm not in a dating mood.'

'Dinnae be like that, they're just a laugh, they always have good gear!' she says.

'Who are they like?'

'They're nice, really nice, we'll pick you up at the gate later. I'm going tae meet them the now. I just thought – you know, we could hang out.'

'Alright.'

'Really?' she asks.

'Aye, I'll see you out there at six.'

Slam my music on – loud as it will go – and find the last of my glittery body lotion, rub it into my arms and legs and neck. Spray perfume over my head and walk through it. I hate these social-work towels; they are so tiny.

I'm still listening to music on Jay's old iPod cos my dock's totally battered – need to get a new one. Skip through tracks until I get to 'Jesus Don't Want Me for a Sunbeam', on Nirvana's unplugged sessions. I love this album. After this I'll play some no-wave. Or Joy Division, 'Love Will Tear Us Apart'. Teresa used to say I was old-school. She said the best movie stars and burlesque dancers, and musicians, dealers, artists and hookers, were all totally old-school. I wish I was a drummer in a really good band.

I've left my brush in the bathroom, pad out of my room and stop. The twins are standing at the end of the hall, holding hands. They're totally identical, curly blonde hair, blue eyes, and they look just like Isla. I love their matching dungarees, and they've both got cute wee welly-boots on; hers have ladybird eyes and his have frogs.

'Hello,' I say.

They scuff their feet and stare at me; they have beautiful wee fat arms and dimpled fingers. Isla comes out of her room with her social worker.

'Mammie!' The boy reaches his arms up.

Isla picks him up and hugs him so, so tightly. The girl wraps her arms around Isla's leg.

'I have something for you both, maybe, if that's okay with Mummy?' I ask Isla and she nods.

Leg it back to my room and haul a long T-shirt on for

now. I only own two lucky things. One is luckier than the other – I come back out with my arms behind my back.

'Pick an arm,' I say.

The wee girl looks a bit curious and freaked-out.

'It's okay, Bethany, go on,' Isla says.

She picks my left arm.

'Good choice,' I say and I pull out the feathered head-dress, and she grabs hold of it shyly.

'What do you say?' Isla asks her.

'Thank you.'

'So this must be for you!' I say to the wee boy, as I whip my black fairy wings out and waggle them like a big beard under my chin. He giggles, snatches them straight away and runs off down the hall making aeroplane noises.

'Thanks, Anais.'

''S alright. Are you taking them to the soft play centre?'

Isla nods and squeezes my arm. Her social worker's away downstairs, waving at her to come down.

'See you later then,' I say.

Close my door to its designated four-inch gap. A lump rises in my throat again. I ache. Don't think about it. Just go out and get wrecked.

Laid out on my bed are a pair of navy-blue shorts, short-shorts, with six buttons at the front and a high waist. I'll need to put tights on under them, cos my legs are so white they're almost blue. It isnae a good look for shorts. Haul on my favourite knickers, matching bra and my oldest band T-shirt – it's totally faded, and it has wee holes in it, but I love it. Slip on four bracelets, pin my hair up at the back until it looks more Sixties. Rub serum between my fingers and smooth it over until my hair is shiny, shiny.

So.

Paris it is.

Paris – offensively rich parents, three eccentric and exceptionally beautiful aunts, a garden with a swing and a sundial. Jasmine flowers. Lilies. A big bedroom with a huge window overlooking the garden. Stuff. Piles of it. All new. All expensive. None from the chore.

Dab foundation on quickly, but not too much. I suit my pale skin mostly, it's just my legs that look see-through in winter, so it's better to hide them. Try my new pink blusher, carefully pencil on cat's eyes with black kohl, finish up with two layers of mascara. I outline my lips with red liner, fill them in, then blot them by kissing the back of my hand. They look like perfect wee cupid's bows – red always make the amber flecks in my eyes pop out.

I glance at where my wings were. Professor True gave me those wings. He bought them in London. Professor True was quite funny really. He loved Teresa and you want someone to love your mum – even if he is a client. It made her happy. He was always bringing her cashmere jumpers, and books, and perfume, and wee things for me. He got the wonky-cock disease eventually. Teresa said it was alright, cos mostly he just liked it up the arse anyway. Gross, or what!

Check myself out – I look like I didnae try, but still hot. Red-red lips, and my eyes are a wee bit green today; 's funny how that happens. You always have tae make sure your outfit is immaculately clean, and ironed when you go out, ay. I'd never walk out the door with something shan on. I'd rather die.

My clothes smell nice – every inch is pristine. I shove

my sneakers on and head downstairs. Shortie's probably waiting at the gate already.

'Hey, Angus.'

'Anais, are you in for the evening?'

'Am I under house-arrest?'

'Of course you're not under house-arrest, young lady – that's a bit of a dramatic way tae describe things.'

'Then I'm going out.'

'Aye, so you'll be wanting your Friday outing money?' he asks.

'Aye.'

Angus rummages around and pulls out the petty-cash box.

'Oh, there's an envelope for you as well.' He slides it over.

I open it up. It's the results from the lab woman.

'They've only got half my results here?'

'You'll get the rest soon.'

'Do they not know what the blood is from?'

Angus shakes his head.

'They want you back down at the station again for questioning. The policewoman's condition is deteriorating.'

My heart misses a beat.

'How can you deteriorate when you're already in a coma?'

'I'm not sure, they didnae say, Anais. You just need tae really watch yourself right now because if the polis can get you locked up, believe me, they are gonnae.'

'Is she gonnae die?'

'We better hope not, and we better hope we can prove you had nothing tae do with it just as soon as possible. We'll find a way, okay?'

'Do the polis want tae speak to me tonight?'

'Not yet, don't worry, go and have some fun. So, twenty pounds outing money, young lady, sign here for that, please. Where are you going?'

'I'm going tae the pictures.'

'Sounds good. What film are you going tae see?'

'That new one.'

'The one about the kangaroo?'

Angus scrawls something down on a file.

'Noh, I'm going to see the one with the girl and the guy,' I lie.

'The one with the girl and the guy, I thought it might be that one.' Angus smiles at me, he looks stoned. 'Well, just you make sure the guy doesnae step out of line, or I'll have tae come downtown and knock him out!'

'Funny.'

'I'm not being funny, Anais, I am being deadly serious. You have tae have someone tae watch your back, and despite what the police are saying about you being a big bad lassie, I think you've nae bad in you at all.'

I feel – shocked. I have never had a member of staff say something like that to me before, and he is just counting my outing money and places it on the table. I sit and look at the religious icons on the office wall.

'You know, you're not the only teenager who has ever been entirely alone in the world,' he says.

'How? Did you come from care, like?'

'No, Anais, I came from worse than that – believe me. I'm just saying: dinnae think you're totally alone, you're not, alright?'

He hands me the money.

'Cheers, Angus.'

'Back by 11 p.m., you have court tomorrow!' he shouts as the door slams shut.

The twins are running down the hallway – chased by Tash. She's wearing a bucket on her head and making zombie arms at them. Bethany races by doing a whoop, whoop, whoop, and scalping anyone who comes near her with a ruler.

I slip out the front door before anyone notices. It's cold outside but it doesnae matter. My legs look skinny in dark tights. This T-shirt is the best, it's my mostest favourite one ever, The Velvet Underground playing in the Factory. It was a present from Pat. She said she shagged their guitarist, or their bass player, or somebody. I wonder how she's getting on with her penis-art? Teresa and Pat were best friends for nearly thirty years. How mad is that? I cannae imagine even knowing someone for thirty years, I probably never will. I really need to go and see Pat soon, I cannae keep avoiding it.

Two blackbirds fly past. Fields of grass sway in the breeze and it sounds like waves. I walk fast and scan the fields, and the edges of the forest, but I cannae see John anywhere. He must be freaking out, and he'll be freezing. This isnae a good time of year to sleep rough.

That was funny Angus saying that, like someone was bothered, like someone would stick up for you. I almost like him – for staff, he isnae that bad.

Get to the gate and the gargoyle is sitting with his back to me, his ears are pointy. I look out and there is no car, not yet, just an empty road. I've not even got Shortie's number to text her and see where she is.

Lean against the gate and light a fag. A bird swoops down low, glides across the fields, it cries out – long and low – and it's eerie. Look again, not one single car, not yet.

I scuff my feet off the wall and watch the bird soar towards the woods. The Panopticon is creepy from up here, the top bit of the watchtower is a sharp peak in the middle of the building, and below that, inside there's the surveillance window, and although the experiment like to hang out there, they dinnae need a watchtower cos they can see anywhere, that's the truth.

14

A LOW heavy bass hums along the road. Fuck, is that Shortie in that motor? It's an old Seventies car, what a fucking death-trap, it is totally pish. She's sat up the front with some guy, the other one's in the back.

'Get in then.' She grins.

'I'm not sitting in the back with him! No offence,' I say tae the guy.

'Totally sound, get in the front,' she says to him and she climbs over the front seat. I jump in the back beside her.

The guy that's driving passes me back a joint, and the car pulls away, speeding right up to eighty, flying past Joan who's trundling up in her old VW. We give her a wave. The guy who's driving is hot, he has the nicest hands I've ever seen on a guy. His fingers are kind of square and long. His hands are twice as big as mine. I love it when a guy is tall like that – it makes me feel petite; I am petite, but it makes me feel more so.

'Anais, that's Ben, and that's Craig.' She nods at the driver.

Shortie flings her arms around the seat in front of her, touching the Ben guy's hair. He kisses her hand.

'Alright,' he says.

'Alright,' the Craig guy says.

He's cute, his wrists are slim – not thin, just perfect. Double-drag on the joint and watch him drive. His hands are like a sculptor's, not a pianist's, more like an artist or an artisan.

'So, where are we going?' I ask, passing the joint to Shortie.

'Dunno,' she shrugs.

'Where are we going?' I ask Craig.

'Poaching,' he says, turning the tunes up.

'What?'

'Poaching!'

'Poaching fucking what?' I ask Shortie.

'Salmon probably. We've done it before, ay, it's a laugh, Anais – you're gonnae love it.'

'D'ye no like poaching?' Ben asks me.

'I dinnae murder fish for fun, no,' I say.

'Anais put a cop in a coma,' Shortie says.

The two guys look back now, the Ben one's grinning.

'So, you'll put a cop in a coma, but you'll no kill a fish?'

'I didnae put a cop in a coma.'

'She did, she battered her with a kosh – all the kids ken about it in all the units. And she burnt down the last place she was in. She's been charged one hundred and forty-seven times,' Shortie says proudly.

'Have you read my files?' I ask her.

'Noh, just eavesdropping on meetings at the office. They're always talking about you, especially Eric, and Angus, and Joan. Mullet does as well, but he's not so fascinated. He just fucking hates you.'

'What does Angus say, like?'

'He's always sticking up for you,' she says.

We drive through some red lights, then turn down a hill heading out to the river. There's a castle in the distance. Some lights are on in the windows. Imagine living in a castle. I cannae believe we are going poaching. I might have tae stage a humanist intervention. Fuck! I am so stoned already.

'I hear you and Shortie had a fight?' Ben asks, grinning.

'Aye.'

'I hear Shortie let you off lightly?' he says, grinning even wider.

She looks away a wee bit sheepish, like.

'Aye, something like that,' I say and Shortie starts giggling, and I do too. Craig keeps glancing at me in the rear-view mirror. I'm glad I came out now.

'So what do youz do then, now everyone knows I'm a fucking degenerate and Shortie's hard as fuck?'

I pass her the skins, and she pulls out a wee rolling mat.

'They're farmers,' she says.

'For fuck's sake,' I say.

'What's wrong with that?' Ben asks.

'I've never been on a date with a farmer, that's all,' I say, trying no tae laugh, but Shortie's laughing, her shoulders are shaking away.

'What kind of farmers are you then?' I ask them. 'Are you sheep-shaggers?'

Shortie cannae roll her joint now for laughing, and the Craig guy's smiling away.

'You're a wide one, ay,' he says tae me.

'We're pig farmers,' Ben says, all serious. 'I dinnae fucking see how it's a laughing matter!'

Me and Shortie are still giggling when we pull into some private estate. There's a sign on the main gates that reads No Entrance.

'I dinnae think we're meant tae be in here,' Shortie says.

'Have a drink.' Ben passes a bottle of beer to us in the back seat, then he opens another two for them.

'We'll not get caught,' I say.

I light a joint. I need this. Fucking pig farmers. Fucking poaching. The night's really pretty out, though, the sky's an amazing dark-blue colour. Craig's driving with the headlights off now, we roll down by the river and then stop.

'Come on then, ladies, after youz.' Ben gets out and opens the door for Shortie.

I get out on my side and Craig's leaning against his door already.

'Alright?' he says.

'Aye.'

Shortie and Ben are kissing over on the other side of the car. I take a drag of the joint and lean against the motor, watch the water glinting – 's all silvered by the moon.

'Have you got a boyfriend then, Anais?' Craig asks.

'Aye.'

'No, she's not, he's in jail,' Shortie says, then starts kissing again.

Craig leans in closer. He smells nice. He's got a square jaw and he's skinny, tall though, with wide shoulders and his hair's quite long, nearly down tae his shoulders. He touches my hair, just lightly, then he pulls a strand off my face and tucks it behind my ear and the world goes quiet.

'Can I kiss you?' he asks.

He leans in, and his lips are soft, and his hair is soft, his neck's warm. There's shivers down my back as he touches my waist, runs his fingers down my side.

'Are we fucking poaching or what?' Ben appears right next to us and I open my eyes. Ben is holding out a hammer tae Craig, and he's got another one at his side, and a torch.

'What the fuck are youz gonnae do? Batter the fish tae death?' I ask.

'Aye,' Ben says. 'Exactly.'

'He's cute, isn't he?' Shortie says.

'I suppose. I thought you weren't the go-with-guys-you-dinnae-know type?'

'He knows my brother. We only ever kiss, they're a laugh, ay. Just decent guys.'

We sit up on the bonnet, listening to music and leaning back to look at the stars. The two of them are wading into the river. I'm really stoned now. I turn on my side and rest my face on the windscreen and watch them raising their hammers in the air.

Thud.

Thud.

The water's splashing like mad, and they're lobbing salmon up on tae the embankment.

'Did you do it, Anais?'

'What?'

'The pig in the coma?'

'Aye.'

'You did, honestly?'

'No, but lately it feels like it'd be easier tae say aye, though. I didnae kosh her, I dinnae think I did anyway.'

'How can you not know?'

'Cos I was so fucking wasted that day, I could have

massacred the mob and no remembered. But, in here – you know, right in here – I just ken I didnae. I keep remembering bits of that day but not all of it. The experiment dinnae care, though.'

I feel the air go funny around us.

'The what?' she asks.

'Nothing.'

'What's the experiment, Anais?'

'Alright, gorgeous!' Ben reappears holding up a dead salmon. He's got blood on his hands and his face, and holds the torchlight up tae the salmon's eyes.

'That is giving me the boak,' I tell him.

'How?' he asks.

'Fuck, get in the car!' Craig shouts and we turn. The estate's Land Rover is motoring towards us, and the police are heading along the other way.

'Someone must have seen us!' Ben slams the door behind us, skidding the car down the gravel embankment, and me and Shortie duck down on the back seat. Craig drives us along by the river with the headlights still out.

'Will they see us?' Shortie whispers.

'They better not, or I'm fucking lifted again, and I'm not having fucking poaching on my record!' I hiss at her.

'Shut the fuck up,' Ben says.

'You shut the fuck up,' I say back tae him.

'Hold on, girls,' Craig says as the police siren leaps intae light and blares. We skid around on the embankment and he plunges the car right intae the river.

'What the fuck are you doing?' Shortie screams.

Water is coming up through the floor and the engine is whirring like fuck.

'It's shallow enough, it's alright.' He grinds the stick down and the car lurches up onto the far bank. The polis car is still on the other riverbank, headlights pointed at us. The policeman is getting out and gesturing to the guy from the estate.

Craig rolls down his window.

'Fucking tossers!' he shouts back.

'That was great,' Shortie says. 'Fucking brilliant!'

15

THE HEADLIGHTS glow, until the car turns left and the lights disappear. Then there is only blackness. I turn away and keep walking silently, letting my eyes adjust to the dark. Fields swish gently in the wind. It's so cold now – my arms are all goosebumps. The lamp posts are orange orbs in the dark, and there urnay many of them. I suppose nobody normally walks along here at night.

I cannae believe Shortie decided to stay out with Ben. Craig asked me to stay, but I cannae. I'm late, but at least I'll not get done for absconding if I go back now. I didnae mean to have sex with him – but he was . . . he was just nice. I dinnae want to see him again, though, I'm not into farmers.

Something flies up out from a field to my left and I shit myself. I'm still buzzy, hyper-aware. Shapes in the hedgerows. Silhouettes in the trees. A cow watches from a field.

There are no cars out. No headlights. Not even miles away. Nothing. Just the swish, swish, swish of fields. The sound of my sneakers hitting the tarmac, me clicking a lighter round and round, a wee flash of flame in the dark.

The Panopticon's a big looming hulk. It's too big, like

somewhere that a giant lives. I dinnae want to go back in there. Stop at the gates and I can tell the gargoyle's been waiting to see how my night went.

'What?' I ask him.

It must be nearly 4 a.m. Surely it'll get light soon? The ground's frosty, they say it's gonnae snow soon, but it shouldnae until November and that's still a few days away.

I wonder if they called the police on me. They will have, I'll be reported missing. I should stay that way. Clouds race the sky. The grass is sparkly.

Feel around the pillar at the base. It's old and crumbly, but there are holds if you get your hand right in. I get my first foothold and grip hard, push up at the same time with my feet. I just cling on, feeling around. Hook my hand over the cat's tail and pull myself up.

The owl swoops right in front of me, then she's away again, over the field, hunting for mice. I sit down on Malcolm the cat's back, put my arms around his neck and lean in, somehow he doesnae even feel cold – I close my eyes.

'Take me tae Paris,' I whisper.

His wings beat – once, twice, we lift up.

'Where in Paris, m'lady?' he asks.

'Fly me tae a side street in the artists' quarter, tae a room above a café where I can look out the window and see the same old man who drinks tea and has cake every day.'

'My pleasure.'

Up, up, up towards the moon. The moon is not quite so terrible tonight; his baldness is luminescent, all his moon craters and valleys stand out. Half-close my eyes as Malcolm's huge wings beat around me. We swoop low across the tree-tops – glide towards lights away in the distance.

I grip his neck, knees holding onto his body. His ears turn and my eyes snap open. The gargoyle stares across at me. He's a demented jester, and someone has put another cigarette out in his mouth. I cuddle into the cat and rest my head on his neck.

The Panopticon windows are lit blue; the night-nurse'll be in now. That building is not a place to live, it's a place to grow specimens. The experiment know I'm back. They're pissed I slipped off their radar for two seconds. They obviously cannae see girls who fly on cats. I'll pretend I didnae go off their radar, but I know I did. If you can do it once, you can do it again, right?

Someone's running across the fields. Fuck, who is that? I duck right down as they get closer, but they lope straight towards me and I can see they are wearing an ill-fitting flowery dress.

'Is that you, Anais?' John hisses.

'John?'

'Fuck,' he clutches his heart, 'I shit myself when I saw you. I didnae think anyone'd be up. Where have you been?'

'I was out,' I say. I dinnae want to tell him I was out with Shortie and some guys – he'd be gutted.

'They'll have reported you missing by this time ay day.'

'I know.'

'Why are you on top of Malcolm?' he asks.

'Aye, about that, Malcolm's a shan name for a flying cat.'

'He's not a cat, he's a liger with wings,' John says.

I slide off Malcolm's back and stand on top of the pillar.

'I thought you were gonnae go for me earlier?' He grins.

'I was gonnae try and drag you off that windowsill, cos I could tell you were gonnae jump.'

'I was wasted,' he says.

'Blatantly. I'm amazed you didnae break anything.'

'My ankle is swollen up tae fuck, I think I've strained it, ay. It fucking hurt when I straightened up a bit.'

'I bet it did.'

'I'd just had shite news – well, Mullet had kept some bad news from me, ay. My mum didnae win her appeal tae get out. She's fucked up about it, and Christmas is coming and she kept saying she wanted tae get out and we could all be together for Christmas, and I just . . . I just needed tae get mashed.'

''S fair enough,' I say.

'Fuck it, d'ye wantae wrestle me . . . girl-on-girl?' he asks.

'I dinnae wrestle, I'd just kick your cunt in.'

'Aye, well, we'll skip that then, ay. I thought you might fancy me in a dress!'

'You make an ugly bird, John,' I laugh.

'Fucking hell, Anais.'

He looks serious for a minute. His eyes are round like he'll cry, and I can tell his anger's gone. That dress is ridiculous. His nipples poke out over the top.

'You like my frock though, ay?'

'Bit slutty.' I grin.

'You'll be wanting tae borrow it then?'

'Aye.'

'Are you coming back tae the unit then?'

He nods down at the big shadow at the end of the drive and tries to adjust his dress, but his paps are still well on show. He places a finger over each nipple for modesty.

'I suppose so.'

I climb around Malcolm's back, then jump the last bit.

We walk on the grass. John limps where his ankle is all swollen. The wee house hidden behind the trees that I saw yesterday is lit up outside, with dim lights on its porch.

'What's that place, John?'

'That's for under-eights, they've got like six of them in there.'

'What, a home?'

'Aye. Most of them are under five, though. They bring them down tae visit us sometimes.'

'That's horrible. D'ye want a smoke?' I pull a joint out.

'Fuck, aye.' John nods appreciatively. 'Follow me,' he whispers and grabs my hand.

'I saw Tash over in that field earlier, looked like she was getting something?'

'Oh, that's their stash,' he says. 'I've looked for it a few times but I cannae find it. They're saving up Tash's earnings from the game – they're gonnae apply for custody of the twins soon as they're old enough.'

'Where's she working, like?' I ask.

'Just on the street. I did it a few times, had one guy used tae pick me up near the bushes by the theatre. There's fucking hundreds of them there. He was alright, just wanted a wee wank-off, then home tae his wife. I get good money when I do – 's cos of my huge cock, ay.' He grins.

'Aye, okay then!'

I follow John around to the back of the wee house. There's a kid's roundabout in the shape of a big sunflower.

'Madam, your chariot awaits!'

I hop on and he spins it; he has to hoick up his dress, and the big shoes he's chored look mental. He's got the joint clamped in his mouth, grinning, one foot on the roundabout, the other pounding the ground.

'So, really, are you alright?' I ask him.

'Suppose.'

'I met Bethany and Stewart.'

'Did their foster-mum bring them in again?'

'No, Isla's social worker brought them in.'

John cracks his knuckles nervously. He hands the joint back to me and the roundabout slows.

Lean back and watch the stars spin round.

'She needs tae stop cutting herself, and have you seen Mullet? He won't go near her if she's cut; she doesnae let anyone but the doctor touch her, like, but Mullet really makes it obvious. I think she's trying tae cut the virus out, ay. She feels so fucking bad that the twins have got it, she cannae take it. There'll probably be a cure by the time they're older, though, and the kind she's got she's probably gonnae live another forty fucking years, ay. It's just shit though. How come the nice people always get the shit luck, Anais?'

'How did she not know she had it?'

'She had the twins at home with her ma, same as her ma had done, same as her granny had done. They never told the school – her ma was scared they'd take the bairns away, and she's away in the fucking head anyway, Isla's ma. They didnae find out until Isla took them for their first immunisations. That's how she found out she had it. Next thing she's hauled in, her ma's hauled in, then her da comes back – says he knew he had it the whole fucking time.'

'Shit! Her dad?'

'Noh, that's not how she got it, no like that; her old

man's a smackhead, he used tae tie her tae the bed when they went out tae score, so she took a shot of his gear one night when he was nodding. Game over.'

'Fucking hell.'

The roundabout's still spinning and all I can see is stars and John's head clear as, with the universe behind him. Every other second we whizz past the wee kid's home again, and a window at the back of the home keeps punctuating the blur of trees, building, window, blur, trees, building, window. A small face peers out from it, then a staff member pops up and switches a light on.

'Shit, John, fucking run!'

He drags his foot to stop the roundabout and we pelt behind the trees and across the grass. At the main doorway I ring the bell.

'You've got stiff nips,' I tell him.

''S it turning you on, ay?'

The door clicks open, and the night-nurse looks at us.

'Your pupils are dilated, Anais.'

'It's dark.'

'Where did you get that dress, John?'

'I nicked it off a washing line, d'ye like it?' he asks her.

'Well, you better take it back again tomorrow,' she says.

'Aye, alright. Night-night, Anais.' He gives me a wink and he's away, up the stairs, peeling off his dress as he goes.

'Have you been out together?' she asks me.

'Noh!' John shouts back as he runs up the stairs.

The night-nurse grabs me by the chin, tilts my head back and pulls me towards the light. She smells of eucalyptus and she turns my face this way and that. The woman sees everything. She sees what you had for breakfast and the kid you punched in primary school. She sees the first thing you ever stole. And the time your baby-teeth fell out and the tooth-fairy didnae fucking come. She even sees the next day when you glued your baby-teeth to the neighbours bike, like they were eyes, and he cried and cried and cried.

'You need to straighten up, young lady.'

'Tell me about it.'

'Upstairs then, Anais. You were both reported missing. Joan will want to see you in the morning.'

Run upstairs, quiet. It's good to be back somewhere with a bed. I would never have thought that a year ago. I would rather have slept in a bush or on a roundabout, or by a motorway, or in a graveyard or the woods, or a doorway, or anywhere but in a unit where the experiment can come in your sleep and take things out of your brain.

Jars lined up in rows. Old labels on them, curling away, but the glass is clean. Each jar contains something – a strand of hair, bacteria, pubes, milk-teeth rattling off glass. Two different-coloured eyes watch from a fat jar. A red bicycle is in the smallest jar, cycling in circles. Malcolm's trapped in the jar next to that, he pounds his wings and the glass vibrates. The Panopticon is in a jar with a red thread tied around it. A man wearing a wide-brimmed hat is in the watchtower, and he keeps banging on the window for me to look up.

'Don't leave your room, don't leave your room!' He rings a bell, warning anyone who'll listen.

I step outside my bedroom door and head for the top floor, where there are three black doors. I'm ignoring the man – let him hammer on the watchtower window all he likes. I go up the steps to the top landing and open the first door.

It's an ancient lido, full of autumn leaves.

The second door opens onto empty space; a sign for Love Lane hovers tae the right. There isnae a path under it, just a sign and nothing else.

I open the third door and step out onto a pier, which juts out so far across the ocean you could probably walk all the way to another country along it. Its wooden planks are dark with slippery moss, and a humming noise permeates everywhere. A black sun has begun to rise.

The door closes behind me. As I walk down the pier masked men turn around, one by one. A wooden boat bobs out on choppy waves. Miles away it is, miles and miles out.

Jars lilt along on the waves. One carries my social-work files, the missing ones. They have been shrunk down to the size of a tablet. Gargoyle holds the tablet and begins to munch down on it; he munches, munches, munches, then chain-smokes. The tablet is getting him high. He bangs on the glass.

Another jar floats by with Chief in it. He's asleep on a red pillow and his scales have fallen out and his skin is so thin – you can see his reptilian heart. Hayley is in the jar behind him: gaunt and stripping. A masked man steps onto the pier. I cannae go around him. Behind me another guy lunges up out of the water, grabs onto the pier and hauls himself up. He's a keeper of the waters of the dead. This is all the water of the dead. The stagnant ocean. The masked men are corpses and their gills flap. They detest the living.

The barnacle-mask man watches me. He knows I'm afraid

and he likes it. They are everywhere, hundreds and thousands of them, all waiting. The masked men have large black disc-like glasses on, and bulbous yellow eyes bulge out behind them. Each mask is covered in barnacles.

'Can I take your photo?'

I am holding my imaginary camera, picturing the prints in my imaginary gallery, and they just stare. Raise the lens and click. Click. Click. Click-click-click.

Masked men lunge out angrily as a boy in a dress races by them.

'John! John, it's me, it's Anais. John, wait for me, please!'

He shouts back, but I cannae hear what he's saying. Someone comes up behind me. I can feel their breath on my neck as they grab my shoulder – shove me off the pier.

Water. Cold. Sinking, sinking, sinking. Keep my eyes open and gaze up towards a murky light as I fall. It's time tae let go. John dives in above me, swims down and grabs my hand, squeezes it hard; he turns, trying to swim back up tae the surface with me. A wee boy swims up towards us; he's tiny, pointy chin. He touches my arm and John lets go of my hand and swims ahead. The little boy turns right back to me and grins. He has hundreds of wee white fangs. He whorls around my head, until water burns my lungs and I'm drowning.

The experiment built me a bedroom to stay in – it looks like mine but it's not. They want me like this. My eyes glow yellow and there's soft hair all over my body: I'm one of them. I bathe in the waters of the dead and I, too, detest the living.

16

IT'S LIKE the fortieth time he's shouted. I wish he'd shut the fuck up.

'Anais, you have court in forty minutes. Can you get ready, please?' Angus calls.

He's on the landing and has been trying to get me up for half an hour. I turn over. My duvet is warm. I snuggle back down inside it – I just want to sleep all day.

'Why's Mullet taking me tae see my ma?' John asks Angus. I can hear them, they're outside my door now. I wish they'd fuck off.

'I'm really sorry, John, but I cannae take you. I have tae get Miss Sleeps-a-lot tae court on time. Hurry up, Anais!'

'Is she in court for the policewoman, like?'

'I cannae discuss that with you, John.'

'How – is the policewoman dead, like?'

'No, she's not.'

'She's gonnae go down.'

I hear John saying the last bit to someone else, and I haul the duvet right off me. I'm fucking pissed off now.

'Is she getting done for it?' Isla asks Angus.

Jesus, there's a whole fucking powwow going on, on the landing. Rub my face. I feel like I slept in a grave.

'No,' he hisses at them, 'she is getting done for half a dozen other bloody things, if that is okay with you lot? Can you hurry up, John, and dinnae wind Ed up again, and *dinnae steal his car*!'

Isla pokes her head around my door.

'Good luck later,' she says.

'Ta, Isla.'

'John?' I shout.

He sticks his head around.

'I hope it's alright seeing your mum.'

'Fucking whatever,' he says and disappears.

Get up. Drag on a pair of jeans, T-shirt, sneakers. Head to the bathroom and brush my teeth. Isla walks past with her school bag slung over her shoulder, Tash behind her.

'Alright?'

'Morning.'

'Have you got court the day?' Tash asks me.

'Uh-huh.'

I drink some water out of the tap. It's cold and tastes like metal, but clean.

'D'ye think they'll do you?'

'No doubt.'

'Well, I hope they dinnae,' Tash says and they disappear down the corridor.

Joan appears in the bathroom doorway. 'Have you seen Brian?'

I shake my head.

'Okay, you'll be having a review when you get back today, Anais. Last night was unacceptable. You cannot still just disappear when you want and think there will be no consequences. Helen's coming in to discuss this.'

'I thought Helen'd left.'

'She has, but you still have your end-of-care review, and she's taking you tae Warrender Institute, remember?'

'Joan, see how Helen left? Like she just quit – it was after she'd spoken tae the police about me?'

'Helen had plans to take some time out from the social-work department for a while, I'm sure. It won't have been anything tae do with you, okay?'

Joan catches sight of someone at the end of the corridor and marches off.

'I'll discuss this with you later, Anais.'

Trudge downstairs feeling rough as shit. Before I was a teenager I didnae get come-downs, not really, I could get as mashed as I wanted then. I've even started tae get hangovers recently – getting old is pish fun. Brian's sat in the living area reading a book. Angus is waiting for me with the front door open.

'Come on, let's get moving, lady, we're late,' he says.

Joan emerges from the left turret and Brian's face falls.

'We need tae talk, now!' she says to him, and he traipses behind her into the interview rooms.

On the top landing the black doors are all closed, like usual. I feel uneasy, like I never really looked at them before. I haven't been back in there to see the snow wolf or the snow bear, and I have this horrible feeling they are gone.

Crunch out to Angus's car. He opens the passenger door and I get in; it smells of wet dog and faintly of good-quality grass. The air's stale and stuffy from the morning sun. It's giving me the boak.

'So, did you have a good time at the cinema?'

'Aye.' I wind down the window.

'I didnae know they did films until four a.m.?'

'They dinnae.'

'So what were you doing?'

'I was getting laid.'

He turns the engine on and just looks at me.

'You cannae say things like that tae your support worker, Anais.'

'I just did.'

'Fuck's sake, just pick a bloody CD,' he says.

Angus drives with one hand, slides his roll-up tin out his pocket and lights one. He inhales and gestures for me tae take one as well. Bonus.

'Have you not got an iPod?'

'I am what you would call old-school, young lady. I would have stuck with tape cassettes if they still made them.'

'Prehistoric.'

'So, what exactly are we in court for this morning?'

I shrug.

'I need more than that, Anais. I didnae get a chance to see the rest of your files, so I couldn't check what all the charges were. I'm a wee bit unprepared, so help me out here.'

'It's nothing too big. They caught me with Valium, or something.'

'That's it?'

'Aye, probably just minor possession.'

'Nothing else?'

'I stabbed a lassie at the back of the chippy on Old Town Road.'

'Tell me that's not what we're gonnae go tae court for, Anais?'

His voice is all high, he's flapping. It's funny. I dunno why he's flapping, though. I think he's wasted.

'Is that why we're going?'

'It's nothing major, Old-School! Take a chill pill, there's nae stabbings, I promise!' I smile nice and he shakes his head.

Flick through his CDs.

'Your music taste is pish, Angus.'

'Dinnae be judgemental. You've probably never even heard half of them.'

My stomach rumbles. I should have had something for breakfast.

'You're different from the other kids, Anais, d'ye know that? And despite what the police, or Helen, seem tae think, I reckon you've got a very astute, intelligent head on your shoulders.'

'Fucking hardly! How come you're doing this job anyway?'

'Well, job satisfaction, and tae meet inspiring people like yourself. Why do you ask?'

We turn right, but Angus wasnae indicating and a car behind beeps us. He gives the driver a wee wave.

'It doesnae seem like your bag.'

'Maybe I'm not that different from you,' he says.

'I fucking doubt it.'

'This is a shortcut, dinnae tell Joan.'

He accelerates the wrong way down a one-way street and gets us through to the other end without anyone noticing.

I slap on an Arlo Guthrie CD and turn it right up. My feet are tapping away on the dash.

'D'ye like music?'

'Only soulless people dinnae like music. I love music, Angus.'

'I used tae play in bands.'

'Aye? I bet they were shite!'

'Total shite!' He grins.

The children's-panel building is grim. They're always grim. Like police stations. Ugly buildings in concrete, all square, nothing nice about them. The only stations that aren't like that are really old ones in wee villages. They can be quite nice sometimes. I'm staying outside as long as I can, under the doorway, so the rain doesnae make my hair go frizzy.

Smoke a roll-up and watch an old man at the lights. The lights change but he just stands there. They change back to red again and he moves forward. A car beeps at him and he staggers back onto the pavement.

Angus seems quite decent. Normally it's all No Smoking here, and boundary issues with clients there. He could almost be classed as a human being. Maybe. I mean he's not Joan and he's not a Mullet. He sticks his head out the door.

'Move it, we're late.'

Great. Door. Corridor. Door. Room. Long table of freaks.

Angus takes a seat at one side of the room, I take the chair in the middle. There are four panel members facing us; three of them have known me since I was ten. At least it's just the wee room today, it's not like a kiddies' courtroom, just a panel room.

My jeans are looking old. I'm due clothing money next week. I desperately need new stuff, maybe a Fifties halterneck. I saw some great star-shaped sunglasses in the vintage shop in town. I've had the white version, but I lost them. The new ones I saw were black, they were classy.

'Anais Hendricks, today's hearing is for,' the Chairwoman runs her pen down a list, 'threatening a staff member with a metal pole, theft and wilful destruction of school property, illegal possession of prescription drugs, possession of marijuana and, the six-month saga of police vandalism you waged against Lothian and Border police?'

Angus shifts uncomfortably in his seat. He looks across at me.

'Anais is aware that she was on a real downward spiral over the summer,' he says.

'Anais is always on a downhill spiral, Mr Everlen.'

'She has been in the past, but I can personally vouch for the fact that she's working exceptionally hard tae rectify this.'

'Are you telling me, Mr Everlen, that there have been no more charges incurred against Anais, since these ones I have read out?'

She knows. How would she? She must know PC Craig, or her fiancé – he's a policeman as well. I bet she knows the fiancé. I'd bet anything.

'Anais is not here today tae answer questions on anything except the charges in hand,' Angus says firmly.

Go, Angus! He looks as crooked as me.

'Well, first on the agenda is the gratuitous vandalism

against Lothian and Borders police department. This included deliberate destruction of police property and costing the police department thousands of pounds' worth of damages. Also, there is the second time that you have stolen a school minibus from outside Rowntree High School, but this time you,' the woman scrolls her pen down the report in front of her, 'drove it into a wall?'

'I drove it intae the wall both times.'

'Something was different the second time, Miss Hendricks?'

She raises her eyebrows, stops, like she's asking a pub-quiz question. The other three panel members look to see what I'm gonnae say.

'The second time it was on fire,' I respond after a minute.

'Correct.'

Brilliant. A correct answer. What do I win? The woman's running her eye up and down the charges again, looking for something. I hate. This chair. Their faces. That shite gold clock on the wall.

What I don't get is this: if they're gonnae lock me up, they should just do it. This pissing around is stupid. She knows I'm accused of it anyway. I keep thinking about that morning, near Love Lane. I was going down by the bus stop, totally fucked, had been out all night and I saw something; it's been niggling and niggling at me, and you know what, I can see it, I fucking can – it was a squirrel. It was a fucking squirrel, half-run-over in the middle of the road, and the morning commuters were driving down from the roundabout and they'd hit it again, but I walked out into the middle of the road and stuck my hand up to stop them. I was already high as fuck. I mind floating down the road in front of the cars, and none of them could get by me, cos it was that narrow bit of road near the bridge.

'And you have just been placed in the Panopticon, Miss Hendricks, is that right?'

'Uh-huh.'

The squirrel wasnae dead. Cars were beeping at me like fuck as I scooped it up, walked over to the green gate and sat down with it in my lap. I cannae believe I couldnae mind that squirrel. I took my cardigan off, and scooped it up off the road. Cradled it like a wee baby. I folded it up right cosy, then I walked up the woods. The cars were still beeping at me as they drove away. I knew I'd remember that day, I knew I'd remember something.

'Yes, Anais moved in a few days ago and is settling in well,' Angus verifies.

'Really?'

'Yes, she has made several friends already, and she has volunteered to take part in the therapeutic arts group.'

What a liar.

'Miss Hendricks was placed in the Panopticon for the suspected grievous bodily harm of a police officer, is that correct?'

The squirrel wasnae dead. It must have been about 8 a.m., so the drivers in the cars were all pissed off, beeping, trying to get to the motorway for work. I sat down on the wall and ignored them, and I opened up the cardigan to check that the squirrel was okay.

'Anais's not been charged for that,' Angus snaps.

The woman chairing the panel looks over her notes. 'Anais has been detained and questioned – is that correct, Mr Everlen?'

'That has no relevance tae our appearance today.'

'Really? You have been detained and questioned for the suspected grievous bodily harm of a police officer who is now in an acute coma, is that right, Anais? I think that is exceptionally relevant. Is that why you are in the Panopticon without permission to return to school – while the police department complete their investigation?'

Her mind's made up.

If I was on death-row – just me and a dead squirrel that couldnae vouch for me – I'd ask for three last things.

First: to fly.

Second: to achieve something.

Third: to look my real mum, or dad, or granda in the eyes, so I'd know the experiment werenae really what made me.

Imagine knowing that you came from people with hearts and souls? That Chairwoman's uptight; she doesnae like me, she cannae stand me actually, I bet she's never loosened up in her life.

'Do you have anything to say about the case, Miss Hendricks?'

Angus sticks his hand out. 'This goes completely against all protocol,' he says.

'Miss Hendricks?'

'No.' Angus holds his hand up. 'Anais is not here to answer questions about any other cases today. I'm not having this.'

The Chairwoman smiles tightly at him. She looks at me. I bet she's never had a threesome. Me and Jay had a threesome once, we couldnae get right intae it, though; well, I couldnae, he could. I'd thought it would be like the best sex ever, but it wasnae really. It was better after, when I thought about it and made it up in my head.

The Chairwoman settles a sheaf of papers back down and sighs. I bet if she saw that squirrel she'd have run it right over.

'Miss Hendricks, I have seen you here more times than I can count. In fact, if there was a place available for you in a secure unit today, we would have you put there right now.'

'You cannae use an unproven case to affect this one!'

'I hope you are not questioning my professionalism, Mr Everlen?'

'If you continue to use an unproven case that should not even be mentioned here, then yes, I will – officially, if necessary.'

'You will be tagged tomorrow morning, Anais, at your local police station. And I'm putting you on a curfew pending further review of your charges. Do you have anything to say?'

Aye. Aye, I do. It's this: here is what you don't know – I'd lay down and die for someone I loved; I'd fuck up anyone who abused a kid, or messed with an old person. Sometimes I deal, or I trash things, or I get in fights, but I am honest as fuck and you'll never understand that. I've read books you'll never look at, danced to music you couldnae appreciate, and I've more class, guts and soul in my wee finger than you will ever, ever have in your entire, miserable fucking life. I wonder if I should tell them about the squirrel?

'Do you have anything to say, Anais?' she asks again.

Paris.

Paris it is.

Paris and its cobbled streets, and a beautiful mother who wears headscarfs and big Jackie O sunglasses and drives barefoot without a seatbelt on. She's a burlesque star. Or a brain surgeon. She's let me drink wine since I was seven. I never get drunk. Just mellow. She reads me poetry and we bake fairy cakes.

'We are aware that the Panopticon has a secure wing opening soon?' she says to Angus.

Maybe a mansion. Maybe a dad who is in government. Maybe he has a mistress, but probably not, because the headscarf mother is so beautiful he is madly in love with her, like every day.

The Chairwoman stares. Fuck off, cunt-pus. Your mind is made up, and I've got absolutely fuck-all to say. I've so much nothing to say that I can feel my throat closing up. It happens like that sometimes. Once when I was four I stopped speaking for six weeks. They said it was a protest but it wasnae.

'It is my belief that you cannot stop yourself, Miss Hendricks. Everything in your record tells me that you will keep offending.'

Angus sits forward and the Chair holds her hand up and continues.

'And, should you be tried for one single offence more, then we have a court order to have you placed in a secure unit and detained until you are eighteen years old, without review.'

'I thought you said you would tag her first?' Angus is standing up and his hands are a wee bit shaky. She is really pissing him off.

'Anais will be tagged, and if she is charged again, then she will be automatically detained for a three-year minimum.'

'For *any* single further offence?'

'Yes, Mr Everlen, for any single further offence – can you sit down please? Thank you. Furthermore, she will offend again very soon; in fact it is my opinion that is exactly what's going to happen. Miss Hendricks can't stop herself, and nobody else appears to have any influence to stop her, either. She is clearly a danger to those around her.'

'No, she's not.'

'With all due respect, Mr Everlen, I've known Miss Hendricks a lot longer than you have. I will personally advocate that she graduates to the maximum-security wing in the Panopticon at the earliest possible opportunity. We have pages,' the Chairwoman brandishes a thick sheaf of papers, 'pages and pages of charges, and this isn't even half of them. Anais, do you want to respond?'

I've nothing to say. I keep thinking about when I went up the woods with the squirrel. I unwrapped it tae set it free and it was still alive, just for a minute. Then its brain fell out. Just like that.

'It is my opinion, Miss Hendricks, that you are going to reoffend. Once you have done so, you will go into a secure unit. And when you get released from there, you will offend again and you will go on – to spend your adult life in prison, which is exactly where you belong, because you, Miss Hendricks, present a considerable danger both to yourself and to *all* of society.'

'This is ludicrous, you cannae say things like that tae a kid. I've a mind tae fucking report you!' Angus shoots up again.

'I've a mind tae report you for abusive language, Mr Everlen. Sit back down! Do you understand me, Miss Hendricks? A secure unit *is* exactly where you belong, despite you convincing people otherwise, and you and I both know it's where you're going.'

The Chairwoman sits back. She has a gleam of sweat on her collarbone. She's underweight. She probably lives on Ryvita, and anger. She looks like she's never laughed – not even once in her whole life.

I bet she doesnae wank, either. Teresa used tae say you cannae trust folk that dinnae wank. They're more predisposed tae murder. I'm feeling panicky again. Count each breath. Inhale one, two, three, four, exhale. I used tae count the places I'd lived. In bed at night I'd count each one, and the things I could remember about living there. Things like bad breath, or poppies in a garden. I remember a wee dog that wore a tartan blanket. Countless foster-brothers or sisters going: *They're not your parents, you know*. A weird cuckoo clock, a purple settee. A car smelling of custard. The dampness of piss on a carpet. A room without windows or doors.

The Chairwoman is still staring like she expects me to say something, or do something, or she's just enjoying knowing in all truth – I'm fucked. Aye. Very good. Fuck you too, Your Honour. Fuck you very much.

'There was no need for that.' Angus glares at the Chair and the board.

'Are we done?' I ask.

'I will ask you one last time, Miss Hendricks. Do you have anything to say?'

I clear my throat and they all look at me again.

'Your brother-in-law is in the police force, isn't he?' I say to her.

'Case closed, until next time, Miss Hendricks.'

'Sorted.'

Walk. Walk while I still can without a tag on my ankle. I'm not up for being trackable 24/7, no way.

I cannae believe I forgot that squirrel. I bet they can tell the difference between squirrel blood and human blood. I bet anything. Maybe my test results will be back soon – the rest of them – and it'll clear all this fucking shite up. I've had enough. I've had so much enough that I feel like I'm falling and I cannae bring myself to care.

There's a play-park down the street. Two kids are on the swings, laughing and kicking their legs out to get higher. Stupid panel. They are stupid as well, and ignorant. They would never fit in, in Paris.

Angus marches out the door, shaking his head. 'She has a fucking problem,' he states and opens the battered car door for me.

'That went well then.'

'How'd you know her brother-in-law was in the police?'

'Something PC Craig said.'

'PC Craig, the policewoman in the coma?'

'Aye.'

Angus rubs at his head again.

'I'm gonnae put in a complaint about that. Officially. It's not on; they can't talk tae you like that, they cannae act like that. None of this is proven, it's all hypothetical. And, I'm getting you back in school. You've had enough time off.' He slams his foot down on reverse and screeches the car around. He's really mad.

'Okay.'

'Don't listen tae what arseholes like that have tae say, Anais. Now dinnae quote me on that – I mean, not the arsehole bit – but they are, fucking idiots. You're not bad in your bones. I've met enough bad people in this life tae know.'

'Have you read all my files yet, Angus? I have been charged a lot, you know.'

'That doesnae make you bad, Anais; bored, irritable, angry – maybe. Not bad, though. And aye, I have been reading your files, and I think you should be a lot more fucked up than you seem, after what you've been through,' he says.

'I am,' I say quietly.

'Maybe, but you've got something! I'm telling you. I've met a thousand kids in homes, and you're different. You could make something of yourself, you really could. You dinnae need tags and time in secure, or any of that. You could be somebody.'

'What, first major female drugs baron in Europe?'

'You're a clever girl, Anais – I am sure you could put your mind tae something better than that. Don't you want tae do anything with your life?'

'I want tae do lots of things.'

'Like what?'

'Own a dog.'

'That's it, own a dog?' he asks.

'I might . . .'

'You might what?'

'Nothing.'

I dinnae say I might paint when I grow up. I dinnae say I'll learn French, so I can read every book in the main library in Paris one day, including encylopaedias and obscure manuals. I dinnae say I'll volunteer to help some old lady with her shopping, and her cleaning, and if I'm really fucking lucky she'll take me under her wing and get tae like me and feed me apple pie and gin – and tell me all her stories about the good old days. Those urnay the things I say.

We stop at the traffic lights. There's a bunch of girls about my age standing there, but they dinnae look like me. They look young. I turn the music up, sneakers off, feet on the dash. I light a fag and look out the window at one of the girls. She's got great legs, really slim but nice. She turns around, laughing tae her pal, and her smile is stunning.

'I'd shag that,' I say and flick my ash away.

17

I'M UGLY today. I am sat on a hill staring at the school, and I cannae believe Angus got them to let me come back. It has been four weeks and two days since I got put in the Panopticon. My days were going like this – get up, fuck about, have the odd half-arsed meeting with Helen before she leaves, play cards with Angus, wait until Isla, Tash or Shortie gets back from school, go and get stoned. It was civilised, but Angus had to go and fuck it up.

The school bell clangs and guppies start swarming out the doors like a virus. Faces. Eyes. Elbows. I put on my star-shaped sunglasses and stand up. I got them from the vintage shop this morning. They are total quality. I have to shake these jeans out, so they sit better. I borrowed them off Shortie; they're baggy, so they hide my tag. If it was on show, the whole school'd be talking about it.

Walk down through the school gates and push in, against the tide of people. They are all heading up the street tae the chippie, or home. I am going to the woods. I get a few hiyas, and glances – a lot of glances actually. I dinnae feel like speaking to anyone.

Last time I got dragged back to school it was by the polis

and I was handcuffed – it was just after lunch on a Monday. The entire Home Ec rooms, and the computer rooms, all watched me being marched by. I went into the computer rooms earlier to try to look up the difference between human blood and squirrel blood. It is different. Molecularly. That means if the police say the blood they have from my skirt is human, then I'll know they are lying. Or the experiment have gone into the labs in the middle of the night and just switched the samples around, ay. Why would they do that? Cos I'm their golden girl, they cannae fucking let me get away. They want to go all the way. Locked door. Square room. One vertebrae. Snapped. I'm gonnae find out what's happened, if the samples are human blood. If they are. Fuck!

If that happens I will need to click my feet three times and find a place far – far fucking away – to call home. Maybe an igloo. I could be the lone Eskimo, friend of whales and seals. Except I dinnae think Eskimos are right friendly with whales and seals. I think they just stab them, skin them, eat them, and wear their skin.

Can you imagine it – a life in a secure unit, then prison. I wouldnae mind if it was for something I'd done! I mean I would, but it'd be different. It makes me burn when I think about it, right inside, like I just want to – disappear. Just like that. That's how it happens. You blink one day and what was there a second ago is gone.

I push through a gap in the bushes, into the woods. It's colder in here and quieter. The leaves have turned to mulch on the forest floor and the boughs are nearly bare. When I breathe out there is a wee stream of silver. Autumn has gone quickly this year and winter is appearing, but she hasn't put on a show yet. Even the weather is still – waiting to see what will happen.

I climb up on my oak tree, let myself fall back until I am hanging by my knees, hair trailing across the forest floor. It's soothing. The trees still have some leaves, all dry and crackly. The rest are mulch. Hundreds of tiny wishes drift through the woods, they sparkle in the dim, and dance up as silver orbs.

I remember Hayley catching a wish for me when we were younger, before she moved away to Singapore and some great life with friends who are rich and clever. Hayley had the most perfect tits I've ever seen. So neat, smaller than mine – more upturned with really pale-pink nipples. I could easy have been her wife. She would have got some fancy job with her dad's company and I would have waited at home, tae love her, and make her some tea, after a long day. Instead I ended up with Jay. Sucking on a mouldy pole – that's what Tash calls it. Hayley was quiet, and kind. Kindness is the most underrated quality on the planet. I feel hollow just now. Hollow where a heart should be. Like when you know someone loves you, but you urnay good enough – that it will go. That you'll make it go, it's only a matter of time.

Take a joint out my bra. Fucking shitty lighter, light again, inhale – that's better, inhale deeply. The forest floor is damp and wild garlic sweetens the air. Somewhere the river gurgles.

There's a newspaper near my head. It's damp, but I can still read the headline.

Nobody Could Prevent Child's Murder.

I have to close my eyes, tears at the back of them, dizzy, let my legs fall down over my head until I feel solid ground. Sink down. Lump in my throat. How can someone do that, ay? And how can someone say – on the front of a fucking newspaper – that there was nothing they could do to stop it?

Seriously. How not? How can you not stop it? If you take a

kid who is in danger *out* of a place where it's gonnae be tortured tae death – well, that kid would not be murdered then. Fact. It was a head social worker said that headline. What kind of message is that to send out to baby-murderers? What kind of apology, or acknowledgement of responsibility, is that?

It's not an apology. It's not an explanation. It's a fucking insult, that's what it is.

It'd be different if it was their baby. You're sure as fucking shit it would be different then. It'd be different if it was some foreign country and they were being ethnically cleansed, or were war victims. But it's no different here, at home, if you've no money. It's no different here. They just let it happen. They say they dinnae, but they do. All the fucking time.

You can stop it. You go in, and you look, with your eyes open; if they have a record of continuous bruises, or bumps, if you visit and they have chocolate smeared all over them – wipe it off. See what is underneath. Dinnae even fucking think about leaving until you do. But they pass by things, don't they, like, professionally. They have never asked me about rooms without windows or doors. Not once.

'How many social workers have you had, Anais?'

'Thirty-eight.'

'Who are the worst to break in?'

'Graduates. They're itching for a good specimen, it makes them feel better about all their student loans, and it makes them believe they're now a grown-up. It's all very serious. They think everything's great. Child abuse. Getting battered. Drug addiction. They fucking love it – makes them feel dead professional and important. Everyone wants to feel important, ay?'

As specimens go, they always get excited about me. I'm a good one. A show-stopper. I'm the kind of kid they'll still enquire about ten years later. Fifty-one placements, drug problems, violence, dead adopted mum, no biological links, constant offending. Tick, tick, tick. I lure them in to begin with. Cultivate my specimen face. They like that. Do-gooders are vomit-worthy. Damaged goods are dangerous. The ones that are in it cos they thought it would be a step up from an office job are tedious. The ones who've been in too long lose it. The ones who think they've got the Jesus touch are fucking insane. The *I can save you brigade* are particularly radioactive. They think if you just inhale some of their middle-classism, then you'll be saved.

Helen's like that. She thought that what I really needed was homeopathic tongue-drops. She said I should take them if I ever felt like I was getting angry.

What she really didnae like, though, was that I wouldnae stick tae the uniform. No hair extensions, no tracksuits, no gold jewellery. That really pissed her off. The first time she saw me in a pillbox hat and sailor shorts, you'd have thought I'd just slapped her granny.

She wanted a case that was more rough-looking. More authentic, so she could take me for meetings at that bistro near hers, where her posh pals would see and think she was dead cutting-edge and that. India's the best place for her. I hope she gets a fatal (yet slow-acting) stomach bug and just fucking dies.

I dunno why I was remembering Hayley earlier. She went. Everyone goes. Everything does. Then we're all just dead. Dead as fuck and there is no heaven. Probably there isnae. Probably there is nothing. Just some gimp sat waiting for you with a bunch of notes.

'So, newly dead person, that time you did that thing – we

have it right here on note 1000000098775f2.987,87. What exactly was that about?'

The watching feeling is getting worse.

I am not an experiment.

I am not a stupid joke, or a trippy game, or an experiment. I will *not* go insane. Something bad is gonnae happen, though. I can feel it. It's in the way that crisp bag has faded from the rain. I am not an experiment. If I keep saying it, I'll start believing it. I have to try. I am *not* an experiment. It doesnae sound convincing. It sounds stupid.

Try it in German. Ich bin nicht eine experiment. My German's shite. Inhale slowly to the count of four, look hard at the tip of my nose and try again. This time I go for an official BBC broadcaster circa-1940 accent.

Today, one finds one is not, in actual fact, a social experiment. One is a real person. This is real actual skin as seen containing the bodily organs of a real actual human being with a heart and a soul and dreams.

It's true that I came from real people once too, and they were a jolly old sort, with no naked psycho-ness in any way.

I, the young Miss Anais, understand wholly that I am just a human being that nobody is interested in. No experiment. No outside fate. I am not that important, and that is just fine by me. I propose a stiff upper lip and onward Christian soldiers, quick-bloody-march! This is Anais Hendricks, telling the nation: to be me is really quite spiff-fucking-spoff, lashings of love, your devoted BBC broadcaster since 1938.

18

'JOAN, I dinnae like boats.'

She's not listening. I've said it like ten times, but she's not having any of it.

'You will like this one.'

'I'll fucking hate it, I'm not going.'

'Your social worker signed you up, Anais.'

'This isnae how I intend tae spend my weekend.'

'Tough titties.'

'You cannae say that!' I look at her, appalled.

'I just did, and you are going, even if we have tae gaffer-tape your hands and wrists and throw you in. You're going. And you'll like it.'

Something is up with Joan. I heard that someone she knows is dying. Like cancer or something. She's been snappy lately.

'Is it a canoe?' I ask her.

'No, it's a boat. You will be in with Tash, Shortie and Isla. You just have paddles and you go around and have fun. You know, like normal people?'

'I'm not normal people.'

'So, enjoy it as someone who is not normal. Just have some fun!'

'It isnae a canoe?'

'It's nothing like a canoe. Now go and get some jeans on, and wear a jumper and a jacket because it might rain.'

Joan jangles the minibus keys; her key-ring is a little monkey with eyes that light up. I cannae believe I have to go to some loch in the middle of fuck-knows-where and float. On a boat. I dinnae like boats. I'm with vampires – they never travel by boat, not unless there is a special hold for them tae sleep in when the sun comes up.

'Is their a hold underneath the boat?' I ask Joan.

'It's a boat, Anais, not a fucking yacht.' She mutters the last bit as she goes back into the office. Cheeky bitch. She sticks her head out of the office door and watches me trailing towards the stairs. I sit down on the bottom one.

'I hate boats.'

'Don't be a scaredy-cat, Anais. Now, Helen is coming tae take you tae Warrender Institute, to meet Mr Jamieson as arranged – did she tell you?'

'Aye. Can you give me money for cigarettes?'

'If you go and get dressed, Anais, and get into the minibus, then yes, there will be some outing money allocated.'

Joan's not stupid. If she gives me cash now, I'll be away. She's getting quite cunning. I'm impressed.

'What did they say about my lab-test results?' I ask her.

'The blood was not PC Craig's blood. Did Angus not tell you?'

'No. Does that mean they know I didnae do it?'

'No, it just means they are now looking for other proof. Do you know whose blood was on your skirt?'

'It was a dead squirrel, I found it down the woods.'

'Did you hurt a squirrel?' she asks slowly.

'Aye, Joan, I koshed a fucking squirrel, ay. Hate the cunts.'

'Dinnae use that word, Anais, it's demeaning tae women.'

'Get a grip. Can you just ask them tae check if the blood on my skirt was human?'

'I'll ask, although I'm not sure they will do that, unless you give them a good reason tae do so. We can talk about it later, now hurry, please, we need tae leave in ten minutes!'

Angus breezes in. 'Morning, Anais, Joan.'

'Morning, Angus,' I say.

Tash is pleating Isla's hair. Brian's sat in front, John is in the back with a cap pulled down over his face. Dylan and Steven are huddled together in the middle. I am standing at the minibus door, smoking a roll-up I cadged off Angus. Double-drag, until I get dizzy.

'Morning, campers, it's going to be a good one!' Angus climbs up intae the front.

'Move,' Tash says to Brian. He scurries to the back and sits two seats behind Dylan. Tash and Isla sit together at the front double-seat, holding hands. Shortie runs out and jumps in.

'I cannae wait,' she says, 'out of this shit-pit for a day!'

Eric is stood at the door like an anxious dad watching his kids go off to school.

'Bye, Anais, have a nice time!' he calls.

I climb in and slam the door.

'Leave it on its hinges, please, Anais,' Joan admonishes and she starts the engine. Shortie slides over and I sit down next to her. She grins happily.

Eric waves at us and wee Dylan sticks his fingers up at him as the minibus pulls away. Joan turns the radio on and everyone opens their windows and pulls their fags out. You urnay meant to smoke in social-work property any more, but Joan's quite good like that. She chain-smokes like fuck.

'Can I have one of yours?'

Shortie grins at me. 'Uh-huh!'

'How many miles is it, Joan?' Isla asks.

'It's eighty miles away.'

'That'll take all fucking day. Can you do a ton in this?' John asks, still under his hat.

'Can we ditch Boner Brian?' Dylan pitches up.

'We won't have name-calling today,' Joan scolds. 'And you and Brian and young Steven will be in a boat with John today. We are looking for teamwork.'

'Seriously, we should just kick him out the back when we hit the motorway,' Dylan mutters.

'Have you got a boner, Brian?' Steven asks Brian quietly, and then sniggers.

'He'll probably rape a fish in the loch,' Dylan says.

'D'ye reckon this claptrap could reach eighty?' John asks, but the staff are pretending not to listen now.

'Can you swim?' Steven asks Brian.

'Who are you gonnae go in a boat with?' Shortie pops her head into the front and asks the staff.

'Seatbelt, please, Shona. Angus and I are there strictly tae supervise. We are trusting you all tae behave yourselves and not let us down today.'

'It's Shortie, not fucking Shona.'

'You all have tae be on best behaviour,' Angus says.

'Right then,' John snorts.

'This will be great, we will fucking tank youz cunts,' Shortie says to the boys.

She opens her fist. It's full of green and blue tablets. Nice. Wee Dylan is looking over and nodding at the new boy, Steven. He watches wide-eyed as I pick out three green tablets and swallow them. His mum's in remission. I hope she gets better and he gets the fuck out of here.

Shortie smiles and closes her fist. I shake my head and tap her hand, so she opens it again. Take three blue as well, just to be safe. She smiles, looking out the window. She's content to just be here with Tash and Isla and me – everything feels chilled.

'Are you okay, Anais?' Angus asks, turning around to look at us all in the back.

'She's fine,' Shortie says.

We turn onto the motorway and the minibus jams in behind a lorry. A school bus overtakes us on the right. Kids are up at the window, making faces at us and sticking their fingers up. Wee Dylan sits up on his seat, pulls down his shorts and flashes them, quick as. Kids on the school bus all fall about in hysterics, then they start to flash back.

'What the fuck's that?' Shortie shouts at them, she shouts it so loud they can probably fucking hear her. She's holding up her fingers like she's trying to find a wee maggot with tweezers.

'And they say our lot are bad!' Joan shakes her head at the kids on the bus.

One of them rubs his jumper over his nipples, then he makes out like he's wanking over Joan. She smiles and gives him a wee *Aw, how sweet* wave.

The bus pulls away and, on the back of it, someone has drawn a huge dick and hairy balls in the dirt.

'Catch up with them,' Dylan shouts.

'We urnay in a race,' Angus says.

Joan hands back some boiled sweeties. Isla rests her head on Tash's shoulder, and Tash strokes her hair. The sky is blue outside and the countryside is green. It whizzes by and I could just drive around like this every day. Watching the green. Watching the whizz. The blues and greens are lush. Shortie opens her window right up and shouts up at a lorry driver.

'Honk your horn then – go on, honk your fucking horn!'

She pulls her arm down to show him what she means, and he does: he honks it and it's a big old blaring horn, a metal one right on top of his truck. He does it three times as the minibus overtakes him.

'Brilliant,' Shortie says breathlessly, coming back in the window, 'totally fucking great!'

We drive around the car park for a second time until Joan spies a car pulling out and swerves for the space; the clutch screeches.

'Oh, for fuck's sake. This bus needs serviced!' she says.

We pull up alongside a family eating sandwiches. The man in the front rolls up his window, casually flicks the lock on his door.

'We should get rid of the Social Work Department stickers,' Angus says.

It's good to open the door and get out. It was getting claustrophobic in there. Everyone piles down, lighting fags. Dylan kicks Brian. He's doing that whenever Angus and Joan urnay looking. He boots him as I walk by. Brian takes a blade out of his pocket and shows it to Dylan as a warning.

'Worried, ay,' Dylan says.

We follow the staff towards the boathouse.

'People are looking,' Isla says.

'No, they're no. Or they just think me and Joan here have had a lot of kids!' Angus insists.

He slaps his hand around Joan's shoulders and she leans into him.

'They must think Joan's a right slut then, cos there's no way we've all got the same dad,' Shortie says. She walks by them, and Joan removes Angus's hand from her shoulder.

People *are* looking. It's the minibus that does it. Our minibus is well embarrassing. It has *Midlothian Social Work Department* emblazoned across it. It's that and the young-offenders aura. A children-in-care aura. A we'llfuckyouandyerweepetsrightup kindae aura.

Two young guys with pit bulls walk by. One of them eyes up John as they climb into a fancy four-wheel drive.

We walk past toilets and a café. There's boats out all over the loch and caravans up on the hill.

On the main desk a young guy is serving, he's cute. Skinhead. Looks like a monk. I bet his pole's no mouldy. He hands over lifejackets to Angus, who hands them back to Joan. She doles them out tae us.

'I umnay wearing that,' Shortie says.

Isla is already fastening her lifejacket around her so the ties are at the front, and knotting them. I put mine on and slump down on a seat by the picnic area. Dylan and Steven run over to the play area and pelt up the slide.

'Okay, troops, we are down here.' Angus points.

This is stupid. I fucking hate boats. Everyone follows Angus to the water's edge.

'Come on, Anais.'

'Coming.'

The sky's grey and there's mizzle. It's so soft on my skin – it's nothing like rain. It's even softer than the lightest drizzle! Lift my face up, so it can kiss my skin.

'I'm not going out if it's raining.' Brian hangs back.

'Away tae fuck, ya wee pleb, yer coming,' Dylan says.

Brian shakes his head and Dylan drags him onto the boys' boat.

'Now, John, as the eldest, you are in charge; and, Tash, you're in charge of the girls' boat. You can see the tags out there, look – up the loch, can you see the red numbered tags?' Angus points.

We all follow where he's pointing and there are wee flags like at different bits of the loch. We nod.

'Okay. So you need tae go around each tag, not just past it. You have tae touch each one, okay? Do you know what I mean by going around?' he asks.

'Calm it, Angus, we're not total retards,' Tash mutters.

'I've got our boat!' Shortie jumps in and grabs an oar.

Tash lifts Isla on and I hop in the back, but those tablets Shortie gave me are kicking in and my legs are going numb. I think I'm gonnae go and see Pat, before I go to the nuthouse next week. If she still knows fat Mick, and he's still living there, he'll maybe be able to get this stupid tag off my ankle.

The laddies rock their boat back and forward until John gives them a look and they stop straight away.

'Okay, so you go around each tag, to the top, and the team that makes it back first wins the first prize of the day!' Angus lights a roll-up and beams.

'Now, two people tae each oar. If you get tired, slow down. Are you listening tae me, Anais? Okay, if you get stuck, use your phone. A lifeguard can be with you anywhere you are within seconds. And look,' Joan gestures at a tiny kid going out in a topper, 'anyone can do this one, okay? It's not difficult, just enjoy yourselves!'

'What's the prize?' Dylan asks.

'You'll find out later,' Angus replies.

'We're gonnae beat youz easy,' Shortie says to John.

Tash pulls our oar back again, but Shortie hasnae begun rowing on the other side yet, so for a minute we go squint. I'm staring at the sky. Shortie nudges me to take the paddle. I'm just watching a cloud.

'Youz'll no beat anyone!' John says.

The boys pull away fast.

'Come on, girls, dinnae let them get a head start.' Joan shoves our boat out.

We're gliding. It feels like flying. I trail my fingers in the water – it's so cold. Imagine what's down there in that loch. Big ugly fish. Mud. Reeds. Some dead witch.

The steady splish-splish of oars is rhythmic. Reeds stick up at the edges of the loch and ducks bob their heads, then dive down and waggle their tails as they look for food. Swans glide by.

A pure-black swan emerges from the reeds. I've never seen a black swan before, he's fucking majestic. Take a photo on my phone, and point him out to Shortie.

'What?' She looks.

'D'ye not think he's stunning?' I say.

'Nope, totally fucking boring.'

'He's a pure-black swan, look at him, he's perfect!'

'Keep your mind on the victory, Anais,' she says.

She points ahead to the flag we need to hit to beat the

laddies. She's getting right into this boating shit, ay. All this space around us feels good actually, now that I'm here. I never knew I liked to be outside so much. I never knew I liked lochs and views and that, but I could seriously handle living in a cottage by the side of somewhere like this.

Those tablets were strong. They're trying to take me up and down at once. We're far out now, the shore looks miles away. Shortie grins at me.

'You're alright, Anais.'

'Aye.'

'Mind when you moved in, and I fronted up tae you, ay?'

Isla raises her eyebrows in despair.

'Like, I couldnae have you just picking on me or that. And tae be honest, I just like a wee fight really, but you like a wee fight, ay, Anais?'

'Not really.'

'You urnay bad for somebody who doesnae like fighting then. I mean, I got you a few good punches, like, but you werenae bad. I thought you'd be taller, and, like, uglier, and, like, you know, more manly.'

'What?' The girls fall about laughing.

Shortie smiles and looks away, waiting for a slap over the head.

'Noh, cos most fighters are just right hard cunts, ay? Oh, come on, Isla, they are! And you are, like, quite hard, Anais. You're almost as hard as me.'

'Shortie?'

'Aye?'

'Shut the fuck up.'

I pass her a smoke and we're sniggering, cos it's stupid, and the water keeps splashing over the boat and we're a bit pish at this rowing shite, but we give it some welly anyway. The laddies are only just ahead, but they urnay high, though. It's an advantage – that's why they're rowing better than we are.

Shortie points at another boat. 'Look at those fannies,' she says so they can all hear her.

A family race by us, wearing matching outfits, and the dad is at the helm shouting at his kids to row harder. Angus and Joan are getting smaller, waving to us away back on the shore.

'Tagged it.' Shortie reaches out and slaps flag number one.

The boys are still ahead. My phone begins to ring. Isla leans back to row. She has fresh cut marks right across her stomach.

'Sorry,' I mumble.

I have to let my oar go tae get my mobile out. I pick it up again quick, and row with one arm. Shortie takes most of the strain for me. Thank fuck. My arms are going like jelly now as well as my legs. I need to snooze.

'Alright?' I answer the phone.

'Alright, gorgeous!'

'Jay.'

'I cannae wait tae see you at the safe-house.'

I dinnae speak.

'What are you doing? Are you naked?'

'Noh. I'm in a boat.'

'What the fuck are you doing in a boat?'

'Floating.'

'Aye, okay.'

'Noh, I am. Listen . . .'

I hold the phone out so he can hear the oars and the water.

'It's quite nice actually. I thought I hated boats, but uhm urnay minding this,' I say.

'Is it a yacht?'

'Aye, the social-work yacht!' I giggle and so do the girls.

Isla is rowing as hard as she can. She's got right into it now and our boat is drawing even with the laddies. As we get nearer I can see that Brian is hunched in a corner of the boys' boat, with his knife out. Dylan's scooping water up with a crisp bag and splashing him in the face.

'Can you call the staff?' Brian whimpers.

'As if,' Shortie snaps at him.

We glide past them in three long hard strokes.

'Call the staff!' he yelps.

'Did that fucking dog have staff tae call – did it, Brian? You fucking freak.' Shortie shakes her head. 'Fucking arse-piece.'

'Loser.' Tash smirks at John.

We put metres between us in seconds. John shrugs his shoulders and keeps rolling a joint. I'm listening to the silence. Jay's listening to us.

'Who's all there?' he asks.

'Just me and some of the other folk from the home.'

'I thought you didnae hang out with anyone in the homes.'

'I dinnae.'

'D'ye think any of your wee pals could bring me in some gear tae the jail, like before I get out? I'm in a wee bit debt, Anais, ay. I could do with the help?'

'I cannae. I'm already in shit with the polis.'

'You know what, Anais?'

'What?'

'I love you.'

He hangs up.

'Anais, are you alright?' Isla asks.

'Aye, I'm fine.'

I feel horrible. I feel like he's crawling under my skin and making it so I cannae not go and see him at the safe-house, but I cannae think about it any more. Today is not about him, and it's not about almost-dead pigs. What if she dies? Will I feel bad then? I cannae say. I dinnae feel bad now, but I probably should, but I didnae kosh her so how is it my problem? I trail my fingers in the water.

These pills are settling in now. It's a nice buzz.

Start rowing again. Water ripples out when the oars dip in. I look back at the boys' boat. Brian's pinned in his corner, jabbing the knife out any time Dylan goes near him.

Way down on the shore Joan appears to be waving, or maybe she's trying to warn them to stop. I squint. It's hard tae tell.

How come they didnae know it wasnae human blood, when they tested the stuff on my clothes? That's the question. That's the thing. The experiment have to raise the game, ay. They have to break you. That's the point, and they've not managed it yet. Everything that has been, every single thing, and I'm not totally broke, yet. They dinnae like that.

19

'LOOK, THEY'RE gonnae drown Brian.' Isla points back down the loch.

'I wish they fucking would,' Shortie says.

'They are, look!'

Brian clings onto the boat from the water. Dylan stands up in the boat and batters him across the head with his paddle. A help-boat is motoring up the loch towards the laddies.

'Let's get out of here,' Isla urges.

'Seven, tag seven, woo-hoo, woo-hoo, tag seven, we are kicking your arse!' Shortie shouts back at the boys' boat.

'Spin on it, ya radge,' John shouts back.

'You're the fucking radge, John!' she says.

'Aye, you wantae come here and say that?'

'Try me!' she hollers and sits down.

We all look at her.

'What?' she says.

'You fancy John.' I smile.

'Noh, I dinnae think so!' She shakes her head. 'Are you gonnae see Craig again, by the way? He keeps asking me.'

'No,' I say.

Isla starts humming a tune. I think it's 'Old MacDonald Had a Farm'. Tash is singing it now, 'Old McShortie had a pig farmer, EE-I-EE-I-O.'

'Very fucking funny,' Shortie says.

Brian's flapping in the water. He's lucky he's got his life-jacket on, cos there's no danger *that's* swimming. He's getting quite far away from their boat now. Dylan leans over the edge and skelps Brian over the head with the paddle.

'Oh, ya fucker, did you see that yin?'

Shortie stands up to get a better look. Our boat wobbles like fuck.

'Stop that, right now!'

A big guy with a beard shouts over a loudspeaker at Dylan. We're giggling.

'I dinnae want tae go back in yet. C'mon, let's get the fuck out of here,' Tash says.

We all lean back and pull the oars, we're getting good now – we've found the beat of it.

The loch disappears around a corner and we follow it around, to another huge expanse of water, and there are all these wee islands with big trees on them.

'We should stop.' Shortie gestures at the island nearest us.

'Are we allowed tae stop there?' Isla asks.

'Aye!' Shortie says. She looks at me. 'We can stop? They didnae say we cannae stop. Anyway, what're they gonnae do – paddle way out here?'

She gestures back at the shore; it is miles away now.

'I suppose,' I say.

'We'll still beat the laddies. If we see them going by, we'll go after them. Please!'

'We'll beat them even if we doggy-paddle the rest of the way.' I look back.

The boys are static now. Totally fucked. The bearded man is hooking Brian out of the water and arguing with John.

'Come on, please, I brought some drink. I have tablets, uppers an' downers . . .' Shortie pleads.

'I've got fags,' I add.

Pat my pocket to check they're still there.

'I've got biscuits, and crisps, and drink,' Tash concedes. She lifts up a plastic bag at her feet. 'Just in case,' she adds.

We row around to the far side of the island, out of sight of the boys' boat. Most of the other boats are further up the loch.

We row right into the island. This is great – we are conquerors, maybe I could name it Anais's island. Or, island El Radgio. The trees are really tall and there's still some flowers. I dunno what they are – like wildflowers, or maybe just weeds. They're pretty, though, ay. This is the last nice day; they say winter's gonnae arrive tomorrow, and that's that.

We float in towards the pebble shore.

'I've got it.' Shortie jumps out.

She lands right up tae her thighs in the water, and we start laughing at her.

'Fuck!' she screams.

'Shut it and pull us in.' Tash hands her the rope.

''S alright for youz tae laugh, you urnay fucking soaking!'

'Take one for the team, Shortie. Man up,' I say, grinning.

She wades us in until the boat crunches onto the pebbles. I'm really comfy in this lifejacket now, it's a portable cushion. I might wear it everywhere.

Tash lifts Isla onto the shore. Shortie kicks off her squelchy shoes and pulls her jeans off and wrings them out.

'Fuck, fuck, fuck!' she mutters.

I'm giggling watching her. Tash is laughing at Shortie as well, and even Isla is falling back, looking up at the trees and letting out a helpless high-pitched laugh. She sounds like a dolphin clicking, which just makes us all worse.

'Very funny,' Shortie says.

'It is that!' Tash walks along the shore.

'Drink – must have drink,' Isla gestures.

We sit in a row. Tash opens her bag, cracks open a can of Coke and pours half of it out, then she tops the rest back up with Bacardi and hands it to Isla.

'Madam's cocktail – we call it the Island Hopper. Ladies?'

'Please, Mama,' I say.

'Okay, truth or dare?' Shortie says.

'Truth,' Tash says.

'How many men have you had sex with?'

'Paid or unpaid?' Tash asks.

'Uh, is it different, like?' Shortie asks, confused.

'Aye, it's different.' Tash looks at me and raises her eyebrows.

'Well, ah dinnae know, I'm not a manky hoor.'

We all stop and look at her.

'Just all of them then!' she says, harassed.

'About nine,' I kick in before Tash batters Shortie. 'I was up for about half, two were debatable, two were out-and-out wrong.'

I hear my voice say that, and I realise I am more stoned off those tablets than I thought, and I reckon I've taken the same amount of downers as uppers, so I'm just swinging between the two.

'What, like, you've been forced?' Shortie looks at me.

'Shortie, are you the naïvist person walking?'

She just looks embarrassed, so I don't say anything else. Shortie must be the only girl I ever met in care who's a virgin. Fact.

Tash lights a fag and studies a cloud.

'You dinnae need to answer,' Isla says quietly to her. 'This is a stupid game, let's play something else.'

'I umnay embarrassed,' Tash says.

'I've done one guy, for a wee while, the twins' dad obviously,' Isla says. 'I didnae like it, didnae rate it, wouldnae thank you for it. It wasnae even a particularly manky pole – just no for me.'

'I couldnae count how many – a lot, though; they like it underage, ay,' Tash says.

'That's true. My adopted ma was always saying the wee lassies were taking all the clients,' I say.

'What – was your adopted ma a prozzie?' Shortie asks.

'Shortie, you're the greenest person I ever met! Aye, she was on the game, so's her pals – that's what I grew up around, which is probably why I've never done it. No offence,' I say to Tash.

'None taken. They only pay above average for schoolies if you're smart, ay. If you urnay, you'll give it away for a bag of crisps and a bottle of fucking cider, while some prick with a wife manages tae brainwash you intae thinking he's your boyfriend. Just him, ay, and his forty fucking cousins,' she spits.

Tash takes Isla's hand. Isla's been crying a lot since her wee ones were brought in for a visit.

'What kind of guys go with prozzies?' Shortie asks.

'Every kind. Bankers. Teachers. Builders. Even blokes on the dole save up their money sometimes. One guy paid me two hundred squids tae piss on him,' Tash says.

'Where? Tae piss on him where?' Shortie's eyes widen.

'In his mouth, while he wanked his wee maggot off.'

'I'd piss on someone for two hundred quid!' Shortie says. She looks so serious. 'Are you kidding me? I'd take a crap on someone for that!'

We all fall back howling and Shortie totally doesnae get it, and the angrier she looks, the funnier it is.

'What? Fucking what?'

'You're a nut, Shortie,' Isla says affectionately. 'I need tae pee but.'

'I'll chum you.'

Tash and Isla wander off to the other side of the shrubs.

'Is Isla okay?' I say.

'Noh, she's not, she's cutting herself like fuck – have you seen it lately? It's doing my head in. She should just stop, but she's all, like, guilt this and guilt that; and the twins. That's what she cannae handle, Anais, she cannae handle that the twins have it.'

'How do you handle that? I dunno how I would, she's still getting counselling, ay?'

'Aye. But she has tae, cos the twins dinnae need a fucking mum that hates herself as well, ay. What good's that gonnae be, if she gets them back? Nae good, Anais. And she's got that fucking ugly thing, you know, when they think they are total ming-bags, body-morphing or body-popping or body-fucking some shite. Now they're giving her Valis and she's just stashing them up and popping them en masse. Then the happy pills, then there's her

HIV meds: have you seen how much she takes? She's worrying me. Seriously.'

'I wish there was something I could do'

'There's not, though, is there? Not fucking nothing. Anyway, how are you? That pig isnae dead yet?'

'Nope.'

'Good, we've got tae stick together now,' she says.

The air is thick then. I dinnae say anything, I dinnae look at her, but I dinnae look away, and I can feel it, she wants to say, because I said earlier and she's probably never heard it said before, but she wants to say now.

'My old dear wasnae about much. My granda looked after me, ay.'

She kicks her heels into the pebbles.

Tash and Isla walk back. We all huddle up next to each other, looking over the loch.

'How many have you shagged then, Shortie?' Tash passes biscuits along.

'I dinnae ken!'

'How not?'

Tash takes the biscuit packet back off her. Shortie has about ten biscuits in her lap.

'You dinnae have tae say anything, Shortie. Shut up, Tash.'

'What – it's alright for her tae interrogate everyone?'

Shortie spits and her hands shake. We just sit. Water laps the side of the boat down on the shore and it bobs up and down.

'I'm gonnae get us enough money for a flat,' Tash announces. 'You two can come and stay with us, if you want.'

'I wish you'd stop. It worries me every time you do it,' Isla says.

'Aye, but in six months I'll have enough money tae rent us a flat when we get out of here. A nice one as well: flash kitchen, widescreen telly, fancy bed-linen. I will get you – anything you want! Anything. There'll be just you and me and an extra bedroom so the twins can visit, and maybe one for these two radges.'

'They won't let the twins visit.'

'They might.'

'They won't.' Isla drops pebbles through her fingers.

'You could study, though. Isla wants to study,' Tash says, all proud and that.

'What?' I ask.

'Child psychology, like, tae work with kids and that, ay. She'd be great at it. Really, Isla, you'd be amazing, you know that. We'll even get married – I'll make an honest woman of you, I'll carry you over the threshold!'

Tash puts her arm around her and squeezes. Isla keeps tugging at her top, cos she doesnae think it's covering her scars enough. I prop myself up on an elbow.

'You look hot today, Isla. You suit halternecks, and they shorts. You look like a model, a short model, like – but a model.'

'Definite,' Shortie agrees.

Isla flushes and smiles quickly. She stops fidgeting with her top. Tash smiles happily and takes her hand.

A curlew flies up from the other side of the loch. It calls out in a low cry across the water. Most of the boats are sailing towards the top of the loch. There's another boathouse up there that does drinks for members, or something.

There's a lot more boats on the water now: toppers and big white ones and one with a red and white stripey sail. Some are racing and some just glide along.

'I could marry youz,' Shortie exclaims. 'You know like how you can become a vicar online now and that; you just, I dunno, fill out a form or something. Though I couldnae fill out a form, not with the dyslexia and that. But anyway, I could marry youz – on this here island!'

Shortie's in earnest and she won't quit.

'I'm fucking serious, fuck it, you dinnae even need a form. God's watching or, like, the clouds are watching. Me and Anais would be watching, ay, Anais?'

I nod.

'I mean, serious, I'll marry youz right now.'

She skids down onto the shore and grabs up a handful of wee blue flowers.

'For the beautiful bride.' She shoves an earthy clump at Isla. 'Now, this is holy and serious,' and she falls to her knees in front of them and makes them clasp their hands together. 'What do youz think?'

'I think you should,' I say.

I'm smiling, cos the two of them look so young and happy, and it makes me hopeful. I dunno for what, like – just hopeful.

'You're just a diehard romantic,' Tash says to me.

I'm already scrabbling up the slope gathering petals and flowers.

'Well?' Shortie asks again.

'I'm in.' Tash grins. Isla leans over and kisses her.

'Right, you're not at that bit yet. Go canny, ay; now, turn around tae face each other.'

Shortie looks to the sky, crosses herself, then opens her hands like they're a prayer book.

'Do you, Tash – light of our Isla's eyes – do you promise to take this woman, our Isla, as your lawfully legal wife?'

'Aye.'

'You are making holy vows before this loch, these clouds, me and Anais – and they swans over there.' Shortie points.

'Okay,' Isla says.

'Right. Repeat after me. I, Tash, will look after, treasure and obey my teenage wifey, Isla, and I will never rug-munch another, as long as we both shall live, Amen!'

'Aye, whatever you said.' Tash takes Isla's face in her hands. 'I do!'

That's real love. That look, right there, that's what everyone wishes they had. Even me.

'And do you, Isla – blushing bride of all blushing brides, beautiful in heart and body and soul and all things – d'ye promise, and I mean *promise*, tae love, honour and obey the love of your life, our Tash?'

'I do.'

'And do you both take these vows until both of youz are dead, for ever and ever and ever, Amen?'

'We do.'

I slip a ring I've pleated out of grass intae Tash's hand. She slides it on Isla's finger.

'I love you,' Isla says.

'Till death do youz part!'

'Till death do us part.'

'Then I declare with the power invested in me by youz, and Anais, and the island – and those swans over there – that you are now wife and wife. You may kiss the bride!'

They kiss, and Isla's teary. I throw petals over them and they flutter in the sun.

'Going to the chapel and we're gonna get ma-a-a-rried,' I begin.

Shortie joins in, 'Going to the chapel and we're gonna get ma-a-a-rried.'

Isla and Tash begin singing as well: 'Gee, I really love you and we're gonna get ma-a-a-rried, going to the chapel of *love*.'

'What the fuck are youz doing?' Dylan stands up and shouts.

Fuck, we didnae even see them sneak up, they're floating just near the shore.

'Have youz got drink?' John demands.

'All gone!'

Shortie turns the Bacardi bottle upside down.

'We're coming ashore,' Dylan shouts.

'No, you're fucking not,' Shortie shouts back.

'Fuck youz then,' John says.

They paddle away for the next flag.

'War!' Shortie hollers.

She launches herself into the boat, we run after her, and the laddies are sticking their fingers up, then trying to paddle furiously away.

Shortie's raging. 'I cannae believe that boat-guy let them go – we cannae let them beat us. No fucking danger.'

'Brian's no in there, he must have been taken back tae the shore,' I say.

'We're kicking your arses!' John shouts back at us.

They're getting far away already. Suddenly there's more boats out around us.

'No danger, you're slow as. Losers!' Isla calls.

I have never seen her look so light and happy – as we paddle like mental, and the sun is high and it's even quite warm, we look healthier already. A bigger boat comes up behind us. There's three birds in it and we slow for a second to let them by, but it means the laddies are really getting the lead now.

Shortie turns around and stares at the lassies' boat, willing them to get out the road.

'Chavs!' the blonde lassie says loudly.

Her pals snigger. Shortie slows down paddling and turns right around.

'What the fuck did you say?'

Isla's still smiling; she kisses Tash on the cheek and grins happily, looking at her wee woven-grass ring. I like it, I did a not-bad job making that.

'Oh my God, it's lesbo chav.' The blonde nods towards Isla.

'Fucking ugly one at that,' her pal adds.

I stand up – paddle in my hand.

'It's angry chav!' her pal laughs.

'You should watch your fucking mouth. She'll kick your stinking cunt right intae next fucking week – ya skanky bitch.' Shortie's livid.

Tash stands up and the boat is rocking like fuck now. Isla's face is burning and she tugs at Tash to sit down. I could fucking leather that posh cunt. She's got stupid designer wellies on, and one of they ski-slope noses. She's a cunt. She always will be a cunt. She's the kindae fuck ye'll meet twenty years on and they just think everything that isnae them is total scum. She is, what Teresa would have called – ignorant as fuck.

I cannae stand it. Isla's fucking embarrassed – she's hidden her hand with the ring on it and she's tugging at her top. The boys have slowed down to see what is going on. Our boat sways as Tash steps forward. Isla nervously pulls at Tash's jeans to get her to sit back down.

'My father owns this loch!' the blonde girl warns us.

''S alright,' I say quietly to Tash.

Daddyownstheloch has shut up; she's smiling. Let her. It can fucking wait. I shove Tash so she sits back down, still speechless with rage.

'Fuckin' posh cunts!' Shortie shouts after them.

'Oh, aye, that really fucking told them!' Tash snaps.

Joan's putting out the picnic stuff on a table when we pull up to the shore. My arms are achey. It's hard work, that rowing shit. We drag the boat up the shore and join Joan at the table. There are egg sandwiches on brown bread. Brilliant! I'm hungry now. I dinnae eat, and then I eat. It's not an eating disorder; it keeps me thin, though. If I didnae not eat – then I'd just always eat, and then I'd be a fat fuck. Fact.

'We fucking beat youz.'

John swaggers along. He winks at Shortie.

'Only by default,' I say.

'Youz were pish, just face it,' Dylan says, grabbing a sandwich.

Shortie tickles him. 'You cheeky wee shit.'

'I'm gonnae pee myself – stop!' he yelps, so Shortie tickles him harder.

Isla is sat quiet on a bench watching the water; me and Tash walk away while Angus attends to a hysterical Brian.

I turn to glance behind us to make sure nobody's seeing us go, and it's alright, nobody's looking. The loch sparkles, and the trees all along it are thick and dark; they sway as the sun begins to fade.

20

ANGUS HOLDS the door open and taps his watch.

'Where have you two been?'

'Piss-stop,' Tash says.

'Lovely.'

'You seem tae have cheered up. I told you, a nice day out on a boat and you'd feel a lot better,' Angus says, quite chuffed with himself.

I grin at him and he slides the door shut behind us.

Brian is in the back-right corner with his fists balled up; he stares at the back of Dylan's head. Brian's clothes are still damp, even though Angus dried most of them under a hand-dryer at the bogs. We could hear them in there for half an hour, blasting the dryer while we sat and ate lunch with Joan.

Dylan is keeping quiet, and Steven seems to follow whatever Dylan decides to do. The minibus trundles out of the car park.

'I had one like that, in the Seventies.' Joan lights up when she sees a pristine VW. 'That's called glamping,' she says tae Angus, cos the lassies at the VW have candles, and wine, and beanbags all out around where they are sitting.

Tash puts her arm around Isla.

'Oh, it's a nice VW. Look, it's got the bay window. God – look at that, someone's smashed it!'

Dylan and Steven turn to look, and Tash just stares ahead smiling.

'Looks like the tyres need pumping up,' Angus adds.

'Has that lassie got a black eye?' Dylan asks.

The posh lassies urnay looking this way. The blonde's holding her bloody nose and her wee pal is shouting down a mobile phone. Angus glances at me in the rear-view mirror and accelerates.

'That was a great day out,' he says.

Joan looks back and opens her mouth to say something, but he blasts the radio.

'Great day, people. Well, except for poor Brian, of course. We'll deal with you when we get you home, Dylan,' he shouts over the music.

Joan turns the radio down and Isla snuggles in for a snooze on Tash. I wish I had someone who wanted me as much as that – like really wanted *me* like that. Maybe I just need a wee dog, and an artist's studio, and a side street in Paris. Not everyone needs people, ay.

I hope the staff dinnae give Dylan too hard a time for trying to drown Brian. They shouldnae be trying to make the laddies take Brian in – he's not their problem.

'Anais, how comes you always look classy?'

'I dinnae, Dylan.'

'Aye, you do. It's not even like you wear designer clothes; you wear some weird stuff. Ay, she wears some weird stuff?'

John nods. So does Shortie.

'But you always look – I dinnae know – like you've got class. D'ye know what I mean?'

'I think so, ta.'

'I'm serious. Like, I dinnae get it. Does someone teach you class, or are you just born with it?'

I want to cry again now. Joan and Angus share a wee glance in the front.

'I bet you even smell of strawberries,' Dylan says.

I turn around and give him a wee kiss on the cheek. He's gonna grow up to be a really nice guy one day. He's flushed, and happy, and I look out the window – there's a world out there, you know. One that isnae here. We shouldnae be here; I shouldnae, I should be in Paris. It's still nice, though. Today. The sound of the engine, the motorway, just a wee band of outsiders, and I feel alright, quite liked. Sort of content.

'You're a fucking crawler,' John sniffs.

'Leave him alone,' Shortie says without turning around.

Amazingly, he listens to her. I could see them together. John leans forward and smiles nicely at me. I smile nicely back at him. He lifts up the long white gold chain from my cleavage. There's five charms hanging on it. One is of a wee yacht. There's also a shoe, a cat, a heart and two red cherries. He swings it to and fro.

'That's a nice necklace.'

He notes the designer stamp on each of the charms. He's toting up how much it's worth. I put my hand under my leg so he cannae see the rings. Tash'll take them into town later and pawn them for some gear.

'Were you wearing this earlier, Anais?' he asks.

'Aye.'

I take it back off him and drop it under my T-shirt.

'Loser!' Shortie says to him.

'Noh, I fucking umnay,' he snaps.

'Aye, you are.'

'Shut it, Shortie, ya fishy cunt. You're all uptight cos you're a virgin. Your fanny's depressed.'

'Shut it, ya clarty poof.'

'You fancy me, ay, Shortie?' He grins.

'I'd rather chew my own fucking arm off than go anywhere near you, ya prick.'

'It's like Scarlett and Rhett,' Joan says to Angus.

The staff snicker up the front like a couple of bairns. Joan passes back her boiled sweeties. I'm hungry again. It must be all that air on the loch. I take one and pass the bag to John. He takes four, then passes it to Dylan. He hands it over Brian's head to Shortie. Open the back window and lean out – feel the wind on my skin.

21

THE OFFICE smells of coffee and stale air from the fan-heater. Angus's handwriting isnae too bad; he's letting me read his files on me. He doesnae have to, but I can apply through the new policies if I want to read them now. Angus reckons all kids should be able to read any of their files, any time, without even having to apply for permission.

He leans back on Joan's chair, puts his feet up on the desk. His boots are off, cos he has a hole in the sole. He's wearing thick fisherman's socks – they look cosy, but totally worn.

'You should buy some new socks.'

'Funny you should say that, Anais. My wife gave me money last week and ordered me tae go and buy new socks, new combat trousers and a jumper.'

'So why are you still wearing that crap?'

'I didnae make it as far as the clothes shops.'

'Too stoned?'

'I spent it on CDs instead, Anais. I cannae bring myself tae buy into capitalist society, just good music, books, and my motorbike. 'S all I need!'

It's funny, he's the only member of staff I've met in years who I really get on with.

'Did you see what Joan put up for you?' he asks.

'What?'

I look up. On the wall, right in between all the religious icons, there is a pagan pentagram and a wee witch with a pointy hat.

'Three-parts witch, Anais. Except on Sundays.'

He's smiling away. Aye. Very funny, Angus. I keep flicking through his notes.

'Are you doing a thesis or something?'

'No, the notes are – well, I dinnae think the social-work department get it right all the time, and I like tae think about that. I might do a Ph.D. on it one day.'

'Have you ever been tae France, Angus?'

'No, I've travelled a lot, mostly the East. I spent four years on a kibbutz in Israel, but no, not France. I did do Italy on my bike, though. Why are you asking?'

'Dunno. I might join the Foreign Legion and learn a hundred ways tae kill a man.'

'They dinnae take fifteen-year-old girls, Anais.'

'Their loss.'

I pick up Angus's next set of notes and skim.

The residents in the Panopticon have publicly stated that they refuse to identify themselves as 'Cared-for Young People'. This emerged during interviews for the 'celebration of diversity' survey. When our student Eric asked the group why they do not identify with the term 'Cared-for Young People', they cited among their reasons that: 'cared-for' was blatantly 'taking the piss' (their words). They also stated that 'Young People' sounded 'shite' (their word). They then refused Eric's possible suggestion of 'Young Offenders in Holistic Rehabilitation' or a return to 'Children in Residential Care'.

Staff at the Panopticon were recently informed that 'Clients' is going to remain the term used to describe residents. Eric informed our 'Clients' of this decision. One girl stated that Clients was inappropriate, as 'Clients have the right to respond'. The residents do not think they have this right. If a complaint is made, it has to be done officially or it is not allowed. This is especially the case regarding historical abuse or social-work department failures. The right to respond is cited in the freedom-of-speech human-rights Act. I propose to explore this area of legislation further.

Several Panopticon residents refer to themselves as Inmates. They say this because they believe they are in training for the 'proper jail' (their words). While this may seem like negative or dramatic terminology, the reality is that up to seventy per cent of residents leaving care do end up either in prison, or prostitution, mentally ill or dead.

I discussed last week's survey and group discussion with my newest 'Client', Anais Hendricks. Anais has been in the Panopticon for seven weeks now; she was relocated from Valleyfield Children's Unit. When I asked what terminology she would use to describe herself personally, she used a term popular for 'Clients' with a background such as hers. The term Anais used was 'Lifer'. The young people who refer to themselves as 'Lifers' do so because they have always been in (care) and/or adopted (with subsequent adoption breakdowns) and they now think they will be in care for the remainder of their upbringing. I suggested to Anais that it was up to her whether that term meant her whole life. On reflection, it was probably rather insensitive of me – it is unlikely that Anais will ever become part of a family unit now. However, the worry is that this term seems to infer a continued institutionalisation after childhood. The effects of long-term institutionalisation are something I hope to explore further. I will continue to collate information as research towards a Ph.D.

Anais is booked for a day out with her social worker tomorrow. She is being taken on a trip to where she was born, to try to help her gain a stronger sense of her own identity. She will then attend an end of 'Client Care' review, as her social worker is leaving. No more situations have arisen within the unit as of 5.07 before changeover today.

Angus Everlen

Put the report back down. I'm feeling edgy. I was sitting in bed last night, feeling creepy – the building was too creaky, and I could hear someone crying and I couldn't work out who it was. The watchtower window had a wee light glowing in it, and the night-nurse came out. She stood there on the top landing looking at all the doors, then she turned around and said something. Like to someone inside the tower.

'See last night, Angus, was it just the night-nurse on duty?'

'Aye, and Brenda, but she was asleep in the staff flat downstairs.'

'So she was in the watchtower on her own?'

'Aye, who else would be there, Anais?'

The experiment, Angus. That is who would be there. They're closing in. I can feel them all the time. The police have been quiet, but they're biding their time, and PC Craig, in that coma, she knows all about them. They are standing around her bed. Five of them. No noses, matching hats, matching trousers, whispering – let go! They're coming for me next.

22

IT IS so weird to step into our lift, to press up, to whizz past our floor, our flat, our stair. I could stop the lift now and go and look at our front door, but then I'd hear other people in there and that wouldn't be right.

What is in our old flat is this: me and Teresa, sitting on the sofa, eating popcorn and watching a DVD. There is no policeman in the hallway, no Pat grabbing me up and carrying me out the door like a wee wizened blank-eyed monkey.

The lift keeps going up. Past the safe-house. Straight to Pat's. I haven't been back to see her – in how long? Years. Look straight up above me and the hatch is still in the roof. I have climbed out that hatch a hundred times, crouched down on the roof and waited in the dark until someone got in and pressed up. Then I'd surf up, arms out, metal wires whizzing by, and when the other lift came up – I'd leap right out.

There's nothing like it. Jumping out into empty space, that wee gap between the lifts where you could fall and die. The buzz is fucking epic. My old neighbour fell one time, but his jeans caught on a metal hook and saved him. He dangled there for ages, with one ear half-ripped off and everyone shouting up the shaft, until the ambulance got here. After, everyone said he should become the face of the jeans company, cos their jeans saved his life.

Ninth floor. Tenth floor. Up. I'm wearing a vintage Dylan T-shirt I bought with my clothes allowance. Wee Dylan asked me who the guy with his name was, cos he hadnae heard of him before. He told me he was named after the rabbit in *The Magic Roundabout*, and he's never listened to music much, let alone old stuff.

Fix my hair, and hum that Dylan song – the one about being on your own. It was Teresa's favourite track. The lift pings open, nineteenth floor. Step out and knock. My nails are really clean. The flat-next-door's telly blares – some old western movie, gunshot rings out down the hall, then hooves pound.

'Oh my God!' Pat shouts at her door.

'Hiya, Aunty Pat.'

'Oh, come in, look at you? Come in, come in. Oh, Anais, aren't you growing up drop-fucking-dead gorgeous! Look at you! Excuse the shit-pit, darling.'

Follow her in, and gangster rap is booming down from the flat above.

'Fucking prick!' she shouts up.

She bangs on her ceiling with a broom, but the music doesnae go down. I think he turns it up. She shoves a pile of wigs off the sofa. Pauline, who used to be Paul, is unconscious on the armchair.

'He's been on a binge, I doubt he'll wake up again today. The bastard keeps nicking my good wigs, and he goes mental if I don't call him her! You should see it when he goes mental – fucking hormones! Honestly, you've never seen the like.

And I don't actually mean it, I've always called Paul, Paul – you know, Anais, I'm not doing it to be contrary! He still looks like Paul to me. They're pert wee tits, though, look.' She lifts up his top. Pauline has perfect silicones.

I giggle. It's good to see Pat, I cannae believe I've been away for so long.

'So, is anyone giving you hassle?' she asks.

'No.'

'Are you in trouble with the police?'

'Not really.'

'Liar, what's that?' She lifts up my jeans and has a gander at my tag.

Avoid her gaze and check out her paintings instead. She's got even more than when I was here last time. They're all over her flat; some are even painted straight onto the wall. There's a stunning black lassie, naked, smiling at something. There's a painting of a parrot on Pauline's shoulder, and another one of her in a red glittery dress. Then there's the penises. All kinds of shapes. Every kind there is. Some have faces on them, or top hats. Lots of them are smoking cigarettes. Each is deformed. They are all preposterous.

'Fat Mike could get that tag off for you,' she says.

'That's what I was hoping. Is he still around?'

'Aye, Mike'll outlive us all!'

We laugh. Fat Mike's a genius of the underworld, but he looks dumb as. He's clever that way – it's how he's got away with it all so long.

'He's cutting hair now as well,' Pat says.

'What?'

'Aye, he was up last night for a doubler: me and Pauline. And he told us – he's decided to find his inner hairdresser.'

Pauline turns over and stops snoring.

'Can you picture it, Anais? Mike cutting your hair with a pie in one hand and a tinny in the other.'

She's pushing my hair back, checking out my clothes and my skin.

'Teresa would be so proud, Anais. You're not on the game yet, are you?'

'No.'

'Good, that's not for you, either. You're built for better, mark my words. This shitty wee life'll not hold you back. I'd place money on it. You could be a model – or a madam. In fact, if you wanted to train in one of the best dungeons in London, I know a lovely one in Shoreditch.'

She rummages in her bag and hands a card to me; it's plain black with just a telephone number.

'They do dominatrix stuff, high-class and kink only. D'ye know how much they make in London for the good stuff?'

'No.'

'You could clean up and buy a place outright by the time you were in your twenties. It's a classy establishment. If you ever consider going on the game, Anais – you go there and you tell them I sent you.'

'Nah, Pat. Anyway, Jay is getting out – in a few weeks. We might give it a go, ay.'

'Jay? He's not coming back here, Anais – I'd be surprised anyway. He's in debt, and I mean a lot of fucking debt. You remember Mark, don't you?'

'Aye.'

'He owes the troll a bomb, that's what I heard.'

Pat rifles through Pauline's cardigan and takes out a wadge of notes.

'Here, you keep that. I'm being serious, take it – you might need it. I feel like you're going to need it, and take these wraps. They're quality speed, so don't take it all yourself. You're skinny anyway, but you could sell it for some cash. And this is premium-quality acid; be careful with this shit, it's very strong! These are some happy pills, they're downers – here, take them, Anais, you can keep them in this.'

She hands me a wee Tupperware tub.

'Thanks, Aunty Pat. I might need tae sell them, though. They want tae put me in a secure unit.'

'They do, do they?'

'Aye. They think I'm bad.'

'That's what the experiment want them to think.'

I go cold.

She's moving around, picking things up and putting them down, and I don't know if she knows what she's said. Pauline looks weird, sleeping through all this. I can feel the experiment in the room, just like that. Watching through the half-opened slits of Pauline's eyes.

'You're the brainybox, Anais, you could get out. Look at me.' She gestures at her paintings. 'Will you see this in art galleries? No, you won't, cos they don't want fucking art – they want ideas. Would you like one of my paintings?'

She looks hopeful.

'Aye – when I get my first flat, though. I wouldnae keep it in a home.'

'You take one whenever you want.'

She pours half a glass of vodka and hands it to me.

'Straight,' she orders.

I drink it down. She refills the same glass and does the

same. It's a tradition; her and Teresa used to do it nearly every night. She first poured me half a tumbler of vodka when I was nine, and I drank it straight then as well – I thought my throat was on fire.

'You know what they don't tell you in this life, Anais, it's this, those . . .' She points at a wall of penis paintings. 'The phallus, the prick, the cock, whatever you want to call it, it's not the most powerful thing in the world.'

'No?'

'No. Like – *they* think it is, *they* build skyscrapers and mosques and big weapons in the shape of penises, to make you think that it is.'

'Why?'

'Gender wars. Absolute domination, over what they fear. What men fear is a cunt, so they try and make the cock scarier. It's why they cut off girls' clitoris, and use rape as a war tactic. It's why the sentencing for rape is so offensively pathetic.'

She pours another two straight drinks.

'Men are scary, sometimes, Pat.'

'Aye, but it's all up here.' She taps her head. 'They want us to think rape's the worst thing that can happen.'

'It's not?'

'Look – I've been raped six ways from Sunday, and it wasn't the worst thing that ever happened to me. It was not as bad as losing my firstborn, it was not as bad as watching my mother die from cancer. I mean it was bad. I am not saying it wasn't bad; it was horrific, it made me stab one guy and I won't even tell you what I did to another. The point is: society's conditioned us, men *and* women, to live in fear.'

Pat must be off her meds, but I dinnae want to ask in case she brings out the bazooka. Last time she stopped taking her lithium she bought a bazooka from Fat Mike's cousin. She keeps it stashed in the airing cupboard, or she used to. The police had to stop her shooting rockets at passing planes last time she went manic; she thought we were in wartime, ay.

'Teresa always knew they'd come for you,' she says, draining her drink.

'Who?'

'The experiment.'

Heart thumping – cannae breathe. Pauline's snoring and I want to get out of here, I want to get out of my face and wake up a different person.

'Penises,' she says. 'Wrinkled wee piss-holes – so fucking what!'

'I better head off, Pat.'

She points at her paintings.

'When men, and women, understand that they are not the scariest things in the world, for *either* sex – it's this!' She taps her head. 'That's when the world's real revolution will begin. I'm fucking telling you. It's your *own* mind that kills you. The most dangerous weapon in the world is a brain. You need to learn to master yours, Anais. It's like a wild fucking horse in there, I can tell.'

Pauline farts. It's a sudden, loud burst of sound. Pat is rocking. I wonder if I could find her lithium and put it in her vodka.

'Do you still see Professor True?'

'Gave him the grater last Tuesday. He likes it rough, that man does. He misses your mum though, even now. I can get him off, but she really meant something to him. He misses that. She had the touch, did our Teresa.'

There's a pipe on the table and from here I can see that the dungeon room has been repainted black and there's a large cat-o'-nine-tails on the wall.

I bet the experiment tune into Pat's flat every fucking night.

23

THERE'S A gap at the back of my drawer, where I can drop the socks down and my hands are wee enough to get them back up. I stuff them down the gap, pull the drawer right out and look. You cannae see anything. I've put all the cash Pat gave me in one sock. It is two hundred and forty quid. The wraps and all the gear are stashed in there too.

Tash is on the landing. She's wearing a skirt and make-up, and her hair is down and curly. She's got more colour in her skin because she's been on the sunbeds, and she's wearing big hoop earrings.

I go out onto the landing.

'Have you ever heard of Frida Kahlo?' I ask her.

'Nope – is she in care, like?'

'No, she used tae be a painter.'

'I've no heard of her. How?'

'You look like her.'

'Good-looking, was she?'

'Aye.'

'Anais – Helen cannae make it today. It's first thing tomorrow now, okay?' Angus calls up to me.

'Okay,' I say.

I feel deflated now. Helen's such a waste of space. I've seen her four times since she's been back, but she is still doing less than fuck-all to help me prove I didnae kosh PC Craig. She thinks I did. That's the fucking thing.

Isla and Tash walk away down the stairs.

'Where are youz going?' I trail behind them.

'Up town.'

'You could stay in and watch telly with me?'

I sound like a fanny.

'It's Friday night!' Tash says.

I watch them walking away. Isla's not happy. John reckons she almost cut an artery yesterday.

'Are you alright, Isla?' I call after her.

'I suppose.'

They walk through the lounge and out the front. Fuck this – I run out and catch them on the drive.

'Anais, your feet are bare!' Tash laughs at me.

'I can give you some cash.'

'I dinnae want your cash, I'll make my own,' she says.

'You dinnae want tae go,' I say, and for some reason I'm almost crying. I dinnae know what the fuck is wrong with me. Even as I'm saying it, I feel like an arse. Tash is just looking at me.

'We could play Monopoly?'

'Anais, calm fucking down – the staff are looking.'

Tash tucks my hair behind my ear and I give her a kiss on the cheek.

'Sorry. I'm just . . . I dunno. Are you taking down the registrations?' I ask Isla.

'Always.' She lifts a pad.

'Will you be warm enough?' I ask.

'See you, Anais.' Tash says like I've totally lost it.

They walk away.

Everyone else is in the telly area or out. I want to make popcorn and snuggle up and watch a film, but Shortie's out as well. I don't feel like sitting in the lounge on my own tonight, not with the experiment – up in the watchtower, tapping on the glass. Trudge upstairs, put on my Chinese slippers and a hoody, and head for the roof.

It's so quiet up here. Malcolm's wings haven't moved for ages. He's given up. I'm giving up. I wish he'd fly over and take me to Paris. Imagine arriving in Paris by flying cat. That would be class!

Dinnae think. Not about penises. Not about Pat. Think about super-powers; of all the super-powers, flight's the best one. Invisibility is okay, but it wouldnae *really* be all that – like you could eavesdrop, and watch people, and steal things I suppose, but you can do most of that anyway. Fuck telepathy. I get that on acid – it isnae fucking cool. Shapeshifting is a bit 1960s. Flying's the one: like in my flying dreams. I've not had one of those for yonks.

The fields go out for miles all around the Panopticon. The branches on the trees are bare, but there's still leaves on the ground. Somewhere a cow moos and birds flap up from the woods. It's like that documentary I watched yesterday after getting wasted with John. We both watched it in the dark, and shared a family-sized bag of crisps.

The documentary was about all these dead bodies in the rooftop of the forests, encased in bamboo cages. In the documentary, people looked up, and right above them in the treetops were all these bamboo cages and each of them had a body inside it – decaying in the breeze.

'What the fuck is that?' John had asked.

'Dead bodies. Up in trees,' I said.

I handed him the crisps.

'I'm gonnae have a whitey,' he said and fucked off up to the toilet to be sick.

I watched the rest on my own. They put the bodies up in the treetops because of the high oxygen content. All that air speeds up the rotting process, then the corpses decompose quickly to feed the soil, return to the earth and make it rich and fertile. I liked it – I watched the whole thing, even the credits.

Pull my hoody up. Brian's walking back across the fields. Wonder where he's been. I lie back and watch the sky. My heart aches. It's every day now this ache, this need to get the fuck away. My tag's bugging me. I went by Fat Mike's, but he was at the dogs. I'll go again. I wonder if the experiment have a little gadge typing it all up – everything that happens to me. Maybe they're faxing back reports, every sixty seconds.

Anais Hendricks's eyes looked to the left – 11.06 a.m.

Anais Hendricks inhaled – 11.07 a.m.

Anais Hendricks took a long shit – 11.13 a.m.

Anais Hendricks is bored – 11.17 a.m.

What if there was no experiment? What if my life was so worthless that it was of absolutely no importance to anyone?

'Alright, ya radge!' Shortie sticks her head out the window and climbs out.

'Hiya.'

I'm happy. Happy to see her. Happy not to be sitting here like a Norma-no-mates all night.

'Did you go and see that monk-guy for your identity crisis yet?' she asks me.

'Not yet.'

'How'd they ken you're having an identity crisis anyway?' she asks.

'Dunno. It started when I was like eight. I told Teresa eventually.'

'What, that you were having an identity crisis?'

'Aye. Like a nervous breakdown, but not.'

Shortie leans back on the turret. She begins to skin up, and the wind keeps blowing her baccy away. I cup my hands around it so it's protected.

'How did you know that's what it was?'

'I don't know. I looked in the mirror and there was this wee lassie who didnae smile, and when I met her eyes I felt embarrassed and awkward – like I'd just intruded on a stranger.'

'That's normal,' Shortie says.

'I used tae bite myself.'

'You should have bit other people.'

'I did.'

'So what did you say tae Teresa?' she asks.

'I told her I didnae know who I was, that I thought I was insane.'

'What did she say?'

'She said: You're eight, you're not fucking meant tae know who you are. That's how I started surfing in the lift shafts.'

'You should have tried knitting, for stress relief.'

'It cannae be much of a buzz – knitting.'

'Probably not, ay,' she giggles.

'Fucking knitting! I'll knit you the now. No, Shortie, the lifts were a buzz! I'd leap when they drew level – then you fly up on the other one, all the way. One time the lift got stuck and I couldnae get the hatch open. I was stuck for fucking ages. I lay down and did big fake snores – pretending tae be a dragon. I was only wee really, ay.'

'I bet it was a class buzz, Anais.'

'It was, until someone grassed me and the school found out and called out a social worker. She arrived in a green Fiat Punto, I remember that, and I brushed my bowl-cut for half an hour before she got tae our flat!'

'You . . . had a bowl-cut?'

'Aye. She came tae explain about identity problems, tae me, and tae Teresa.'

'What was her explanation, like?'

'That was the funny bit, she had a flowchart, on like a stand, and a marker pen – and she explained what psychotic schizophrenia was.'

'What?'

'Aye. She reckoned my biological mum was some schizo they found naked outside a supermarket, so she draws this cat on the flowchart, then another bigger cat – with a bib on.'

'D'ye want a blow-back?'

'Aye.'

Shortie leans in and blows the hot smoke into my throat and it burns like fuck.

'Aye, so she divides the flowchart page in half with a green line, then she points at the big crap cat she's drawn and says it's a lion,' I say.

'A fucking lion?'

'Aye, and I was like: It doesnae look like a lion, it looks like a crap cat!'

'What was your mum doing?'

'Chain-smoking – she'd had tae cancel all her afternoon clients, so she was fucking raging. The social worker was all like: This is what a schizophrenic sees; like you see the small cat, and everyone else sees the small cat, but a schizophrenic looks – and they see a lion.'

'Trippy shit.'

'I asked her if I'd get tae be a schizophrenic when I grew up.'

'What did she say?'

'She said, maybe. Then Teresa went mental, kicked her out. I sat rocking in front of the telly and she belted me across the pus, said if I wanted everyone tae think I was fucking mad – I should just keep rocking.'

'Fuck, that's harsh.'

'I know. I just thought it sounded cool – seeing stuff others people couldnae see, like something out a book. I mean, I also wanted tae be a fucking dinosaur. They didnae seem so worried about that.'

Shortie looks freaked out. We sit, quietly watching the light change over the fields. I wish I'd never said a thing.

24

'WHAT'S WRONG, Isla?' I ask her.

'Tash didnae come back.'

'What?'

'She got intae a punter's car last night, and she didnae come back.'

I feel sick right away. Step into the office where Isla's sitting, and Angus is on the phone to the police station already.

'It was a blue Escort, I've got the registration.' She points at her pad.

'Isla, have you been out all night?' Angus asks.

He holds his hand over the phone; she nods tae say aye, she has. She's pale and shaky.

'What happened?'

'I waited where she left me, near the docks – I took down the number, and I waited, then I rang her phone and it just kept ringing.'

She's crying again.

'How long did you wait?'

'All night. Till seven this morning – then I got the bus,' she whispers.

Her hands are freezing cold and I get that knot in my gut. Tash wouldnae leave Isla there all night – not a fucking chance. We stare at each other, and I can hear a car door click shut. Click, click, click. It feels like someone is pouring lead through my veins.

'The other lassies on the dock were going mental at me because I wouldnae move. They were shouting that I shouldnae be there if I didnae want business.'

Angus clicks the phone down.

'Okay, the police have traced the registration – it's a missing car. It was stolen last week in Rochester. We need to go down and make a statement, Isla. Anais, you have tae go; Helen's waiting for you.'

Isla grips my hand.

'I'm going with her, Angus. She needs me with her.'

'No, sorry, Anais – you going tae the police station is not a good idea. Isla, you are stuck with me until we get back.'

Bad. Bad feeling. Bad in the gut. Bad in the air, and just like that – wee faces flit across the walls, exactly the same as the concrete ones, but these ones are in plasterboard. It's like someone has half-flicked a light switch, so you can see that the spirit world is actually always there, watching us live our lives.

'Anais, you have tae go now. Helen's waiting in the car.'

'I'll be fine,' Isla says, blowing her nose.

'You're sure?'

'Aye, go.'

I dinnae like this. Bad, horrible feeling, knowing that Tash is somewhere out there right now when she'll want to be here. Cold skin. What if she's got cold skin? What if she's staring at the sky and the clouds are in her eyes?

I watch Angus lead Isla outside.

Helen's car reeks of nail polish and aromatherapy oils – bergamot, to be precise. She's got a wee bottle of it sitting on the dashboard. I can taste spring-onion crisps. They're all I wanted for breakfast. I hope I umnay pregnant to a pig farmer. I wish I hadnae eaten – I want to be sick every time I think of Tash stepping into a blue Escort. Door shuts. Guy presses lock on all the doors – click, click, click. She turns around, looks him in the face.

Dinnae think. Not about cars. Not about Tash's earrings, or her hair, or her laugh, or how you want desperately – to see her again.

It's dull out, and there's frost everywhere. We drive in silence, out in the country, down the motorway, until we are at the big crossroads in town. People are standing at the traffic lights looking just like people, living normal lives.

Click, click, click.

They'll find her. They will. Do not think about it. Don't, or you'll start to panic.

It's weird driving through the city after being surrounded by farmland for weeks on end. I cannae believe I've been in the Panopticon for over two months now. It almost feels like home, cos of, like, Shortie, and Isla, even Angus, and the roof. It's a long time since I've wanted to stay anywhere. Helen is breathing, just in, and out. Her nostrils flare. Her fingers are long and bony.

'So you're leaving – tae, retire?' I say.

'I'm taking a gap year.'

'But, you're what: fifty?'

'I am thirty-seven, Anais.'

'Same difference.'

Helen grits her teeth.

'Wouldn't you like to take a gap year, Anais? Go and help people less fortunate than yourself, or work in a sanctuary to save elephants?'

'No, I fucking wouldnae.'

'Some day you won't feel so smart about things. One day you'll realise it's up to you, and you alone, to make something of your life.'

'Fuck off, Helen.'

'Be rude if you want, it's not my problem any more. So, today, I want to go through this with you. Focus. Anais, are you stoned?' she asks.

'Just a wee bit.'

'Right. You were born in Warrender Institute, as you already know, and I have finally managed tae find your adoption certificate – well, a copy of it. It was taken in with the rest of Teresa's documents when they were investigating her murder.'

I flinch at the word. And now all I can see is Teresa's kimono on the floor in our bathroom. I could slap Helen sideways.

'Mr Jamieson is really looking forward to meeting you. He was there when you were born, and he remembers it well.'

'What? He saw me, and my biological mother?'

'That's what he said, yes. He's actually been at Warrender longer than any other resident.'

'That's promising, the longest crazy they've got!'

'Don't say crazy, it's not a positive term.'

'What would you say, like?'

'I would say, people like your mother are obviously fragile to the pressures of life and, sadly, those pressures can make them ill. That's maybe what made your mum run away from the hospital.'

'If it makes you feel better.'

'You are fragile, Anais.'

'Am I fuck!'

I go quiet and think about the iguana in that guy's flat a few years ago. What was his name again? Chief. He was a right weirdo.

'Angus said you thought the blood on your skirt was animal blood, and you had them checking it out at the lab?' Helen breaks the silence.

'Aye, I picked up a squirrel, I didnae know it had blood on it. Why, have they got the results yet?'

'The tests came back saying it was definitely human blood, Anais. The police think you're just – trying to halt the investigation with this squirrel story.'

'Do they now?'

Clever experiment. They are smart and relentless and wholly fucking brutal, and in my heart I'm raw, and scared, and nothing. I feel cold, shivery. I want tae get in a bath and put my head under the water.

Click, click, click. Tash turning around – looking at the guy, him saying something to her. What does he say?

Some day, aye, you will walk into a room, or a car, or an aeroplane, or a toilet, and you won't know it right then – but you will never get back out again. Exit only. Fact.

You might go home and put your shopping down and turn on the telly, and all the time you dinnae realise that the next time you go back through your front door it will be in an ambulance, or a body bag.

'You must remember something about that day?' Helen asks.

Shrinking. Shrinking, shrinking, shrinking.

It was a squirrel – it wasn't PC Craig's blood, I know it in my bones, and so do they, but they don't care. They dinnae. The experiment *want* me to know that they'll have me in a secure unit for life – for something I dinnae do. How else can they break me?

Helen's serene. The city is ugly. People. Cars. Buses. Trees. Buildings. Then the motorway again, and silence. A turn-off. We drive by a car broken down by the side of the road, then a wee bit later a man walking along with a can of petrol. We whizz past a garage and down a track in the woods, through wide-open gates: Warrender Institute. It's a big building – like the Panopticon, but less imposing. Huge windows, like the ones in my dream.

The nurse greets us and we all turn to wait for an old barefoot man who's walking down the corridor. This place stinks.

'This is Mr Jamieson, Anais. He was living here when you were born,' the nurse says.

The old monk stops about a metre away; he nods his head a lot – and looks totally pleased to see me. His eyes have a right agitated sheen, and the left one is milky and bloodshot. I think he must be totally blind on that side. The other one is a watery pale-blue colour, and it doesnae look much better.

'Hiya.'

I dinnae know what else to say. My hands feel really far away, and my arms and my legs dinnae feel like mine.

We walk along to the day-room. The monk sits in his chair and I take a seat across from him. He isnae saying much. The nurse gives me weak orange juice in a plastic cup. I put it down on the table and check the place out. There's a woman in the corner dozing; her T-shirt has Happy Place written on it. Her handprints are in green paint underneath and there's spittle around her mouth.

It smells like saliva in here. Like when you go to the dentist, or to get your eyes checked, and the man comes right up into your face and you can smell the saliva in his mouth – it's gross. There must be a café or something through that door as well. I can smell bad school dinners and bleach.

The monk smiles and smiles, and nods his head. He's kind of cute, tiny and wizened and I dinnae have a clue what to say, so I just sit. After a while he begins to look sad.

My face flushes, and I feel embarrassed. Helen is out in the nurses' office chatting – she's probably telling them all about elephants in India.

Someone should wipe the spittle from that old pill-head's mouth; every time she exhales a strand of it expands out.

'So you saw my mum?' I ask finally.

'Aye.' He grins.

'But you cannae really see?'

'I could see quite a lot then,' he falters.

'What did she look like?'

'Nice thatch.'

I dinnae think he's taking the piss but I cannae be sure.

'And a winged cat, lovely it was, great big wings.'

He spreads his arms wide to demonstrate. Shivers up my back. A winged cat and a woman that jumps from a big arch-shaped window and never stops falling.

I'm not looking at the walls, cos I dinnae want to see faces. I cannae imagine a woman in this room giving birth to a baby, but that doesnae mean she wasnae here. He said she had a flying cat and he even drew it for me. My arms are prickling.

'She flew in on it. It followed her around, and it padded right down this ward. They didnae see it, of course. Oh, it had lovely black glossy wings.'

A cat that flies – Malcolm. There's a coldness in me. The hairs on my arms are really up and I look around the room as hard as I can, as if this cat will materialise for me to see it, but it doesnae. The faces are there briefly. Just like a tracer.

'My mother flew?'

'Uh-huh, flew in – flew away. They didnae see anything.'

The monk leans across to me.

'They dinnae see much, though – do they?' he says.

Glance towards the office. Helen and the nurse are drinking tea.

'So. You're saying you saw *my* mother.'

'Aye,' he nods.

'And she flew in here on a winged cat?'

'Oh, aye. He was braw, he had a thick coat. His wings were huge! Your mother flew in from that side of the building – the orderlies thought she was walking, but they didn't look down, her legs were *not* touching the ground! She glided right down that corridor on him, then through this door. He waited for her, while she gave birth tae you – and that took quite a while! Then she smashed that big arched window right there, then she jumped. Well, the cat picked her up, down by the woods, about five minutes later. I saw them flying east.'

'Right.'

He's so schizo it's hopeless. Weird thing is, I totally believe he's never told a lie in his life.

'Your mother was massive with you in her tummy.'

'What colour was her hair?'

'Black, like yours.'

Helen's still chatting in the nurses' room; they're all laughing about something.

'What did she smell like?'

'Eggs, and death.'

'I hate eggs. So – let me get this straight: she flew in on a big black winged cat, and she gave birth in here?'

'Aye.'

'In this room?' I ask him.

'Right there.'

He points to the window. I look, but all that's there is a fake rubber yucca tree.

'And she smoked cigarillos,' he adds.

'She smoked wee cigars?'

'Aye. She was a cigarillo-smoking Outcast Queen.'

He is taking the cunt.

'They're lovely, they are – sensational girls, the Outcast Queens. D'ye not know of them?'

I rub my head, and undo my ponytail and shake my hair out. My scalp feels too tight, and this is the single weirdest conversation ever – it tops ketamine. Maybe the experiment have already got me, maybe I'm in a cage somewhere right now, drooling down my chin.

'Oh. Well. There were only ever three,' he says.

He seems disappointed in me.

'What's an Outcast Queen?'

The monk smiles queerly and my tummy flips over – he is freaking me right out.

'You dinnae seem mental,' I tell him.

'I was in the army before this, Anais. I went to boarding school first from the age of four, all the way until I was a young man – then straight in the army. Both are quite extreme institutions in their own right. They got me early. It's hard when they get you so young.'

I'm sweating. I need to get out of this room.

'I couldnae be in the army,' I say.

'Me neither – in the end, it was too late, by the time I came here.'

'What do you mean?' I ask him.

He just stares at me. His white eye's moving with the other one. I want to believe him, I want to believe that I was born here – not in a test-tube. I dinnae want to have started life as a fucking experiment.

'What colour were her eyes?'

My heart's pounding and the shrinking's coming in. He can fucking sense it.

'They were just like yours,' he says.

My mother had eyes and they were the same colour as mine. A nurse comes in with a medication tray for the drooler – she holds her hand out and swallows some tablets down. I want to take them off her. I'd pop anything I could get my hands on right now. The drooler waves at the monk and goes back to sleep.

The monk takes out a worn domino, its numbers four and four – he gestures at me to take it.

'It's my lucky one.'

'We better leave now, Anais.' Helen appears.

The monk quickly hides the domino; he doesnae like Helen, and she can tell.

'Thanks for speaking tae me,' I say.

I walk away and my legs are like fucking jelly.

'You'll come back and play me at dominoes?' he calls after me.

'Aye. Okay.'

'D'ye promise?'

'Aye.'

It's snowing outside, just lightly, and Helen's spraffing shite, but I dinnae hear it.

As we reverse out the car park, the monk comes stumbling out the doors. He's not fast. His bare feet slap off the stones and his pyjamas flap around his skinny body.

'Stop the fucking car.'

'Anais, we should just go, our appointment time is over.'

She slows down and I wind down my window, feeling protective of the monk although I dinnae know why.

'It was snowing, Miss Anais!'

He pants as he reaches the car and grabs at my window.

'It was the prettiest snow I have ever seen – it began tae fall just as you were born. It was the biggest snowstorm for fifty years that winter. The snow was so thick, it covered everything and it sparkled and the moon was full, Miss Anais – a great big one. I remember, cos hardly anyone was asleep. We all heard your first cry, you sounded *so* fierce!'

I let him see my tears, it's important – I dinnae know why, but it is.

'I looked out the window, not long after she jumped. That big one right over there, see. I looked out the window tae see where she went, but she was gone, and her footprints were filling up with snow, they disappeared by the light of the moon. It was such a big moon,' he whispers.

'And she was gone?'

'Aye.'

The monk grasps my hand. He's frail. He'll not be here much longer, he's on his way out. I'll look it up when I get back: snow and a full moon, the coldest snow in years is bound to be on record. Maybe there's even a photo. The monk slips the domino into my hand.

'For luck,' he says.

'Good to meet you then, Mr Jamieson. We need to go!' Helen says.

I turn and glare at her. If she starts on him I'm gonnae fucking slap her.

'They dinnae own you,' he whispers.

'Bye then,' Helen calls loudly.

I turn the domino over in my hand, and slip it in my pocket before Helen can see. The car begins to reverse and

I stick my head out of the window. The monk steps back and stamps his feet together hard.

'Good luck, daughter of an Outcast Queen,' he salutes me.

All the way down the drive I watch him recede. Still saluting. Still barefoot, standing in his pyjamas.

25

WINCE AT the light in the living area – that watchtower seems bigger than ever. The night-nurse has just come on duty. I am watching her tae see if she speaks to anyone in the watchtower again. I can imagine her up there, while we're asleep, doors locked, playing chess with the experiment, all of them naked. Playing for our souls.

The boys are in the pool area. John is wearing new clothes – Shortie says he's moving out soon.

'Where have you been?' the night-nurse asks me.

'Up town,' I say.

She grabs me by the chin and tilts my head up into the light.

'I am a hundred per cent certain your pupils are dilated.'

'D'ye want tae let go of my fucking chin?'

'Do you know I haven't *once* seen you with undilated pupils, Anais Hendricks!'

'Aye? Well, maybe I've seen you!'

'Seen me what, Miss Hendricks? What have you seen me do?'

My mouth tastes like dog-ends. The night-nurse snorts. Tonight's interrogation is over. She's wearing a blue suit and her soft albino hair is neatly tied up at the back. She sashays away.

'Upstairs then, boys,' she says.

'Have you seen Isla?' John asks me.

'No, I'm going tae see her now.'

'I cannae believe it about Tash, ay?' wee Dylan says. He looks scared – I give him a wee kiss on his cheek. It's horrible for everyone knowing she's still out there. I cannae even remember the last time I sat down and ate, or anything.

The kitchen's still open – someone's forgot to lock the larder door. Sneak in, quiet as. There's a catering-size block of chocolate in the larder, it's the length of my arm. Shove it up under my jumper, grab a few bags of crisps and some vanilla essence.

Imagine being the daughter of an Outcast Queen, imagine being a daughter! Imagine if flying cats were real and you were special, not just a total fucking no-mark.

They say the devil's best trick was to make everyone believe he didnae exist. Maybe God's just a scientist. This is *all* an experiment gone wrong, every single one of us, just wonky as fuck because of some chemical cock-up that was meant to produce something less faulty.

Click, click, click. The car doors all close, Tash looks in the side rear-view mirror, watches Isla get further away.

Everything's fucked.

How do I know I'm not an experiment? I dinnae. Fact. And the other fact is this: nobody knows, cos we're all just wandering about with no fucking idea what the universe is, or what death is or what happens after you die. Maybe I'm just going schizo.

But, if nobody knows anything about anything, then who's

to say there's not an Outcast Queen who smokes cigarillos, and sends out winged cats to watch over her daughter?

What if schizophrenia makes you believe in flying cats? Probably it does. That, and it makes you see faces where there urnay faces – next it'll be voices, then it'll just be me and the monk playing dominoes until the meds run out.

Back in my room I open the top latch of my bedroom window and stick my head out – it is such a relief to see her face.

'Hey, Isla.'

'D'ye want first on?' she offers.

'Nope, I've got something better to smoke. D'ye want some?'

'Aye, sound.'

Tie a hunk of chocolate and some grass together and swing it along to Isla. Her eyes are red and puffy.

Shortie snaps her window open and sticks her head out on the other side.

'I have a delivery for you as well,' I say, and I undo the knot on my shoelace with my teeth. Swing a parcel along to her.

'You are saving my life, I thought I was gonnae end up straight for fucking ever. I'm gonnae skin up.' Shortie's head disappears.

'What can you see?' Isla asks.

'What?'

'Out there, fucking look.' She gestures across the lawn and she's almost shouting.

It's the Prozac that's making her aggressive and weird and totally non-Isla-like, and the police still haven't found the car that took Tash.

'All I can see is the dark,' I answer.

'The lawn,' she points.

Look down, but all I can see is dark, and fir trees silhouetted against the sky. Bare oak trees. There's a frost out, and there's been snow. Our lawn sparkles.

'Tash used tae see clocks there, on the lawn. She'd say the whole lawn was full of them. Big old grandfather clocks and grandmother clocks, and that their hands were spinning and they were all tick-tick-tick-ticking away.'

'I remember you saying that when I moved in.'

'She said it so often, Anais, that I began tae hear them.'

I light a match and it goes out. Light another one and it goes out as well. Curve my hand around the third and it catches.

'Then, today, they just stopped.'

Tash is still not home and it's been four days. I saw her photograph on a poster at the train station tonight. Click, click, click. Car engine. Door. Locks. Trying the handle, fan heater on hot, a porno on the floor, the man's hand reaches out. Tash turning to try and get a blade out of her pocket and stab him.

'Yup, they've gone now. The clocks have stopped ticking, Anais.' Isla strains to hear something.

'Tash'll come back, Isla.'

'Dead people dinnae come back.'

That's true, dead people don't come back, not even for a second, not for one word or one whisper or one tiny bit of human touch. They go and it's cold, and it stays cold and you cannae ever change it.

'The clocks have fucking stopped, Anais.'

My heart stops, then it thuds back in.

'They put a poster up, in the train station, it's got her name and photo on it. She'll see it, Isla, she's just – getting wasted. She wouldnae leave you.'

'I know she wouldnae, you know she wouldnae, we all fucking know she wouldnae, so where is she?'

I dinnae know why I'm lying, and trying to say Tash'll be alright and she'll be back soon. This night is too big and too strange and too dark, and it unfolds out around us, all the way out there – dark streets and dark fields and dark car parks. I cannae take this.

'When my babies were born, Anais, they came quick, just like that. No big fuss. No drama. My mum had them in my arms before she even cut the umbilical cord. I put them right on the breast. Fed them myself. That's how they fucking got it.'

'It's not your fault, you didn't know. You have tae think of them, Isla. They need you.'

'The first thing I said tae my babies was, *I love you*.'

The trees rustle. It's so cold out that it stings your skin. Winter's come to claim the world again, the sky is clear and the stars are bright.

Isla disappears in her window. Look down at the lawn. Imagine all those grandfather clocks there? Tick-tick-tick; cuckoos and big old white ones and skinny brown ones and tiny ones. Grandmother clocks, and shiny brass bits and cogs to make the pendulum swing. I can almost see them, but I cannae hear them. Isla pops her head out again and she is holding a half-empty bottle of vodka.

'D'ye want a drink?' she asks.

'No, I just want tae smoke myself fucking senseless. Ta, though. I could come through tae your room?' I say.

'Night-nurse won't let you, the doors are locked.'

'Aye. She'd only go on about my fucking dilated pupils!'

We giggle. It's so good to hear her laugh. She downs almost the rest of the bottle. I light another joint. I dinnae know where the fuck Shortie's got to. Maybe she's tried to sneak downstairs to see John. We all know she doesnae want him to leave.

'There's soul-stealers out there, Anais. My old man's like that, even before the Aids, he'd sell my mum. He once sold her tae the guy upstairs. He would have sold me; that's why she wanted me in care, it's safer.'

Her hands are shaking.

'I'm gonnae get the night-nurse tae come and see you, Isla.'

'Dinnae. I'm just gonnae crash. Tomorrow I'm gonnae ring up, ask for a visit to see the twins.'

'Are you sure?'

Shortie pops her head out her window – with a humongous spliff clamped in her gob.

'Ladies!'

She brandishes the beast, sparks her flame-thrower. We laugh at her. She grins and double-drags it. Isla downs the dregs of her vodka and lobs the bottle across the lawn – it thuds on the grass.

'Tae absent friends, may they soon return,' she says.

'Absent friends,' we echo.

'Pass the joint then, Shortie.'

She swings it along to me.

'What did the old guy say at the hospital?' Isla asks me.

'Nothing much.'

'He must have said something.'

'He said I was the daughter of a cigarillo-smoking Outcast Queen, one of only three cigarillo-smoking Outcast Queens. He said she flew intae the nuthouse on a flying cat.'

They're both silent for a full minute.

'Sounds about right,' Shortie says.

We smoke and listen as fields rustle in the quiet. A crescent moon sits all lopsided above the forest, leering at us in the sky.

26

THE DARK is too dark.

Sleep won't happen.

Clocks won't tick, no matter how much I wish they would. The night is sinister. For some reason I'm remembering ski-slope Julie who cried in primary One, cos I told her the social worker brought me, not the fucking stork.

Ski-slope never swore; I did, I was five but I swore. I bit. I kicked. I didnae sleep, hardly ever. She called me a liar and I smashed her apple off the playground, then I ate her strawberry rubber – while she stood crying her eyes out. She told everyone I was evil and they believed her.

She had a gym outfit and could do a cartwheel. I was three weeks late for school; I was always arriving from somewhere. I had a wee suitcase, and my teddy. It's manky, that teddy; it's no wonder, though, I always kick him under my bed wherever I live. I wouldnae speak at first, whenever I went anywhere new to live. I just watched. Waited to work out who the people were that I'd moved in with, and then if I thought I could relax, I'd start gabbing away and probably never shut up. Teresa said when I did start speaking she cried in the bathroom for half an hour.

There are long low hoots from outside. It's one of those nights, where all you can do is watch the shadows on the wall – until it gets light.

Extra-big bowl of cornflakes. Icy-cold milk. Perfect. The chef's voice grows louder and louder from the kitchen.

'It was a big bar!'

'Maybe someone ate it?' Joan asks.

I can see him through the hatch. He's looking at Joan's big belly and wondering.

'Noh, it was a great big fuck-off bar,' he says.

'Please try not tae swear in front of the clients!'

'They only speak in swear-words, Joan! Those wee pricks are fucking feral.'

'Aye, well – they dinnae get paid tae be here; we do.'

Go, Joan!

'That chocolate bar was big enough for twenty sponge-cakes, Joan. I only got it in the last delivery.'

She sticks her head out the hatch into the dining area. I keep eating my cornflakes. They're covered in sugar and drenched in milk. Shortie's over by the telly with her feet up, watching cartoons.

'Have you seen a bar of chocolate?' Joan asks me.

'A big huge bar?'

The chef interrupts her, sticking his head out to take a look at me.

'A big huge bar of chocolate, Anais?'

'Nope.'

Push my bowl through the hatch.

'Any toast?' I ask the chef.

He shakes his head. 'You're the girl who wants vegetarian meals?'

'And?'

'They've not authorised them. What are you living on in the meantime?'

'Good looks and fresh fucking air, pal!'

He looks like he wants to machete me, in the face.

'There's no need for that attitude,' Joan calls after me.

There is a need for that attitude – I tried being nice to the chef, but he cannae stand us, so fuck him.

'Where's John?' I ask Shortie.

'He's at the shops.'

'Where's Isla?'

'She's in her room.'

'Where's Dylan?'

'He had a visit arranged with his uncle. Watch this, Anais, this is great!'

Shortie bursts out laughing at the TV again. I scuff upstairs.

Morning, beautiful. Can you come on Friday? Please, please, please? I just want tae hang out like old times. I've got gear for you as well.

Jay has sent me, like, ten texts making sure I will be there on Friday. I forgot to ask him about what Pat said about his debts, but he'll no doubt tell me when I see him. He hasn't been as nice as this to me since I was like twelve, and it's soothing to have something, *anything*, nice right now.

Okay x.

My hands stink of vanilla, I like it. I pop my head around

Brian's door and he pushes his glasses up his nose and rubs his hands on his shorts.

'Do you have any money?'

'No.'

'Dinnae fucking lie tae me, you wee prick.'

'I dinnae, Anais. I dinnae get any until my clothing allowance comes in.'

'Aye, well, stay away from the Lane, Brian. If I find out you went in one old person's cottage and ripped them off, or worse . . . I'll chop your fucking dick off.'

My room's a shit-pit; it reeks of vanilla, so I open my window. The staff do room-checks tomorrow so I need to make sure I double-hide the money, and the speed-wraps from Pat, and the other gear. I'll deal with the gigantic brick of chocolate later.

Isla's vodka bottle is still lying on the lawn. I need to go and see if I can catch Mike this time. I want this tag off; I could do it before I go and see Jay. I wonder if Jay's changed much? Eighteen months, it's a long time to spend inside. Brush my hair and pick out what I'll wear to go and see him. Isla might chum me up town later. We need to take our mind off Tash, at least until there is news.

'Isla, d'ye want tae go up town?'

Swing my leg around her door and twirl burlesque-style into her room.

The floor hits me.

Her left hand is open, and someone is screaming.

'Fuuuuuuuuuuuuuuuuuuuuck!'

I am on my knees, but I'm still falling. Her hand is out, like she is waiting for Tash to come, but she's not here and

I am up, lifting her under her arms, cradling her, pushing her hair back, trying to clean her face.

Footsteps pound up the stairs.

'Fuck!' Joan drops tae her knees, her face white, and she tries tae take Isla off me, but she can't. Click, click, click.

'It's okay, Anais, it's okay, just let me check her over.'

Adrenaline floods my veins and the faces are there on the walls, but I don't care. I don't care about faces, or the experiment or that watchtower staring down. I'm roaring now, really fucking open-mouthed gut sobs, and Joan is feeling for Isla's pulse – placing her down on the floor. I'm doubled over and I cannae breathe. Her eyes are open.

Angus is at the door, on the phone, in clipped tones, calling for an ambulance. I lean over, tuck Isla's hair behind her ear.

27

EXPERIMENT – 2. *Us* – 0.

'Time of death – 8.27 a.m.'

The ambulance man says it quietly upstairs, but we can all fucking hear it. None of us are allowed up there. Dylan's just back. Steven's in. Brian's in. John's in. Shortie's shaking like fuck.

The ambulance man takes a big plastic bag intae Isla's room and I am still crying, but I dinnae care. I feel like someone keeps battering me. Every bit of my body aches.

There are cups of tea on the dining tables – and packets of chocolate biscuits.

'Have another cup of tea, Anais,' Angus says.

'No.'

'You're in shock. You need sugar.'

'I want tae see Isla,' Shortie says.

'No, you cannae go up, Shortie. I'm really, really sorry, but we need tae let these men do their job. Okay?' he says.

Shortie won't let go of my hand. The two ambulance men come out with a long black bag but no stretcher.

'Where's the stretcher?' I ask.

'They dinnae need one,' Joan says quietly.

'Put her on a fucking stretcher!'

My hands are shaking like fuck, adrenaline is making me buzz and there's flashes of faces on the walls. The ambulance men stop and look down over the balcony. The glint's in the room, it's dense as fuck. The staff can feel it, and we can feel it, and the fucking ambulance men can feel it – we are ready to take them all out. Every last one.

'It's okay.' One of the ambulance men stops and speaks over his radio to someone outside. 'Can you bring in a stretcher, please, Jim?'

Joan opens the front door.

'Anais, do you want tae sit down in the office?' Angus asks me.

I shake my head.

'Thanks, Jim, bring it up here,' the ambulance man says.

The stretcher is laid out on our landing. The ambulance men lift Isla carefully onto it. She's straight now, her back is straight, and she's not being taken out like the rubbish. I want to wrap her in something soft, take her a pillow and a teddy.

Angus stops shoving a mug of tea at me and puts it on the table, and the ambulance men walk the stretcher along the landing and downstairs. Shortie is crying so hard her face is red. Brian's in the telly area staring at a blank screen. His programme is normally on just now. He has a wee pile of biscuits by his side. Joan opens the front door for the ambulance men and follows them out.

My skin is hot.

It is teatime, and I am in the train station. I just scored some grass and I am walking past a missing-persons poster, and a face is looking out from a photograph and the name reads Natasha MacRae, fifteen years old, and all the commuters are just walking by.

Click, click, click.

People dinnae want to look. They dinnae want tae see. Nobody will ask.

'Where did Tash go?'

'She just went.'

'Went where?'

'She just went, Your Honour, got in a car.'

'Who was driving?'

It could have been anyone. It could have been some sick cunt with a space in his sex circle. It could have been the devil, or the experiment. Probably it was just an average psychopath, Your Honour.

Disappearing. It happens when you blink. It happens as you write down the registration number for a car pulling away. It happens when you ask for the payment and the guy reaches into his coat, and you just know in your bones he's not going to pull out money. It is happening right now as the ambulance men secure the stretcher with straps, so they can lift it onto the ambulance.

I have to go.

The roof has been discovered. Angus knows we come up here, but Joan doesnae yet. We need this roof, it's the only place the watchtower cannae see us. I keep imagining Isla and Tash, petals in their hair – kissing on the island. Laughing. Till death do us part. Then her hand, just open like that. And somehow now all I can see is Teresa, an empty bath, her kimono on the floor, and I really need tae drink until I cannae see anything any more.

'I knew you'd be here.' Shortie sticks her head out the window.

She climbs out onto the turret roof, takes my hand. She's chewed her nails off. Her fingers are stubby and raw. She tries tae put her arm around me. I'm rocking, just enough to hold the shrinking back.

Down in the car park, the resuscitation equipment is brought out. They put it away and the ambulance waits with its back doors open. One of the medic guys is talking to Joan. He smiles and pats her on the arm. The ambulance looks like some square metal ladybird – throwing its wings right back, ready to fly away.

Shortie clenches and unclenches her fist. Her jaw is white and tight. That lump in my throat is so big I cannae breathe. I'm wheezy. There's a knot in my gut that's been there how many years? It's moving up as well. I lean forward and retch. I retch and retch, but it's just liquid. Shortie holds my hair.

Police arrive and the next staff team drive down in their cars. There'll be a changeover now. Today's team will inform the relief staff of Isla's death. Her social worker will arrive soon. They will write down words on files. Isla will lay in the morgue on her own and we will not be allowed to go and hold her hand.

28

SHORTIE COMES back from the shop with a wee bottle of Bacardi.

My mouth tastes of bile. I accept the bottle and drink half of it straight.

'This is gonnae break Tash's heart when she comes back,' she says firmly.

Dinnae say anything, not one word. Shortie begins to cry. We sit up here, away from everyone – lunch comes and goes. Eventually we smell dinner cooking. Cars are pulling in and leaving downstairs. More police arrive, then the lab woman.

'That's the one that done my swabs.'

'They always call her in,' Shortie says.

Sun pulls itself across the fields. Stars come out and we throw our crisps at the wood pigeons nestling in the eaves. They're right fat bastards. Noisy as well. I can recognise three new birds on sight. The small tawny owl, starlings and a kestrel. The kestrel's out just now. It hovers over the farmer's field, then swoops.

Shortie climbs back in the window and disappears down

the turret. I stand up on the edge of the ledge and look down. That's all it takes – just one step forward.

'Here, Anais, take this.' She re-emerges, panting, and shoves her duvet out the window.

I take it off her and wait until she climbs back out, then I wrap it around the two of us like a wee nest tae snuggle in. She giggles.

'What?'

'We're like two fucking chicks, waiting for somebody tae come along and feed us.' She grins, then she's crying again and I hold her in as close as I can.

The staff are shouting for us outside. Angus has not told them that we keep escaping up here. He's a good guy, one of the best I've met in care. Downstairs Brian is slinking out the front door, then he's away – running over the fields.

'What's that?' Shortie's looking out.

'What?'

'Listen.'

I listen. It's a hoot, just faint, then another. Britney glides across the fields, her white-tipped wings are glowing in the moonlight. The staff are still shouting and the wind is picking up.

'We better go back in,' Shortie says.

It's even more baltic in the turret – I touch the stone wall and it's like going back in time, like this building has always been here and it doesnae care. It's freezing: our breath curls out, wisps like ghosts, curling away from us. We stand staring at them for a second, then Shortie leans forward and kisses me on the mouth, and I kiss her back. We scuff downstairs holding hands.

In the main room the blue light's already on, and the night-nurse is on duty.

'Up to your rooms then, girls, it's past bedtime,' she says.

We follow her up the stairs, and Shortie's crying again. We walk past Tash's bedroom door, then Isla's. Someone has stripped Isla's bed. Her posters are still up on the walls, though.

We don't want to let go of each other's hand, we just stand at my bedroom door and the night-nurse looks at us, then she has a quick scan downstairs.

'Just for tonight, until things settle down,' she says, and she ushers us both into my room and pulls the door almost closed behind us.

I give Shortie an old T-shirt – she hauls it on and curls up at the bottom of my bed like a wee cat.

There's a spider with a steel web; it weaves quickly, and Isla is in the middle – stuck. Each steel wire slices her. The spider casts out more and more threads of steel in an intricate pattern. I want to kill the spider, but she's got my head. She rubs her legs together ready tae spin my body further in. She will cocoon me; my legs are still twitching, but soon they will be paralysed.

I wake – drenched, my heart batters off my chest. Shrinking. Shrinking. Shrinking. I'm a wee fucking pinprick.

The curtains sway to and fro on the wall. I am still falling and the floor is swaying – everything is swaying, and this isnae a flashback, it's the other side. The veil's getting thinner. Every year it gets less hidden, that other world – it's always there, waiting, until eventually we see it.

There's patterns all over my walls, Victorian swirls with

delicate bars across them. Tash and Isla are in there – wrapped in each other's arms. Isla reaches out from the wall. She wants me to know that this pain is good, that I *have* to feel it.

Peel my top off and push my legs down and hit something soft. It's Shortie; her chest rises and falls. She's so wee, and her skinhead is growing in – her fringe is all tufted up. I brush it back. Her forehead is hot and her skin is clammy. She took some of Pat's Valium earlier, to stop her shaking.

There's a lump in my throat, a pressure pushing up, that's been there for how many years? Sobs begin in my whole body, spasms head-tae-toe. I clamp my hands over my mouth so I dinnae wake Shortie. My mouth is wide open, and I'm crying so hard I begin to silently retch. Hours pass. The sun comes up. I cannae see. My face is swollen and I cannae stop sobbing. Shortie's still asleep. I nudge her. Nothing.

'Are you asleep?'

I'm shrinking to a tiny pinprick, I'm so wee that I can hardly hear my voice as it says something I have never, ever heard it say.

'I just want my mum.'

Shortie bolts up. Just like that. Like she's waited there quiet all fucking night, knowing I had to say something and I'd never fucking say it if anyone else was there to hear it. She knows just like I do, this is the *only* time in my entire life that I will say those words out loud.

'It's okay,' she says, pulling me in close and holding me, while I sob.

29

'WHY DOES your room smell of vanilla?' Joan asks me.

'I don't know.'

'Is it a perfume?'

'Probably.'

'You took vanilla essence from the kitchen, didn't you?'

'Nope.'

Joan is jittery – they cannae get me to speak half the time lately, but she knows I want the rest of my clothing allowance, so now she's pushing me for conversation. She's not fucking stupid. I need more cash, I'm getting out. I am not leaving here in a body bag, not here, not John Kay's. Not anywhere.

If I can get the rest of my clothing allowance then I'll have three hundred quid. Click, click, click. Jay wants me to go out there in about an hour; we can get totally and utterly fucked up. I've already started on Pat's wraps.

'I was speaking tae Jamie at your last unit,' Joan says.

'Aye.'

'He said you'd started a lot of riots there.'

'So.'

'He said you were a total nightmare. I told him you have been as good as gold in here.'

'When's the funeral?' I ask her.

'Monday.'

'What's the coroner doing with Isla?'

'Just verifying all the details. Try and not think about it, Anais.'

'You do know Tash's dead?'

'Why'd you say that?' Joan looks at me. She's got big bags under her eyes. She looks like shit.

'She wouldnae have left Isla.'

'We don't know that, Anais.'

'I do. What did Isla's mum take earlier?'

'She just collected some of her old possessions, teddies and things like that.'

'Do the twins know?'

Joan nods. She kneels down at my chest of drawers. She's relieved to hear me speak, she doesnae like it when any of us go quiet.

She opens my bottom drawer and lifts up a T-shirt. Shit! A brick of chocolate falls out. Joan picks it up. There are bite marks all over one end, where I've been eating that instead of meals.

'Anais, what is this?'

'I dunno.'

I turn away because I'm smiling.

She stands up with the giant chocolate block in her hands.

'Seriously, what is this?'

Jesus – I cannae believe I forgot to hide that!

'It's a protest, Joan. Bring it up at changeover. I am protesting at the lack of vegetarian options; also at enforced menus by the chef; also at the way we have tae live here – watched by that fucking thing twenty-four fucking hours a day!'

I point at the watchtower. Joan takes the big bar of chocolate and the T-shirt it was wrapped in – I swear she's trying not tae smile.

'You'll get this T-shirt back once it's been washed.'

'Cheers.'

'Are you going tae read something at Isla's funeral?' she asks.

'No.'

I am not going to read anything. It's not my place; it would have been Tash's, but she's not here and I cannae speak for her.

If Tash was murdered, they've not found her. She must have been murdered – it's that wee horrible grain of truth that you just know in your bones. When I found Teresa in the bath, I couldnae see where the blood had come from, I couldnae see if she'd done it herself – but I knew she hadn't. You just do.

You do strange things when you find someone you love dead. I walked through to the living room and got her cigarettes. I thought I'd take her one, and maybe a glass of gin. In the living room I looked out from our window, down to the car park, and I saw this black dot, moving away, a big black dot. I kept watching and another one appeared behind it, and an arm appeared out from the black dot, and it gestured to the other one.

They looked up, and saw me, two men, black wide-rimmed hats, empty spaces where their noses should be.

30

I'M BEING watched through the trees, but it doesnae bother me. The woods are almost empty now it's winter – just the odd dog walker and nobody else around. I come out by the wooden stile and cross the road.

There's a wee jeweller's right up the top of the village – I'm going there first. I have to pass by the gate where Tash and Isla would sit for a smoke. In fact, I'll avoid it; I'll go past on the way back.

The jeweller's shop is all lit up and the doorbell chimes when I walk in.

'Hello.'

'I was wondering if you could put a hole in something for me?' I ask the guy.

'What's that, dear?'

The man puts his specs on and I slide the domino across the desk. Double four.

'Oh, I see. It's a well-worn one, isn't it? Yes, I could put a hole in the top if you like.'

'Ta, can you do it now or . . . ?'

'Come back on Monday.'

He writes a receipt for what it will cost and hands it to me.

Walk through the car park by the village hall, and light a fag when I get near the woods. I can hear shouts – someone's getting totally leathered further down. Great! That's the last thing I need tae see. That speed Pat gave me is well strong, I shouldn't have taken a whole wrap in one go. I want tae avoid going past them, all jeering at some fight inside their circle, but that would mean going the long way.

Keep walking. I'm gonnae have to go right by them; fuck it, it's only kids from the local school. There's a big lassie lifting her leg – she's gonnae stamp on someone's head. She better watch it, you can easy kill someone that way.

It's starting to drizzle, and all the street-lamps are like orange orbs. I walk by the crowd surrounding the fight, and my stomach lurches.

'D'ye still think you're fucking hard now?'

The big lassie lifts her leg again to stamp on Shortie's face.

'What the fuck d'ye think you're doing?' I shove in and the group parts, then closes around us, so nobody walking nearby can see.

'She fucking started it!' the lassie says.

Shortie's crumpled on the floor; she's trying tae kick back – but she's woozy. She grins up at me. Click, click, click. There's been more than one of them at her. Click. Click.

'She stamped on my face.' Shortie looks up at me. One of her eyes is swollen and closing up already.

'I'm gonnae fucking do it again!'

The lassie thinks she's hard as fuck cos she's battered a girl from the home. I grab her by the back of her neck, pull her in, like I'm gonnae snog her face off. *Crack*! Bone off bone. Someone boots me in the back and another one's dragging me down. Nails. Punches. This isnae pain – it's not what pain feels like. I catch Shortie's eye; she's grinning at me, woozy, but she's still got the fucking glint. It passes between us – dark as night and just as true.

'Fuck it, Anais, ay; fuck it, and fuck them, I fucking love you.'

Scrabble upright, stagger back – then turn, fly through air. CRACK, she's down, out; drag her back up by the hair, smack her in the pus – once, twice – a tooth flies through the air. Skelp her fucking sideways, and she's pushing her feet along the ground, pleading and trying tae get away.

Click, click, click.

There's a faint voice somewhere, it's saying again and again: *If you dinnae stop her – she won't stop!* And someone steps up behind me, their whole body moves in behind mine. They are grabbing my arms, slowing them down as I keep punching, and Shortie is whispering into my ear, I can hear her, under the roar.

'She's had enough, Anais, that's it – stop, you're alright. I've got you.'

My arms slow, my body relaxes into her hold, my heart is pounding and everything is coming back – louder than before. A siren screeches close by and Shortie is taking me by the hand, leading me over the road, and I'm looking back at them. Someone's picking the lassie up off the deck.

'I didnae mean it,' I whisper and I'm crying, and she's dragging me on.

It's misty out now; cars down on the road put their fog-lights on. The ground in the woods is wet – we're running, and I slip. Shortie drags me up again.

'Dinnae look back, dinnae. Just keep walking,' she says.

I'm shaking. I'm really fucking shaking; my teeth are clattering, cos I've never wanted to hurt someone as bad as that.

I cannae see the lights behind us any more, we're right in the forest now.

'It's alright, Anais. Here, stop a minute – just breathe.'

Shortie pushes me against a tree, and she's panting as well. She pulls her cigarettes out, lights a fag in shaky hands and passes it tae me. Then she leans in and kisses me, and I hold onto her, because there is nothing else – no air, no sky, no ground.

31

HOLD SHORTIE's head over the sink while blood swirls down the plughole. She pushes a wet roll of tissue across her eye and climbs into the empty bath. I dry her face, her neck. I won't try to brush her hair, cos her scalp will still be too sore. We placed a towel along the bottom of the bathroom door so nobody can tell that we're in here.

I clean myself up quickly. The police will be up here any minute now. If the lassie I battered identifies me, then I'll be straight into a secure unit tonight.

Jay, I got held up . . . do you still want me to come?

This is what they wanted. That's what the police said: one more charge, and they've got me. It won't be a secure unit near here; upstairs is never gonnae be finished. They'll take me to John Kay's.

Aye, but come now.

Keep dabbing at my face in the mirror, wiping the blood away, but all I can see is dead pigs, and dead Islas, and a dead Anais – hanging in a cell. One vertebrae. Snapped.

There's a knock on the door.

'Who is it?' I ask, trying to make my voice sound even.

'It's Dylan – let me in.'

'Not just now, Dylan, what d'you want?'

'Brian's down in the office, he's grassing you up!'

'To who?'

'He's grassing you tae Angus and Joan – he says you've just battered a whole bunch of lassies down in the village. He's saying you broke one girl's legs.'

'Shit!' Shortie looks up at me.

'The polis are on their way, the staff had tae ring them. They're looking for you the now – they dinnae know you're back here yet.'

'Dylan?'

'Aye?'

'Go downstairs and, if the staff look like they're coming this way, do me a favour and stop them.'

Are you coming right now? I need tae know, for definite?

Okay A Xx.

Shortie gets out of the bath and opens the door a crack.

'Can you manage that?' she asks Dylan.

He nods and she opens the door to let him see that I'm alright. Shortie's black eye is already swollen up to fuck, but I've cleaned up quite good. Dylan looks scared – I dinnae like it.

'We're alright. Cross my heart,' I tell him.

'Can you keep the staff outside? Cos Anais will be put away, if the polis get her,' Shortie says.

'Aye, I can do it.' He turns away and clomps down the hall.

Shortie gets me out the back interview-room window. She smashed it out with a stone and her jumper wrapped around it, so they wouldnae hear it. I drop to the ground, and look back up at her.

'You better come back,' she says.

'I will.'

Then I am running, down towards the woods. I can see a police car pulling down the drive behind me, but their lights dinnae reach out over the fields. The wind is fucking freezing and I didnae even have time to grab a coat.

Darkness feels safer than daylight. How many times has the dark been my safe place? I begin tae count all the places I've slept: bus shelters, graveyards, old cottages, holiday-let caravans in winter when the park is shut, in the woods, disused buildings, a burnt-out car, under a bridge, on the beach, the viaduct. I once slept on a roundabout in the middle of a dual carriageway. I watched the cars all night – it was winter, so I kept my knees tucked up in my top, and newspapers crumpled up and stuffed under it for insulation, and I breathed – with my head inside my jumper, so as not to lose any body-heat. D'you know what that's called? Resourceful. Stupid. Fucking idiotic. I am not sleeping rough again, not for anyone, it's not fucking safe and it's not fucking funny. The woods thin. Nobody is around at the village main road, thank God!

The bus-shelter timetable says forty minutes until the next bus. That's enough time. The bus'll stop by the old row of cottages over the road. The cottages are all hunched in a row, their letterboxes set in a grim grin.

I just want Jay to hold me, and stroke my hair. I want the night tae just become us and a bed, and the shadows on the walls. I need to get fucked up, properly.

Tension gnaws my gut, and the adrenaline won't let me

go, I cannae get it out my body. I took two trips when we got back to the unit. I was saving them for a moment like this – I need to see clearer. I had half an E from Pat's stash as well.

Walk across the road, down to the village high school and go around the back. There's one minibus that's always parked here. I find a chib – a rusty pole. I'm ramming it in the minibus door when two laddies walk up the hill.

They come and watch: one is buzzing gas, and the other one's doing tricks on a yo-yo. The road is empty and orange and wet.

'D'ye want some?' The kid holds out his gas for me.

'It's bad for your lungs,' I tell him.

The front door cracks open.

Hop up into the driver's seat, rip out a plastic box under the dash and grab the wires. Fuck. Fuck. Fuck! My heart's going mental and the trips are kicking in now. It's hard to see what's brown or red in the dark. The ignition catches. I pull my foot up right gentle on the clutch and ease it into first.

'Get in then,' I say.

The laddies climb up into the back, and I reverse the minibus fast.

'What are you doing?' one boy asks.

Slam my foot down on the accelerator.

'Fuuuuuuuuuuuuuuuuuck!' he screams.

It echoes. That fuuuuuuuuuuuuuuuuuuuuuuuuuuck echoes.

Bang! We hit the gym-hall wall. Impact! Bring it. Powwow-wow-wow-wow. Reverse again. The laddies are laughing their arses off as we drive into the wall a second time. There's a screeching from underneath the minibus and smoke's coming out the front. Fucking great! We just sit here for a minute, grinning, then something big falls off the back; it clatters and the sound spooks me.

Click, click, click.

'Where's Tash?' I ask the laddie.

'Who?'

'Aye, you ken,' I say, and I stagger down the step, feet on the tarmac – I dinnae feel right.

'That was fucking amazing!' the smallest laddie says.

I run up to the corner and the bus is just pulling out. I catch up with it and bang on the door – he stops. Thank God he's stopped.

'A half tae town.'

'Are you a half?' he asks.

'Aye, I'm a half!'

He puts it through. Twat! I dinnae look at the folk on the bus, with their long noses, and their stares. I'm going cross-eyed – those trips are way stronger than the last I had. Wobble down the aisle. There's condensation on the windows and everything smells like wet dog. Fuck, fuck, fuck! I just need to make it to Jay's. He'll have something to bring me down, Valis or smack or anything, I dinnae fucking care what.

Glance out the window. The polis urnay following, just the experiment – four black rimmed-hats, a car overtaking, one looking up. Fuck them. They can fucking try me! I'm not taking it, not now.

My nose. Look at in the window, and it's so fucking long. Keeps growing. Rain spatters outside and the experiment speed up and cruise ahead. Paris. Think of Paris. I bet the rain in Paris is way nicer than this. Imagine if there was an Outcast Queen in Paris, flying to work on her cat; maybe she sent Malcolm to bring me to her, but the experiment turned him to stone.

I need tae get milk.

I hate it when this happens. I can hear people's thoughts – all the way down the bus, I can dip into each passenger's head and hear what they're thinking.

I cannae be bothered ringing, she'll just moan. Wish this bus would hurry up.

Look at the back of the passengers' heads and try to work out which person each thought comes from. I cannae switch them off, they lilt in and out – most people's thoughts are so boring I could die, but I dinnae want tae be dead, staring away with no light in my eyes and my hand held out and scissors on the floor and blood on my cheek.

Fuck, fuck, fuck! I'm panicking. Shit, shit, shit! I wonder if the police are tracking me right now from my tag? I need to get it off.

I can hear a siren somewhere. I feel fucking sick. Shit, it's getting worse, palpitations and colours like worms everywhere – shit, shit, shit!

Just, hold, on. Rub at the window. Stare. Stare. Stare. I grip the seat in front of me and I'm sweating, and everything looks the same outside the window, and if everything looks the same how am I gonnae know when to get off?

Eventually they appear – five huge fingers pointing at the sky. The high-rises are like one hand that holds hundreds of people's lives. There's five blocks and Jay's safe-house is in my old staircase.

I ring the bell. There's a woman in front of me.

Need tae get Jack a winter coat. A tartan one. Need tae get his injections from the vet.

Woof, woof – I growl as I walk by her. The bus doors open and I soar down the steps.

The cold air stings, and it's misty when I breathe out – cars blare their horns at me as I cross the motorway; ribbons of light unfurl from their headlights. And I remember watching gymnasts when I was wee, with coloured ribbons and coloured leotards. The experiment – Beeeeeeeeeeeeee eeeeeeeeeeeeeeeep.

Fuck. Fuck. Fuck! 3–0 to the experiment. They have Teresa, Tash, and now Isla, but you need four queens to make a deck. They drive by and one lifts up his hat, so he can stare right at me.

'You're next,' he mouths.

The lift stinks of pish.

This is where I stood in cords, holding a social worker's hand, going to see my new mummy. And this is where they took her away, and this is what I have to do. Now. I press floor fourteen. Wait. Crack my knuckles. Wait. The lift pings open and it is sat there. Door 73F.

Step up to the door and knock, just lightly.

I bend down on my knees and the acid is putting trailers everywhere – my fingers are elongating, and I open the letterbox and peer in. There's a light on in the hall. At the end of that hall is the living room, and that hole in the door has been there for about ten years. Our carpet is a different colour than it used to be, though, and there is no clock on the wall. Whoever lives here now doesn't smoke, because all I can smell is air freshener and nothing else.

I'm sorry.

I whisper it through the door and turn around and march straight back into the lift. Jab – up, up, fucking up! I'm getting out. Fuck it. That's what Teresa would tell me to do.

She'd want me to have something better: to go to Paris and paint naked boys and read every book in every library and walk by the river and never look back. I am getting out. They'll want me in John Kay's when I get home. Later. They'll get me in there this week. Unless I go. This is my floor. Ping.

Mike opens his door.

'Hello, Anais – a vision indeed!' He has a tinny in one hand.

'Mike, can I come in?'

'Aw, Anais, away and come in, hen, aye, come in. Fuck, how are you?'

'Alright.'

'I've not seen you since your ma, well – we all miss Teresa, you know. She was quite a woman.'

His hallway's rammed with magazines and boxes of knocked-off PlayStations and MacBooks and mobiles.

'D'ye need a laptop, hen?' He points.

There is a stack of about forty laptops on one desk; the other wall has stacks of boxes of dog food, then beans, Xboxes, porn DVDs. He has a Christmas tree up and the light bulbs are those coloured ones that nobody ever gets now. On the top of the tree there's a Barbie;

she's smoking a spliff and she looks like she's wearing bondage gear.

'No, Mike. What I really need – is tae get rid of this?'

I show him my tag.

'Aye, hen. That's no a bonnie bracelet for a wee looker like you, is it?'

'No, it's not.' I'm laughing, and Barbie is parting her legs, sliding down the top of the tree, up and down on the top of the tree, and I'm leaning against something inky. Fuck – it's the money press. Beside me on the floor's a wee mountain of fake twenties.

'Are you alright, Anais?'

'Aye. I'm gonnae go and see my boyfriend, ay. I've not seen him for ages.'

'He's a lucky laddie. What's his name?' he asks as he goes into his kitchen.

'Jay.'

He comes back out with a welding gun-type thing and plugs it in tae heat it up.

'Ye might get a wee burn, is that alright?'

'Aye. It's fine.'

'Jay that's inside? He's no out for ages, Anais. His door's marked – d'ye ken that? He owes a fucking wadge ay cash out, and no tae nice people. Can you not meet a nice laddie? A banker, no some wee piece ay pish fae round here.'

'A banker?'

'Or ken somebody straight!'

I must look confused. Barbie has got her tits out and she's go-go dancing in the reflection of the baubles, and I can remember laughing with Teresa, I can remember that. Jay's probably just not telling anyone he's out, if he's in that bad a debt. I'm not saying anything.

Fuck! The heat on my leg is unbearable, and the gun buzzes and everything's far away.

32

THERE'S WEE witches on the inside of my eyelids when I blink. They are always the same ones – they're quite cheery like, until they turn. If the experiment put an implant in my head, could they see the witches?

Sometimes I close my eyes when I'm tripping and I can see wee Pac-Men eating the dark, turning everything fluorescent.

Get into the lift, press down. My ankle is red fucking raw fae that burner – but nae tag. Nae fucking tag! My arms feel grimy. I should have wore a coat, cos it's so fucking cold, but I dinnae, I never do. I dinnae wear coats or extra jumpers, cos it never looks as good.

My T-shirt is damp. I mind sleeping rough last year, and when I ran out of clothes I robbed a clothes line, but because it was winter all I could find was rows and rows of frozen jeans, and frozen jumpers and knickers and towels. I unclipped one pair of jeans and carried them away like a cardboard cutout.

It's all buzzing too loud: the light in the lift and Isla and Teresa and Tash, all telling me – what?

The lift pings open. Four doors just stand there. A darts

commentator is making his low speech in someone's living room. An audience claps. It smells like Fray Bentos pie on the landing. Teresa wouldnae let me eat processed food, apart from the only thing I *can* cook – Kraft macaroni. She would make an exception for that. Usually she got all organic stuff from the butcher. He would bring us chickens, or steak and chops – when he came around for his shags.

Hands shaky, and my legs. I just want tae get in bed with Jay, and watch cartoons, and smoke myself blind. I keep feeling like I'm gonnae pass out, cos I've had too much, but I want more. I want to forget.

I tap on the door, but there's no answer – tap again.

'Alright, Anais?'

Spin around. It's troll. Troll Mark, who sells the shan wraps.

'Alright.'

'Jay's expecting you, Anais, has he not answered? He's fucking wasted, ay. You are looking great, by the way!'

He passes me a wee bong; it's neat, really pretty green glass. I drag hard on it – and my spine goes numb.

He knocks on the door five times, then twice more.

'Man, you're growing up!' he says.

'Aye.'

'Have another smoke, finish it!'

I inhale again, twice, hold it, then drag the last bit of the bong. My throat is burning and my legs are heavy as fuck. He knocks exactly the same way again, and I see it then. A big deep cross gouged into the door – somebody's done that with a big fucking knife.

'It's marked?'

I turn around and the door is open and nobody is there.

'Aye, it's fucking marked!' He slams his fist out and drags me in.

SLAM.

The hall is black; fear in my gut, I want tae go, need tae fucking go – now! He pushes me against the door and there are voices down the hall, and I dinnae ken what was in that bong, but it's all falling away, the floor, my legs.

I'm being carried down a hallway. I know it's a hallway because it echoes the way they do in the high-rise flats when there's nae carpets on the floor.

The living-room door opens and it's bright and there's four guys. Four. One, two, three, four, and Mark makes five. One bald guy comes right up to take a look at me. He opens my mouth.

Fuck.

Fuck.

Fuck!

'I need tae use the bathroom,' my voice says. I cannae-fucking-breathe.

'Dinnae waste your time, Anais. The door's fucking locked.'

Shit! My heart pounds. Dinnae let them know you're scared, try to smile – maybe I'm just reading this wrong.

'Sit down, have a smoke?' The bald guy shoves a joint in my face.

Try to focus. Who's in here? Count. There's Mark, a skinny guy in a tracksuit, the bald one, an Asian flashy bloke and a short stocky bulldog fiddling with a webcam.

'Nice ay ye tae help Jay oot with his debts, hen. You must be a right good girlfriend, ay?'

The windows are covered with bin liners, and I know for

fucking sure Jay's in his cell. He's in his fucking cell. I'm woozy, shit! There's the floor, underneath me. I'm lying back against the wall, but I'm still dropping back, back, back. I can hear them, but I cannae lift my arms now, not even an inch. Fuck, fuck, fuck!

'What did you give her?'

'Everything: smack, roofies. She only smoked half, but she was fucking pickled anyway.'

I'm shrinking – there are colours everywhere so I cannae see clearly, but I can hear everything in here, I have crystalline audio vision.

Whoooompf. I need tae not float like this, along the ceiling, cos that strange wee body down there – I'm sure it belongs to me.

'D'ye like movies, hen?'

The bulldog's pulling my T-shirt off and I'm numb – the experiment are here. Watching, and they are clever and I am nothing.

'D'ye hear that, lads – she likes movies. Nod your fucking head, hen. D'ye like movies, ay?'

'Take her fucking bra off.'

'Hit my fucking hand away again, hen, and I'll rape your arse so fucking badly you'll bleed for a fucking week, ya fucking cunt!'

Black. No colours. No light.

'She's gone.'

'She can still hear – look, she's listening.'

I've got a brand-new bike. It's red and the wheels go round. If you were a flying cat, would you eat the eggs of kestrels?

Zip rips my gut – intae lurch.

'Turn her fucking over.'
'Fucking cunt bit me.'
'Turn her fucking over!'

33

THERE ARE caskets made out of bamboo and they swing along the forest roof.

The trees are tall and thin and there isnae a lot of leaves up there, so you can clearly see that each casket is open, and the bamboo's woven in wide circles so you can see through them. Each contraption is about six and a half feet long by two feet wide. It's the best way tae rot a corpse – did you know that? A bamboo cage at the top of the trees.

'It's very comfortable, Anais, you should join us.' Teresa smiles down at me from a lovely old bamboo cage.

'Where's Isla?'

Teresa points along. There's Isla, her mouth's open. A centipede crawls out.

'Mother Teresa?'

'Aye?'

'I dinnae feel well.'

'You're not well, Anais. Not at all. Dinnae be scared. You'll stop breathing soon.'

Her kimono sleeves are so wide. Each inch of silk costs more than the person who made it can earn in a year. She's holding my bone cigarette holder, and smoking, and reading a book – she flicks her ash and it falls all the way down through the trees.

My neck is getting sore looking up. John's in the basket next tae Teresa. She's shifting her kimono so he can see her tits. He begins to wank frantically.

'Nae offence, Anais,' he shouts down.

The canopy of baskets sways. The monk is there. So's Jay; he's become a skeleton, but I know him by his shoulder blades.

'Why?' I'm croaking it out, but he cannae hear me. 'Why the fuck did you do that?' I try again.

The twins are playing with a feather headdress and a bouncy ball. Their basket is a double; it's taller than the others, so they can stand up and play clap-a-hands.

I'm so tired. Lie down and stare up, my eyes are getting heavy.

'Is it alright tae go tae sleep?' I ask Teresa.

'Aye. Just give intae it. Dinnae fight it. Just let go, Anais.' Her teeth are gone.

I'm sinking into the foliage on the forest floor, and a giant centipede crawls across my stomach, but I dinnae care. I dinnae feel it, I dinnae feel its feet; just a tiny pin, jabbing into my forehead. Then another. It hurts. It's fucking sore! I open my eyes. Someone is dropping something on my head, sharp enough tae puncture my skin. I touch where one has hit me and, when I take my fingers away, there is blood.

A basket above me is shaking – it's Tash. She's shaking her cage and her moustache unfurls – it curls right out through her bamboo cage and all over the sky until it's dark. It hooks itself around the moon and drags it out the sky.

She's shouting.

'Wake up. Right *fucking* now, Anais. WAKE the fuck UP!'

Dry eyes, sour mouth – there's burnt spoons on the floor and black bags taped over the windows and the room fucking stinks.

Where are they?

Push myself up. Fuck, I can smell vomit, it's on my hand. Top lip's burning, coldsores, cankers in my mouth; my tongue is huge, swollen, and I'm shrinking.

Get up, get fucking up! They're not here, they've gone, the webcam's away. Shit, retching, lean over. Stop. Stop it! Get fucking up: now, Anais. One foot up, then the other one, use the wall. There's my jeans. Pull them on – fuck, it hurts! Wrap my arms around myself and sink down, sobbing.

Fuck, fuck, fuck! Stop crying, get up, finish pulling your fucking jeans on. That's it, pull them up, dinnae touch the bruises, dinnae stop; get out the fucking flat, now. I rip one of the bags off the windows. Look – there's still a world down there, there are matchstick prams and Lego dogs. A wee speck of a laddie swings a lead.

Jay. I hope someone kills him.

There was five of them. There was five. There was a webcam. There was five. It's one of those where a lassie looks all fucked up and underage. Fuck! I can smell them. I can smell them on me. Piss rises up from my jeans.

Toilet. Pull light on. Nobody's in the flat now, just me. It's just me, but I need tae go now. One minute, though. One minute. The water's cold in the taps, my hands are shaky as fuck. There's a tracksuit top on the floor. Pull it on.

Clever experiment.

I fucking, hate!

I was dreaming of Teresa – she was giving her old punter a hand-job and John was watching and wanking.

Tash kept dropping wee clocks on my face.

Tick.

Tick.

Tick.

34

I DON'T know how long it took me tae get back here. I cannae remember most of it. Angus was shouting and saying the polis were gonnae be able tae lock me away now, and Shortie was just standing on the stair staring at me.

This is life. Breathing in, and out. The bathroom is white. My legs are purple bruises. There isnae anywhere I dinnae ache, and I think if I died now, it would be peaceful. Tash would meet me, and Isla.

I want tae just slip under the water – but instead I am pulling myself up, and undoing the lid on nail-varnish remover, and cleaning varnish off my toes. I'm cleaning myself as careful as if I were a newborn.

I would rather do anything than be around people like that again. I want out. I want to watch a fire-breather as dawn comes up on the solstice. *They* cannae have this soul. They have taken everything else and it's the only thing left that I own. I'm not telling Shortie what's happened, or anyone else, but especially not Shortie; she's had enough tae deal with. What would be the point of her feeling hurt as well? Nobody's gonnae catch those guys, and the polis fucking hate me anyway. What would they do? Clever experiment.

I go back downstairs, into the office, and Angus is still arguing with PC Arnold.

'So tag her again!'

'I dinnae think so, Mr Everlen.'

'Anais, are you okay? You look really pale,' Angus asks.

'I'm fine.'

'Are you going tae tell us where you have been, Miss Hendricks?'

'No.'

'Well, I have no other option than tae take you down the station for questioning,' PC Arnold says.

'Come on, look at her – she's not well, and you cannae take her straight down there and off tae secure, Mr Arnold. She is allowed special consideration, if a family member has died.'

'Aye, but that wee lassie wasnae related tae Anais, was she?'

'That's not the point. The girls develop unusually strong bonds in here, they are a family.'

'Aye, but they urnay related, are they? We have an order here tae put Anais in John Kay's. She'll be kept there until she's eighteen, I reckon, and that is that!'

'But PC Craig has improved!' Angus is almost shouting.

'Aye, but Anais battered an *innocent* schoolgirl from our village, Mr Everlen. If that family decide tae pursue it, she won't be done for grievous bodily harm; it will be attempted murder. She needs locked up.'

'Tag her – I'll take her tae school personally, and I'll go at four o'clock and collect her at the gate. You can monitor where she is: and the rest of the time she'll be on total house-arrest. We let her go tae the funeral on Thursday – and then she's all yours!'

'I dinnae think so, Mr Everlen.'

'Well, your sergeant said I could legally push for extenuating circumstances tae be taken into consideration, should we prove that Anais was in a state of extreme shock when she got in that fight.'

'That's what my sergeant said?' he asks.

'Aye, pretty much. And you better check with him before you take her anywhere, or you might be the one who gets in trouble,' Angus says.

'I'll check that with the station.'

'You do that.'

Angus shows him out.

I walk out behind them. Shortie runs up.

'So are you gonnae tell me where you've been yet?' she asks me.

'No.'

'Fuck off, Anais, what's the big secret?'

'I umnay going tae John Kay's.'

'How? Are they letting you off? Are they letting you stay here?'

'No.'

'Then, what?'

'D'ye think Dylan could break intae the staff safe?'

'Aye. How?'

Shortie squeezes my hand and she doesnae need me to tell her. I'm getting out. I dinnae care how. If I don't, then I will only ever have been nothing, and no-one, and what is the point of surviving this – for that?

'Anais?'

'Aye, Angus.'

'I have an order here, I got it from the head of the social-work department. Dinnae ask. He knows someone I know. Anyway, they are going to make sure that you can stay until the funeral – you have special consideration. I am meant tae take you to school tomorrow, but I trust you tae come back, and on Thursday we will go and see Isla off, okay?'

I well up, and he squeezes my shoulder.

'D'ye want tae talk about it, Anais?'

'No. But, Angus?'

'What?'

'Thanks.'

I am wearing all warm clothes. They call it dressing for the weather. I've never bothered before, but right now I want tae be warm, and safe. Head down the woods. Dinnae let the experiment see you planning.

This is what's different from yesterday – I've got my hair cut into a bob, I dinnae want to smoke, I dinnae want food, but I will eat, and not just chocolate. I will eat soup, and bread, and cheese, and I will stop having a day on and a day off tae stay skinny. I will comb my hair, and brush my teeth and learn how tae be nice to me.

Run and catch the first bus; it gets me into town and then I get the second one. Folk from school are on it. It's stuffy in here. I cannae believe they are making me go in for one day. I sit up the back and have a smoke, just so I have something tae do with my hands. I'm late for school, by like what . . . a few months?

There's Christmas decorations in windows and trees,

and the lights are on when you go through town and it is so beautiful, a wee fairytale kingdom with old-fashioned rides and doughnut stands and hot mulled wine. I had that once. It was fucking minging. The bus turns right, out into the residential streets, and I look down into a garden of gnomes and reindeer. Santa's climbing up a chimney.

It's the 16th December. I opened the square on the advent calendar this morning, and there was nothing in there. Nae chocolate Jesus. John ate the lot, seeing as he cannae help himself but nick things, and he laughs every morning when it's someone else's turn to open it and there's fuck-all there.

I'm wearing my lime-green mini-kilt, thick tights, a jumper and a jacket with a wee dragonfly on the lapel. I put loads of extra conditioner in with my clothes, so everything smells super-clean. I washed my hair twice. I'm wearing my oldest Converse. They look so shit and worn, but they're great. I put gloves on, and a scarf. I'm dressing myself like I'm somebody else's bairn. Carefully. Like it counts.

I have a letter in my pocket. I addressed it tae the head of Jay's prison. I have another one for the guy in Jay's cell – he told me his name was Rod. I just addressed it to Rod, I dinnae know his number, but I put Jay's cell number on it. I don't know if his cellmate will get it. I hope so, though. They dinnae like paedos in jail.

Kids all around me talk about school and what they watched on TV and who's shagged who. Drift downstairs, get off the bus and wander through the school gates with the crowd.

Through the door. Down the hallway. Into my classroom. Sit down.

'Anais Hendricks! Nice tae see you're present,' the reggie teacher says.

'Not really present!' Someone behind me mutters.

Take two Valium out my pocket – chew, swallow, breathe. There's a late assembly. I follow my class out and down another hall and into the cafeteria, where all the assembly chairs are. Take a seat in my year's row. Loudness. Voices rattling over each other. Eyes and faces and hair and bags – it's all glaring. It's funny: Pat reckoned rape cannae kill you, but she is wrong.

'Did you take a trip after the October break? You've not been in for ages, ay?' the girl next to me asks.

Smooth down my skirt. I feel stupid. Awkward. I dinnae want tae shrink here.

'Aye, I did.'

'Where'd you go? We went tae Florida again, but just for the October break, ay. You didnae miss much over the last few months. English is boring as ever. History's still shit,' she says.

She sticks her legs out and admires her tan. The headmaster comes in, takes one brief sharp look at me and begins.

In afternoon science class a Van de Graaff machine is brought in. A teacher I shagged once on Ecstasy is taking this class. Kids say the other teacher had a nervous breakdown. I place my hand on the Van de Graaff and my hair rises straight up and out. The laddies are watching. What if they've seen it? What if the porno is online? It would have gone online. Where else would it go?

There are still bruises. I touch my own hand really gently, under the table, so nobody can see. Almost like I am holding my own hand. Is it sad tae hold your own hand? If nobody was looking I'd hug myself. Arms around me, holding me in, holding on. I've been doing that on the toilet in break-times. What a fucking idiot, ay? The laddies giggle, and in the shiny dome of the Van de Graaff there's a girl who looks sad.

Paris.

Imagine Paris. Imagine being born a beautiful, lucky wee girl with a beautiful mum, who I'd met, who I lived with; one who made pancakes, and drank gin, and listened tae jazz. One that loved me so much I grew strong.

Imagine a name that is not this one. I have tae finish it now.

It's the only thing that belongs to me – the birthday game. I have spent far too much of my life dealing in truths, too many truths to mention.

Some truths are so heavy they weigh the whole world and the sea. We did Heracles and Atlas in history. Atlas held the weight of the world; Heracles was a bent fuck. Atlas knew what truth was. Truth is something that laps its way in with the tides, and it returns night after night – until it washes you away. The moon brings it. The tides deliver it. When they leave, the tides steal from the shore. They steal grains and shells and stones. They steal cliffs and rocks and stiles and trees and fields and houses and villages and wee countrified lanes. Then they drag it all out to the bottom of the seabed.

The tides won't stop until they've taken everything. One day everything will be at the bottom of the sea. Maybe people will grow fins again? Maybe swimming feels like flying if you have fins and live in the sea?

Paris it is. Maybe one sibling? A brother. Gay. Overly protective, smart, funny, ridiculously attractive. And three aunties. One in Florence. One in New York. One in Iceland. Mandatory holidays to each every single year. It's a *total* fucking chore.

35

THE STAFF finished their meeting and they've called all of us into the lounge. A new girl with blue hair has already had a scrap with Shortie. Shortie's glowing. The new lassie has a black eye. We're being briefed about the funeral. Me. Shortie. John. Dylan. Steven. Brian. The new girl.

'So we thought you could draw a memorial to Isla on the tower?' Joan suggests.

I'm not even answering that. Shortie is wearing a trilby, fitted trousers and braces. She looks great. I'm wearing a yellow dress and black leggings and no shoes. I'll wear furry boots when we go out, and I'm buying a really warm coat for the funeral. It is Twenties-style. Angus will take me to the shopping centre later. I'm wearing one of those Russian hats with the earflaps, and fur lining as well. You could sleep rough in this hat in the winter and not die.

John Kay's rung. They are looking forward to signing me up for group therapy.

Fucking freaks!

'Anyway, we can maybe work on some ideas next week, once things have settled down,' Joan says.

'We want you all tae feel like you can say goodbye tae Isla in a creative way,' Angus says.

'What about Tash?' John mutters.

'Who's Tash?' the new girl asks.

'Some of you have applied for special circumstances to attend Isla's funeral. Shortie, Anais, John, Steven and Dylan – you will all be collected in the morning, okay?' Joan says.

We nod. She's holding a large card.

'If you all want tae sign this, please, we will have a wreath for Isla, and this card from everyone. We will all be here for the wake afterwards, which will be held here in the main room.'

I've packed my bags for the secure unit. Three bin bags. No matter how much shite I accumulate I always seem tae have three bags. Joan checked them. She can check all she likes, the only things that are important to me, urnay in there.

A social-work minibus trundles down the drive – great, it's the wee kids coming in for a visit. Fucking hell. It pulls up and five of them jump down.

'I thought we could do some crafts with the residents from the small children's unit today,' Joan says brightly. 'Especially you, Anais. If you want tae attend tomorrow, you can take part in something that isnae just about you for once!'

'I'll do crafts with them!' John grins. He's totally monged on something.

The front door slams open and the wee kids run in, ahead of two support workers.

'Can we see the games room?' one asks.

John shows the wee laddies the art on the watchtower,

and they start taking crayons out of a box and drawing onto it. John is drawing a peace symbol with feet. Two wee lassies run around me and Shortie.

'Come on, Anais, let's show them.' Shortie's grinning.

'We've got a games room in ours, but we dinnae have a pool table.' A wee red-haired girl tugs my sleeve, pointing at ours.

Joan brought her record player in and some vinyl – it's prehistoric stuff, but it's surprisingly good; she obviously looks squarer than she is.

'Can we put a record on?' her wee pal asks us.

She's got short hair and she's wearing an Elmo T-shirt. Too cool for school – nothing like the brown cords and brown shoes the social workers used tae dress me in.

'I cannae be arsed with this,' I say to Shortie.

'Anais, you cannae say that!' She drags me over to the pool table, then helps a wee lassie put a record on.

'What's your name then?' she asks her.

'Alice.'

'I'm Shortie, and that's Anais. Pleased tae meet you.'

The little girl comes over to me and I shake her hand solemnly. The record kicks in and she gets all excited and starts jumping about.

'C'mon, let's shake it,' she says.

'Shake it?'

'They watch music videos all the time, duh! Come on, shake it, Anais.' Shortie grins.

'Fuck off!'

'Ooh, you swore! Fuck off, fuck off, fuck off,' Alice parrots.

Jesus fuck!

'Puh-leeeeeese dance with me?' She folds her hands in prayer, then begins busting out demented chicken moves.

'I need a fucking smoke.'

'Anais!' Shortie says.

I shake my head at her and walk off.

'I'm gonnae go for a fag too.' Alice runs after me and takes my hand.

Joy.

'No, you're not,' I tell her.

'Aye, I uhm.'

'No, you wait here. You're too young to smoke!'

'I'll just sit with you then,' she says happily.

We sit on the front step, up where it's not so frosty. It's cold out, but I'm warm enough. Alice is wearing a hat too.

'Are you cold?' I ask her.

'Nope!'

She chatters away. I forgot this. Whenever I meet wee kids in homes it's the same: they chat and chat. They tell me all about their lives. Even the older kids do; they've been doing it with me for years. They'll come to my room and they just know there's nothing they can say that will make me pity them or look at them like they're cheap or dirty, or crap or ugly or hideous as fuck.

The wee girl squeezes my hand, drags me back to the winter sun.

'I remember you,' she says.

'I dinnae think so, Alice.'

'Aye, aye. I saw you playing on our roundabout in the middle of the night. You were with that guy back in there. He was wearing a dress.'

I laugh.

'Aye, that was me. The guy in the dress is called John.'

'So d'ye get tae leave soon and get a house?' She squints up at me.

'Hopefully.'

'Why hopefully?'

'Well, they want me tae stay on a few years, maybe until I'm eighteen.'

Alice is horrified. 'Why?'

'Cos. I did some bad things.'

'Did you say some bad words?'

'Aye.'

'Like shit?'

'Dinnae say that!' I laugh at her.

'Like fuck?' she asks me, her eyes going round. 'Did you say cunty-balls?'

'Uh-huh, stuff like that.'

'I bet you didnae mean it, though,' she says, and picks up a stone and throws it. 'I can tell you didnae mean it. D'you want me tae tell them for you?'

'No, it's okay,' I say.

She leans in against me.

'Maybe you could just leave and, like, get a house and I could come and live with you? I'd like that,' she says shyly.

'That would be cool, ay?' I say and wipe my face.

'Can you bake a chocolate caterpillar cake?'

I shake my head.

'Oh well. Could you learn tae bake a chocolate caterpillar cake?'

I squeeze her hand and she puts her arms up, so I let her clamber over me. I hug her. We rock like that on the porch. I can feel the strain in her. Her muscles all tense and her mind always searching around her to see who's safe and who's not. She knows about rooms without windows or doors. She knows I do as well – it's not a thing you need tae say.

Snow begins to fall, light as ash. Alice sticks her tongue out to catch it.

'Yum, yum, yum,' she says.

'Have you seen Britney?' I ask her.

'Who's Britney?'

'You've not seen Britney? You haven't seen our resident owl? Well, that's shocking. Next thing you'll be telling me you've never met a flying cat?'

'Cat's dinnae fly, silly!' she says.

'Oh, they don't, do they? C'mon, let's go and see who we can find first: Britney, the gargoyle, or – Malcolm, the Panopticon's secret flying feline!'

She's grinning and totally excited to meet a flying cat, or an owl. I pick her up, sit her on my hips and we walk down the drive to see Malcolm.

36

SHORTIE WENT to the jeweller's earlier and picked up my domino. I've hung it on a chain and it's hidden under my dress. I keep checking it's still there. I bought my Twenties coat, and a new dress. I now only have £517.26 left. I got my allowance, Pat's cash. Shortie sold some deals for me at her school, and John must be turning tricks again, cos he gave me two hundred and told me he'd stab me if I didnae take it. I'm almost ready. I ate chicken at dinner tonight, I dinnae ken why – I think I'm losing it. Nerves, ay. It was fucking minging. I'm never eating dead flesh again.

John Kay's rang the staff earlier. They've reserved me a single room. There's eight people in the unit, an intensive anger-management course every day, group therapy, gym class, lessons, and if there's nobody tae take you for weekend release, you dinnae get out.

Wee Dylan is booting the head off a snowman on the lawn. Me and Shortie are eating popcorn and watching from the window. It's dark out there, and the lights from the porch are illuminating the wee circle where the snowman is, but everything else is dark.

'D'you think Tash will be there tomorrow? She might make it back, ay – she might have heard?' Shortie asks.

I shake my head.

'How'd you know?'

'I just do.'

Angus comes along with some chocolate bars.

'What are you two cooking up?'

'Fuck-all!'

'D'youz want some chocolate?'

'Aye.'

It's great to watch Dylan being happy, kicking the fuck out of a snowman. Steven is out there as well, but he's not bothered about kicking anything, he's getting out next week. His mum's cancer is in remission. Dylan is gonnae be lonely, he'll be one of the only ones in here at Christmas.

'John cannae wait tae move intae his supported accommodation place in town,' Shortie says.

'Aye?'

'Aye. It's dead good. It's like a bedsit, but it's his own.'

'Sound.'

'He's gonnae make me a meal,' she says.

'Is he now?'

'Aye.'

My heart flip-flops, and I think about the last time we kissed, but she doesn't look at me; she's looking out the window.

'Good. So. We're agreed then?' I ask her.

'Exactly how we said,' she says.

John comes swaggering downstairs.

'It's never too early tae start,' Shortie whispers.

'What have you done?'

'Angus!' the night-nurse hollers from somewhere.

'You know how Brian grassed you – for battering that cunt in the village, ay?' John says to me as he kisses Shortie on the cheek. She takes his hand.

'Aye,' I say.

'Well, we thought that was naughty of him.'

The night-nurse emerges out the front and Angus follows her out there. We go out and look up. Brian is hanging upside down from the bars of the top turret window.

'What are you doing, Brian?'

'He's just hanging about,' Shortie says.

'How did you get up there?' Angus calls.

'We have to get him down! I've called the fire service,' she says.

'Noh, you dinnae, just fucking leave him,' John says.

'Joan has the only keys for that floor. I dunno how he got in there,' Angus says.

'Can you get Joan in, with her keys, then?'

'She's away on a training course!'

'We called for help. Just hang on, Brian!'

'What the fuck else is he gonnae do?' John snorts.

'You know what this reminds me of?' I grin at Shortie and John.

'What?'

'A few years ago I used tae nick the Christmas lights off the tree outside the church. They were all different colours and we'd put them in the rooms in the home. We were lit up like a fucking fairground in there that Christmas.'

A fire engine rolls down the drive. Firefighters put ladders up the front of the building, and two unfold a net at the bottom. The other firemen go to see if they can try to drag Brian up into the building – they appear upstairs.

'Just chop his thing off while you're there – do the world a favour!' Shortie shouts.

'That's enough,' Angus says.

'We're gonnae have tae cut through, or it'll be the blow-torch!' the firefighter says.

'Ooh, get the blowtorch,' Shortie shouts.

'Blowtorch, blowtorch, blowtorch!'

'Inside, all of you, now,' Angus snaps.

We shuffle inside. I am so tired. I keep thinking about Isla in the morgue, and Tash. Click, click, click.

When I get into my room I look out my window. A red light flashes on and off from the fire engine and I can hear them firing up a blowtorch. A few minutes later sparks fly by – I guess the cutters didnae do it after all.

37

'THEY'VE SAID you will be driven to John Kay's after the wake, Anais, okay?' Angus says.

'Aye.'

I didnae eat breakfast this morning. I dinnae think anyone did, other than Brian and Mullet. The chef made porridge and most of it is congealing in a big plastic tub on the table. I didnae sleep last night. I thought about how Isla used tae smile, and how she never let anyone feel sorry for her; she'd be taking her HIV meds and visiting the twins and worrying about Tash – but she would never worry anyone. She'd never lie. She'd always try. It was just the cutting, she couldnae stop, then she cut too deep. I miss her. It still doesnae seem real that she's not here. I keep expecting her to stick her head out the bedroom window at night, or to see her and Tash walking back from the village.

I posted the letters to the prison this morning. I came back to the unit and dressed all in black. Black leggings, black polo neck, black shoes, black jacket. I have black sunglasses. I'm wearing just a touch of mascara and lip-gloss and my hair is pinned back. I've cried every night since I got out of the safe-house. I keep having nightmares about it, but I umnay blocking it out. Not with grass, or pills, or anything.

'It's been good tae work with you, Anais,' Angus says.

'Is that all?'

He nods. We go out to his car. The social-work cars drive out first, then me and Shortie in Angus's car. John, Dylan and Steven are in with Joan. The twins, Stewart and Bethany, are with their foster-mum in the car behind us. Isla's social worker is there and some woman counsellor Isla used to see.

'Why's Isla's mum not coming?' Shortie asks.

'I dinnae know, Shona.'

It's not a big cemetery, the headstones urnay flash – it isnae like the ones in town. There's trees, though, and birds singing. Shortie and I walk behind Angus. I am holding Shortie's hand and so is John, and I cannae cry.

'Dylan did it, ay.'

Shortie squeezes my hand and passes me a package, a stiff envelope. The staff urnay looking just now, so it's the ideal time. I slip it into my pocket and thank God that Teresa wanted tae take me abroad once upon a time.

'When did he do it?'

'When the staff were trying tae get Brian down. Dylan kept it hidden for you, cos he knew Joan would be in your room packing.'

At the top of the cemetery is an open grave that's just been dug; there's no headstone yet. Everything feels swirly: the sky, the air, the wind. Isla's coffin is waiting to be lowered. I dinnae know what a good coffin would look like, but this one looks cheap. They have only buried her because the foster-mum and the social workers said the twins should have somewhere tae visit her when they are older. Normally she'd just get burnt. This is better, I think. Is it better? None of it is better really, there is nothing good in this, for me. Not one thing. I want her back.

There are six sashes. We wanted tae hold one, but they wouldnae let us. The staff are doing it, and some folk from the church that Isla didnae even know.

We stop when we get to the grave, and a leaf falls from a tree. Most of the trees are bare, but that one still has leaves. It spirals down as the Minister makes his speech.

The experiment are here. In their car, waiting. They will follow the police car with me and PC Arnold, for four fucking hours all the way up tae the northern isles.

John is jittery. So's Dylan. So's Shortie. The Minister turns the page and continues to talk.

'What did you give them?' I ask Shortie, and she shrugs.

'Everything,' she says.

'In my whole stash?' I ask.

She nods. I try to add up what was left in my stash, but I cannae mind. It was a lot – and it was Pat's industrial-strength shit as well.

'They took it all?'

She nods.

Dylan is staring at the Minister. Steven is as well. All it would take today would be a speck of dust falling, but they're ready, I can feel it.

Bethany and Stewart throw flowers onto the casket. We have one each tae throw down as well. I cannae believe Isla is in there; it doesnae seem real, but it is. The sun is bright over the graveyard, and it begins to snow.

'Isla knows how tae make an exit. That's the prettiest snowfall I've ever seen,' John says.

Shortie takes my hand.

'So we will return now to pay respects and thanks, Amen.'

The twins are pelting after a rabbit – their wee legs are getting stronger, they're not as chubby now.

Joan chats to the Minister as we walk back towards the cars.

'Was that it?' Shortie asks.

'That was it,' I say.

'Your boyfriend's waiting,' John says to me.

He points at the police car – we look across, give him a wee wave. He is pissed off. John Kay's is not even on the mainland; it's on an island they dinnae tell the public about because they dinnae want press, or vigilantes, turning up.

I dinnae see anything on the way back. I hurt, really fucking ache, for Isla and for Tash, and for Teresa. It's all catching up with me, I feel fucking old. We drive through the Panopticon's gates, and I take one last imaginary photograph. I'll put it up in my imaginary gallery later. It's of Malcolm, and he's wearing my star-shaped sunglasses.

There is food on tables, and the watchtower is glittering, and we are reflected in it, as always. The Minister is standing up in front of everyone.

'It's so good of you tae come out and say something, Minister,' Joan says.

'Not at all. It's times like these where we all have tae do our best, and what we have tae think about in this hard, difficult time is the light – we have tae be able to strive for the good, not for the darkness.'

'Tell her now,' I whisper to Shortie.

'Today is a sad day for all of us. When someone is taken away so young, it is hard to understand that this is God's will, and God's will alone can decide when it is our time to go. We must have the courage tae let Jesus guide us in our hours of sadness!'

John's legs are jigging up and down like mad, and he is clenching and unclenching his fist. Shortie grins at me – she's got really bright eyes now – I can feel her watching me without even looking back. Look at the watchtower: look at it! Watching all this, it's sick. The experiment are behind that glass, drinking tea, waiting for me tae leave; they are taking us out one by fucking one. One raises his mug of tea.

'God knew what was best for Isla, a lost sheep in his flock.'

The glint's here – in the room, passing around the kids, one by one, Angus sees it first. And the twins' foster-mum is walking out the door with the twins. Shortie has warned her tae go, to take them out of here now. This isnae something for them to see.

Now it's just the staff, the Minister and us.

'God is with Isla, as he was always with Isla.'

'Was he with her when she fucking died, on her own, up those fucking stairs?' John says.

'Ssssh,' Joan admonishes, and she's looking up too, catching it. Angus is trying tae see where I am, but the kids have closed around him and Joan.

'We must ask God tae walk beside us!'

'Fuck – you're God!'

Shortie raises a chair above her head, just as Mullet clicks that the screws that are normally holding all the furniture down urnay there.

'Joan, watch out!' he shouts.

'FUCK YOUZ!' Dylan screams.

A chair crashes through the window. John tears a pool-cue off the wall and smashes out the strip-lights. Dylan is taking a run at Angus, and I am running up the stairs two by two – behind me the new girl has a fire extinguisher and she's battering in the office door. Windows are being smashed all around the main room. Joan is on John's back, restraining him, and I am reaching into the bathroom where I stashed it, picking up a glass bottle – lighting the rag with a match. It catches.

'Shortie!'

I raise the lit bottle tae her and launch it – up, up. It turns once, twice, arcs towards the surveillance window.

'This . . . this is how we fucking say goodbye tae our own!'

Shortie raises the telly above her head and lobs it through the last unsmashed window, and they are chanting, smashing, punching, it's going around – *This . . . this . . . this is how we say goodbye to our own!*

Smash.

The whole surveillance window shatters, and I see them – turning on their fucking tails – the experiment, for a fraction of a fucking second: exposed.

38

YOU HAVE to do the first things first – you have to begin at the beginning. This is the last time, I will never do this again.

Begin at the beginning, pick a birth. You have tae do it like it is important, like it counts.

How about a birth just like this: an ordinary baby is born, on an ordinary day, in a hospital just outside London. The labour takes fourteen hours, the baby is eventually delivered by Caesarean section. The mother cries – the father cries. Everyone is happy.

Pull my hat further down, tweak the rim so it turns up, it's a 1920s-style hat, with a wee pin and a cherry on it. It matches my 1920s coat – and shoes. The train pulled into King's Cross at 10.22 a.m. I didnae travel in the toilet. I didnae think I was dead; in fact, I have never felt this alive – every single breath feels like a first chance.

Next is the biological mother: Claire. She was the eldest of three sisters; her younger sister died in a boating accident and she passed on a few years later from ovarian cancer. Biological father: had a stroke and died six months later.

Now I'm an orphan. There are far worse things a girl can be.

'How much are your lilies?' I ask a woman on a flower stall by the river.

'Four for a fiver, love.'

'I'll take them.'

'Just four?'

'Aye.'

The lilies are flat, so they'll be easy to float – the river is calm. Walk down some steps to the shore. A wee laddie up on the pathway watches me. Down by my right a man is making a sofa out of sand. His wee dog runs around him and people throw coins down. They clatter into his bucket and some just land in the sand.

I unwrap the flowers and kiss each lily in turn. They smell that sweet way. The river is grey and they will disappear in seconds, but it doesnae matter. I place them on the water one by one. One for Teresa, one for Tash, one for Isla, one for Anais.

The tide whorls them away.

It took me ages tae walk down here, all the way past the tourist sites. Big Ben. Parliament. The wheel. The trees, the Christmas lights, the boats, the Christmas market and performers on stilts. And not one person has looked at me twice.

The buses here run all the time. In the village I'd wait for fifty minutes if I'd missed one. Here there is an LCD that tells you: due, 2 mins. I walk along to the steps and run up them, to the bus stop. A bus comes straight away and I get on, sit down next tae a man who is wearing a wee black skullcap. His sideburns are curly. The bus stinks. I breathe into my scarf until we pull up outside St Pancras.

I've got it straight now, in my head. I know how I began.

I cannae think of the unit, or anyone I've left behind. I dinnae look left, or right, just straight ahead, and there's no queue at the sales booth, so I walk right up.

'A single ticket,' I say.

'No return?' the woman asks.

'No. Thanks.'

I put the ticket in my pocket.

It is what it is. Some people are blonde, some people are poor – some people get up and die on a day when they were gonnae go dancing. I've been playing the birthday game for years, and this is it: game over. There are no brothers, no sisters, no palazzo in Italy – no free perfume from Harvey Nichols. Just a plain ordinary life, the only one I will ever own.

I have to run for the train: the man's putting his whistle into his mouth as I jump up onto the carriage. My heart is going pit-a-pat as I scan the platform, but there's no-one there; no polis, no Angus, no experiment.

Weave down the aisle – this is it, just breathe, it's all you have tae do.

I am in carriage F. My seat is 64B, opposite an elderly guy. I take my coat off and fold it neatly, place it down on the seat next to me and sit down. There are eighty-four seats in this carriage. The carpet has a swirly pattern, yellow on blue. The train is racing away from the city, out into the green. A hostess trolley rattles down our aisle; she stops at our table.

'Can I get you anything, sir?'

'Tea, please, no milk,' he says.

The woman pours, and the man smiles – and I smile back, but just quickly. 'S alright. Sometimes you can just tell the goodness of a person by their face.

'What's your name?' he asks me.

Tuck my hair behind my ear, look up.

'Frances,' I say.

'That's a nice name,' he says.

And it is. It's a nice name, if you look up its origins: it means freedom.

Paris.

Paris it is.

I am Frances Jones from Paris. I am not a face on a missing-person poster, I am not a number or a statistic in a file.

I have no-one watching me.

All I own is a lipstick I stole this morning, several hundred quid – and a lucky domino. This is it: no more experiment, no more meetings, no files, no straight to a secure unit, no giving up, no giving out, no beating up, no getting fucked, no looking over my shoulder, no locked cell, no broken vertebrae.

Paris – it is.

If you go there, you might see me working in a café, watching the people go by: smoking coloured cigarettes and patting my wee dog.

I'll learn French and get a room on a back street – maybe I'll walk my rescue-dog by the river four times a day. I'll go to galleries, and read everything in their libraries, even the manuals, even the papers. I'll eat chocolate croissants for breakfast. And I won't take any lovers for ten years. I'll wash my hair in lavender shampoo. I'll browse couture shops, and junk bazaars. I'll go to the Moulin Rouge. I'll write poetry in the back of dark bars. I'll watch live sex shows, and wank forty times in a row.

I'm just a girl with a shark's heart – Frances Jones. You wouldnae know me from anyone else if I walked by you. This is it, I'm getting out. So, Vive freedom. Vive Paris. Vive le mad artists and drunken whores. Vive le girls with tits and hips and perfumes and perfumers. Vive absinthe and cobbled streets, vive le sea! Vive riots and old porn, and dragonflies; vive rooms with huge windows and unlockable doors. Vive flying cats and cigarillo-smoking Outcast Queens! Vive Le Revolution. Vive Le Dreamers. Vive Le Dream.

I – begin today.

Acknowledgements

Thanks, and appreciation (in no particular order) to:

Jason Arthur, Tracy Bohan, Ali Smith, Joseph Ridgwell, Cherry Smyth, Suzanne Dean, Freddy Chick, Kevin Williamson, Liz Hope, Darran Anderson, Laurie Ip Fung Chun, Michael Langan, Rosie Gailer, Adelle Stripe, Mark Burgess, Emma Finnigan, Dave Oprava, Arts Council England and Iona Davis.

I would also like to thank everyone at William Heinemann and the Wylie Agency.